# The Architect of

Rafe McGregor

© Rafe McGregor 2017

Rafe McGregor has asserted his rights under the Copyright, Design and Patents Act, 1988, to be identified as the author of this work.

First published in 2009 by Robert Hale.

This edition published in 2017 by Endeavour Press Ltd.

Table of Contents

1. A Vision in Violet	5
2. The King's Detective	13
3. Henry Marshall, Esquire	20
4. Murder in Bohemia	27
5. The Penang Lawyer	34
6. What the Boy Said	41
7. Colonel Frank Rhodes	49
8. Doctor Morgan Drayton	55
9. Lieutenant Francis Carey	63
10. Confession of Faith	69
11. Hugh Armstrong, Esquire	78
12. Death by Misadventure	86
13. Agent Provocateur	92
14. Intrigue at the Zoological Gardens	100
15. The Holme	108
16. The Doctor's Revelation	116
17. The Maltese Tiger	122
18. Devil's Acre	129

19. The Colonial Secretary's Accident	137
20. The Shikari's Lair	144
21. The Russian Connection	152
22. Monument	159
23. Empire Day	166
24. Rendezvous in Shad Thames	176
25. The Empire Loyalist League	183
26. Cat-and-Mouse	190
27. Supper at Simpson's	198
28. A Riverside Duel	205
29. The Seventh Conspirator	213
30. Doctor Leander Starr Jameson	222
Epilogue	230

1. A Vision in Violet

I'm not sure why I decided to return to London when I did.

I learned of Ellen's accident the day before the Boer surrender, more than a week after her death. I resigned my commission forty-eight hours later, but by the time I boarded the Union and Castle steamer in Cape Town, it was already six weeks after her funeral at St James' Church, in Piccadilly. There was no practical reason to come back, and certainly no need to have left in such haste. Perhaps it was because I was sick of the war and wanted to get as far away from it as possible. No matter my motivation, the two day delay at Freetown had been intolerable, and I couldn't wait to disembark at Southampton. Now, on my second morning in London, I wasn't quite sure what to do with myself.

After an early breakfast, I was toying with yesterday's *Times*, rereading Mr G.E. Buckle's call for 'officers' diaries to shed further light on the military operations of the war'. My finances were in a dire state, and even though I'd selected a modest establishment in the Windsor Hotel, I would shortly require an income of sorts. What with my Victoria Cross at Ladysmith, and the lengthy service of my adopted regiment, I was sure Mr Buckle would accept a submission. He might even offer a small advance, which would be most welcome. On the other hand, I wasn't sure if I wanted to talk about the war, let alone have my experiences laid bare before hundreds of thousands of readers.

A knock at the door interrupted my contemplation.

I opened it to find the hotel's upper-attendant accompanied by a smartly attired young woman about ten years my junior — nineteen, or twenty at the most. She was pretty, with fair hair a shade darker than mine, a pert mouth and a button nose. Very pretty, actually.

"Excuse me, sir, but you have a visitor. Miss Paterson is the lady's name."

"Thank you, Green."

He left us and Miss Paterson stepped forward and offered a gloved hand. "Captain Marshall?"

I took it gently, but she squeezed very tight. "Yes, I'm Alec Marshall. Miss Roberta Paterson?"

"Yes, sir. I'm very pleased to meet you."

"No, the pleasure's mine, Miss Paterson. I only arrived in London yesterday and I intended to call on you this afternoon to thank you for your kindnesses. Perhaps you'd be more comfortable in the hotel parlour?"

"I would not."

A New Woman, just like Ellen. "Then please come in and make yourself comfortable. Would you like some refreshment?" I asked as she entered my small sitting-room.

"No, thank you."

I admired her violet tailored suit and velvet hat with a black feather as she arranged herself in an armchair with small, prim movements. I closed the door and sat in the other chair. "Thank you very much for the telegram — and the letter that followed."

"I'm so sorry to have had to resort to such an impersonal, brutal method, but I thought you'd rather know as soon as possible."

"There was nothing brutal or impersonal about it at all. You did receive my reply? It took a while for the wire to reach me; I was on patrol in the veldt."

"Yes, I did. But there was something I didn't tell you in the letter. Something that I need to tell you in person."

Her creamy complexion became flushed, and despite the painful subject matter, I couldn't help noticing how attractive the sudden display of emotion made her look. "Then please tell me now."

She sat up very straight, and took a deep breath to steady herself. "I think Ellen was murdered."

"Murdered?" I was completely dumbfounded.

"Yes, well, maybe... no — oh, I don't know! It was all wrong. It should have been referred to the police. What happened wasn't... it wasn't right... that's all I can say."

"You have some evidence of this?"

"I *knew* you were going to say something like that. It's so typical of a man, all intellect and no intuition. Have you any idea how accomplished a rider your sister was? You may take that as your first piece of evidence if you insist."

"When Ellen visited me in Natal the last year before the war, she rode better than me. I take it she didn't ride side-saddle in London, either?"

"Certainly not. And you are perfectly correct, she rode as well as any man — better than most. That's why I can't believe she fell off and broke her neck — it's balderdash! She loved animals, and she knew everything there was to know about horses. Ellen was a veterinary surgeon, after all."

I still wasn't sure what to say, so I held my tongue and nodded, hoping not to offend Miss Paterson by my lack of commitment.

"It doesn't make any sense, Ellen falling off while cantering in Regent's Park. Nonsense, utter nonsense." She shook her head so vigorously, I feared she'd dislodge her hat.

I said nothing for a few moments, choosing my next words carefully. "One of my men, Sergeant Dicks, was with me for the last eighteen months of the war. He was in the thick of it at Groenkop, Kalkkrans, and a dozen skirmishes — maybe more — all without a scratch. Five days after the Treaty of Vereeniging was signed his horse was startled by a snake. It reared up, he was thrown, and the fall broke his back. Dicks had spent his whole life in the saddle. These things... they happen." I tailed off.

She bridled instantly. "Captain Marshall, you are speaking to me as if I were a child. I am quite twenty-one and I know much more about life than you give me credit for."

I raised my palms. "I'm sorry, I didn't mean to offend you. It's the last thing I wish."

"Well, you have. And you didn't let me finish. It's not just Ellen's proficiency in the saddle that makes her death suspicious, it's who she was with when it happened."

"Lieutenant Francis Carey?"

"Yes, exactly!"

She spoke as if it ought to mean something to me, but it didn't. Yesterday, out of curiosity, I'd looked him up in *Who's Who*. Born in 'sixty-eight in Charlestown, Nevis; he'd served with the West India Regiment in Africa, been mentioned in despatches in Gambia in 'ninety-two, then left the army to hunt professionally. Carey was renowned as the most successful heavy game hunter in the Empire, he was a Fellow of the Zoological Society of London, and frequent donor to the Zoological

Gardens. Ellen had been the assistant to the veterinary surgeon at the zoo, so I'd assumed that was where she'd made his acquaintance. "The shikari?" I asked.

"You don't take him seriously either, do you?"

"I can't see how Carey is significant to Ellen's accident, no. Is he?"

"Yes, of course he is. Lieutenant Carey may be an officer, but he's no gentleman. The man's a complete blackguard. A rake, a criminal, and it's even rumoured a traitor as well."

"Really?"

She added gesticulation to her nodding, becoming more impassioned as she continued. "Yes, yes! You wouldn't know, living in the colonies, but Lieutenant Carey has a dreadful reputation in London. He's very secretive about his family and it's said he worked on an illegal slaver as a youth. He's believed to sell his skills as a shootist to anyone who's unscrupulous and wealthy enough to employ him. He's even rumoured to have worked for the Russians in Afghanistan — Lord Curzon expelled him from India."

If any of that were true then he obviously wasn't the sort of man I'd like my sister to have passed the time of day with, but it was hardly enough to suspect him of murder. "No, I knew nothing of his character," was all I could say.

"You don't think it's relevant?"

"I...why would he want to kill Ellen? I assume — I hope — they weren't close."

"Of course they weren't — and what's that got to do with the price of tea in China!"

"Unless he's possessed of some sort of homicidal mania, he would need a reason to murder. If he is a lunatic, he's unlikely to have killed in a manner so subtle as to evade detection. Assuming he isn't, he therefore must have stood to gain from Ellen's death. Cui bono is the first rule of a murder investigation. The second is that most people are murdered by relatives or close friends rather than strangers."

"How horrid. No, Ellen certainly wasn't close to Lieutenant Carey. He's a Fellow of the Zoological Society, that's where she met him. He captures wild animals for the zoo."

"Had Ellen been riding with Carey before?" I asked.

"Once, I think, some time ago, but this was the first time they had been out alone. He asked Ellen the day before, on the Wednesday."

"She told you this?"

"Yes, she did."

"What else did she say?"

"Ellen was amused. She thought he had an ulterior motive, but couldn't work out what it was."

"Not that he had... intentions... honourable or otherwise?"

"Well, they were hardly likely to be honourable with Lieutenant Carey. I've already told you the man is a Lothario."

"So why did Ellen accept?"

"Isn't that obvious? She was curious."

I wasn't convinced there'd been any foul play, even if Carey was the Devil incarnate. "Miss Paterson, I know Ellen was your very dear friend, but —"

"I'm not finished yet," she declared. "The inquest was incredibly quick. Ellen died on Thursday evening; the coroner's court was on Monday. He recorded a verdict of death by misadventure on the same day."

"I'm surprised there was even an inquest. My father has a considerable amount of money and influence, and I'd have expected him to exert himself in order to avoid any hint of a scandal. Not that I'm suggesting there was anything untoward, but if Carey has such a poor reputation, then I don't expect my father would've wanted it known that Ellen was alone with him."

"It was your father who insisted upon the inquest."

I doubted it. "Are you sure?"

"Of course I'm sure!"

"Did Carey give evidence?"

"Yes, he was the only witness."

"In Regent's Park, on a May evening?"

"They were riding in the grounds of The Holme. Ellen had permission to ride all over the park. She was so popular; everyone knew she was the real surgeon, not that disgusting Mr Gibbs. People even called her *Doctor* Marshall out of respect. She was a celebrity in her own right... such a lovely... " Miss Paterson faltered and her eyes misted. She dabbed them delicately with a handkerchief and continued. "It was twilight when she — when he killed her."

I sat back in the chair and stroked my moustache, thinking aloud. "You want me to do something about this?"

"Really, Captain Marshall, your attitude is disgraceful! I was under the impression you loved your sister." She jumped to her feet. "You ought to be ashamed. Ellen spoke of you every single time we met. The day your Victoria Cross was announced was the happiest of her life, even more than her qualification as a veterinary surgeon. You were the world to her, and I'd expected you to display at least a modicum of brotherly love in return. Good day, I shall see myself out."

"Wait!" I stood up and she turned back to face me.

"I'm not accustomed to being spoken to like a servant."

I noticed that her eyes were a very dark blue. Exactly the same as my own, except they were burning with a fierce intensity where mine seemed to have lost their lustre of late. I looked down into them without saying anything, but she held my gaze defiantly. "Please accept my sincere apologies. I was only considering how best to set about my inquiries."

Her demeanour changed instantly. "You agree with me! You think the lieutenant murdered her?"

"I haven't formed an opinion yet, Miss Paterson, but from what you've told me it's obvious that I need to find out what happened for myself. You may rest assured I'll pursue the matter until I discover the truth. So, once again, please accept my thanks."

"I don't suppose I can ask more than that."

"Please sit down. Won't you have a cup of coffee — or tea?"

"No thank you. I'm on my way to work. That's why I called so early."

"How did you find me so soon?" I'd been meaning to ask for some time.

She smiled, and was beautiful with it. "I'm a journalist, Captain Marshall. It's my job to find things out."

"A journalist?" I raised my eyebrows.

"You disappoint me, sir. I expected you to be at ease with professional women. Do we intimidate you?"

"No, I've met several lady journalists, just none who are 'quite twenty-one'." She coloured again. "And, while it's very kind of you to address me as 'captain', I don't use my rank anymore. I'm not in the Reserve or on half-pay, I've left for good. May I show you out?"

"You may."

We descended the stairs. "With your permission, I'll call on you tomorrow. You're in Wimpole Street in Marylebone, aren't you?"

"Why not telephone instead?"

"Er... yes, I shall. How will I find your... number?"

"In the London telephone directory." She pointed at the reception counter. "There's one over there."

I'd not used a telephone before, but I didn't want to reveal my ignorance. "Would you like me to hail you a cab?"

"That won't be necessary, I instructed my driver to wait." She held her hand out again, and we shook. "Good morning, *Mister* Marshall, we'll speak tomorrow."

"Good day, Miss Paterson."

I watched her leave. She hadn't convinced me that Ellen had been murdered, nor even that Carey was a rogue. I imagined it would be very easy to acquire an evil reputation in the stifling formality of London society — particularly if one was used to the relative freedom of the colonies, as I was. There was only one fact that didn't ring true, and that was my father's conduct; requesting a public inquiry was completely out of character for him.

I took out my watch: a quarter to nine.

I'd spent the whole of Tuesday attending to the routine matters that must naturally accompany a return to one's native land after an absence of eleven years, including a visit to Ellen's solicitors; she'd appointed me her executor, but I'd been told that the earliest I could be accommodated with an appointment was next Wednesday. I'd made every excuse to put off a visit to my father, and was relieved at another reason to procrastinate; in any event it was too late in the morning to find him at home as he'd probably already be on his way to the City. My only other plans for the day involved placing a fresh bouquet of flowers on Ellen's grave, but I decided it was time Carey and I met.

I knew he kept rooms off Grosvenor Square and was a member of the Travellers Club. I was wondering which address would be the better to leave word for him when I noticed the telephone directory and thought I should familiarise myself with — what was for me — the latest technology. I approached the counter at the same time as another chap, a tall man with a fine set of moustaches.

As I picked up the directory, the stranger spoke to Green. "Good mornin', I'm lookin' for Major Marshall. I'm — "

"I'm Marshall."

"Good day, sir," he saluted. "I'm Sergeant Lamb, from Scotland Yard. Superintendent Melville sends his compliments, and requests the pleasure of your company." He produced a card from his coat pocket and handed it to me. It read: *William Melville, Superintendent, Criminal Investigations Department.*

"And when would Superintendent Melville like to see me?"

"As soon as is convenient, sir. He instructed me to wait."

"You mean now?"

"If that's convenient, sir," he said with a grin.

I removed my homburg from the hat-stand. "It is. Lead the way."

"Very good, sir."

What could the King's Detective possibly want with me, I wondered.

2. The King's Detective

Lamb had a hansom waiting outside; apparently everyone did this morning. We set off up Victoria Street, our progress extremely slow in the heavy traffic. The first thing I'd noticed upon my return was how much more crowded the streets were than in the summer of 'ninety-one. It was the noise that alerted me to it, the continual clatter of hooves and wheels on the granite sett. I was sure there were more omnibuses, carriages, and carts competing for the same space. The second thing I'd noticed was the dirt. Not so much the filth on the streets — they were in fact cleaner than I remembered — but in the air. I felt as if I could taste the dust and the smoke of kitchen and factory fires in the close, cloying atmosphere.

It would probably have been as quick to walk the short distance rather than drive it, which fact led me to suppose that Melville was concerned to make a favourable impression. This, in turn, made me conclude that he wanted something from me, though I couldn't imagine what. Eventually, we passed my old school, in Dean's Yard, and then the gothic grandeur of Westminster Abbey. Our progress was further impeded by the workmen erecting covered stands next to St Margaret's Church in preparation for the coronation, three days hence. We passed the Palace of Westminster — the secular match to the sacred Abbey, juxtaposing it across Old Palace Yard — and turned right, as if to cross Westminster Bridge. Before we reached the bridge, however, the driver stopped opposite the clock tower and Big Ben struck nine as we alighted. New Scotland Yard, distinctive with its stylish brick corner towers, stood in front of us.

I followed Lamb into the headquarters of the Metropolitan Police Force.

William Melville had been one of the most famous policemen in the British Empire when I was growing up. He was one of the original Special Irish Branch, established to counter the Fenian bombing campaign, and had played a part in foiling the Jubilee, Balfour, and Walsall Plots. He'd also been personal bodyguard to the Prince of Wales, the Shah of Persia, and the German Kaiser. It was claimed that while anarchists and nihilists traditionally regarded London as a safe haven because of the British government's reluctance to repatriate them, 'Melville's Gang' was so effective that the violent extremists had all left for greener pastures.

Lamb led me through a labyrinth of corridors and staircases until we reached a door with Melville's nameplate. He knocked twice and we entered a compact office with a pleasant view overlooking the Embankment. There was a display consisting of two revolvers and two truncheons above a walnut mantelpiece; the only other decoration was a large framed photograph of King Edward the Seventh. Two upholstered easy chairs were arranged in front of the large pine desk, and a third — occupied by Melville himself — behind it. The desk was cluttered with umpteen piles of paper, four speaking tubes, and a telephone.

"Major Marshall, as requested, guvnor."

"Thank you, Lamb, that'll be all for now."

"Guvnor, Major," Lamb took his leave.

Melville rose and approached me. He was in his early fifties, above average height and portly. His ash blonde hair was receding, and he had a fleshy face with a thick, grey moustache that made me think of a walrus. His movements were crisp and his eyes sharp as he extended a large flipper. "I'm William Melville," he said in a faint Irish brogue.

"Alec Marshall." We shook. His grip was strong.

"Do make yourself comfortable. May I offer you some refreshment, a cigar? No? Please accept my apologies for your perfunctory summons, and my thanks for your swift response. I wasn't sure if you would honour me with your presence at all."

We both sat. I noticed he moved quietly for a big man. "How could I refuse a request from the King's Detective?" I smiled.

"Quite easily I'm sure, Major."

"In truth, sir, I've been an admirer of yours since I was a boy. If you don't mind me saying so, you're probably one of the reasons I decided to become a policeman. I've always wanted to meet you."

"You flatter me, but if that really is what brought you here, I'm delighted, because perhaps you'll lend an old man a sympathetic ear. I'd hoped to appeal to you as one policeman to another. I know you arrived from Cape Town yesterday. Might I ask what your immediate plans are?"

"My sister died in a riding accident at the end of May. I came back to put her affairs in order and — well, that's why I'm here."

"My condolences on your loss."

"Thank you."

"Will you return to Africa once you've completed your fraternal duties?"

"No."

"May I assume you'll be seeking employment of sorts?"

"I have a testimonial from General Broadwood, under whom I served in the closing phase of the war. He suggested that if I present it to the commanding officer of his old regiment, the Twelfth Royal Lancers, my application for a commission might be favourably received."

"Is this what you intend to do?"

"I'm not sure yet."

"I know you resigned your commission, Major, so it doesn't take a detective to deduce that you're tired of soldiering."

I'm not accustomed to sharing my innermost thoughts with strangers, but Melville was a man I'd admired from afar for some time, and he spoke as if the regard were mutual. "I am. I'm tired of killing men with whom I have no personal quarrel."

"I believe I construe your meaning, but — if you'll forgive me for saying so — you seem to be rather good at it." He shuffled several of the sheets of paper on his desk. "Major Alec Marshall VC, Natal Mounted Rifles. Elandslaagte; wounded at Ladysmith; volunteered for the Natal Composite Regiment; wounded again at Groenkop; Kalkkrans; South Africa Medal with two clasps; honourably discharged thirtieth of June 1902."

"You know a great deal about me, sir."

"You're right, I do."

"Not many people know about the VC."

"No, it was misprinted in the *London Gazette* as 'Lieutenant Alexander Marshal' wasn't it? They amended it in a subsequent supplement, but no one ever reads amendments. You spoke of coming back to London, but you are not an Englishman, are you?"

"No, sir, I'm Scots."

"And I Irish, which doesn't make either of us any less loyal to his Britannic Majesty, or either of us less at home in London. And *I* don't even want to blow any of it up." He chuckled. "How would you feel about doing some work for me while you make up your mind, Major?"

"Doing what, sir?"

"Do you know what my job here is?"

"Not exactly, but I know you were in the Special Irish Branch, and that you keep watch on the anarchists and protect the Royal Family."

"That's right, my men do all of that, and also protect visiting royalty and heads of state when they're in England. My problem at the minute is that I have precious few men, and a surplus of royalty — not to mention the colonial premiers. Sir Edward, the commissioner, has already recalled more than five hundred pensioners for service. Pensioners, can you believe it!" He laughed again, his cheeks wobbling. "That's how desperate we are for men to police the coronation. And what do you think happened a week ago? Well, I suppose if you knew, I wouldn't be doing my job very well! The Home Secretary, the Right Honourable Mr Akers-Douglas, instructed me to keep an eye on a certain Dr Drayton." He paused for effect.

"Dr Morgan Drayton?"

"The very same, private secretary to Dr Leander Starr Jameson. I don't have to tell you of all gentlemen that Dr Jameson was the intimate friend and confidant of the late Mr Cecil John Rhodes, the most substantial man in the Empire. Mr Rhodes was very particular as to what happened to his money after his death, perhaps because he had so much of it. As a matter of fact, he was so particular that he made seven wills and several dozen amendments to them by codicils. You'll know that Mr Rhodes died on the twenty-sixth of March, shortly after your promotion. In the two weeks before his death he made two amendments to his final will, and there have been some… irregularities… which have resulted in the delay of its execution. Do you follow me, so far?"

"Yes."

"Good fellow. Because of these irregularities, all the witnesses to the last two amendments have been summoned to appear and confirm various details before the will can be executed. By the time these irregularities became apparent the two gentlemen in question, Dr Drayton and a young bank clerk by the name of Eric Lowenstein, were already both in London. Instead of returning to Cape Town, as you'd expect, they both remained here.

"At the end of May, Lowenstein disappeared, and Drayton has been conspicuous in his attempts to find him ever since. A missing person naturally concerns the police, especially so in this case, as it's believed some harm may have come to the fellow. Up until last week, however, it didn't concern my section. Now, with my meagre resources stretched well past their limit, I'm told to put a man on the job. What man?" He lifted his arms in a show of exasperation.

"But then I hear that one of our war heroes is on his way back to London. I've dozens of war heroes to choose from, if I wish, but this one spent eight years as a policeman, and the last three of those as a detective with Superintendent Alexander in Durban. In addition, he is already acquainted with Drayton, was once even close to him. How could I not avail myself of the opportunity, Major?"

"What do you require of me?"

"I would like you to renew your friendship with Drayton, and find out what in God's name is going on."

"Drayton and I met in Pitsani," I responded, "in the Bechuanaland Protectorate. He arrived as the new locum a few months after I was commissioned in the Border Police. We often worked together and quite naturally became friends. We had only one major difference of opinion between us; the British South Africa Company. Drayton approved of Rhodes and Jameson, and the extension of their rule by whatever means necessary — I did not. By the time Drayton and I shared digs, Rhodes' dominion was already larger than any other colonial territory in the world. He boasted that if he could reach the planets, he would colonise them as well, and named a country after himself. I thought the man was a megalomaniac, Drayton thought him visionary."

"You do not approve of the Empire?" Melville asked.

"I did not approve of Rhodes' private empire. The man was a law unto himself out there. Manicaland, Gazaland, Mashonaland, Matabeleland... he and Jameson took their Company Police, conquered first, and asked permission from the Crown afterwards. Rhodes served himself, not the King."

"An interesting observation. Please continue."

"The Jameson Raid was the end of my tenure in Bechuanaland. Rhodes pressurised the high commissioner in Cape Town to cede the eastern part of Bechuanaland to his Company so that Jameson could use Pitsani to launch his unauthorised invasion of the South African Republic. My squadron of Border Police was incorporated into the Company Police. I resigned and left Bechuanaland for Natal; Drayton went to work for Jameson. That was just over seven years ago, and I've not seen him since. We did not part on friendly terms."

"Yes, 'Jameson's dash into the Transvaal' was a fiasco. It rather caught the popular imagination though, however rash and unlawful it may have been." Neither Melville's face nor his voice betrayed any emotion, and it was impossible to discern his own opinion.

"I don't doubt it, and yet here we are with 20,000 soldiers from all corners of the Empire lying dead in the veldt. All, I suspect, so that men like Rhodes and his ilk can take possession of Paul Kruger's gold mines."

"You may be right, but you haven't answered my question. Are you prepared to renew your acquaintance with Dr Drayton?"

"It appears that I'm uniquely qualified for this particular service to His Majesty," I looked up at the photograph, "so I'll gladly undertake the task."

"Good fellow!" Melville was up in a flash, pumping my arm again. "Let's have a cigar to mark the occasion, they're Henry Clay."

"I prefer my pipe, but I left it at my hotel in my haste."

"Never mind, they're very smooth on the palate." He continued as he cut the two cigars with his penknife. "I don't expect you to find Lowenstein. Official and private detectives have already spent more than two months without success. What I would like you to ascertain is Drayton's opinion of the reason he disappeared. When our men asked the doctor, he claimed it was a mystery. Find out if that's true. More important, however, I'd like to know why Drayton is still in London. Both he and Lowenstein are required in Cape Town to prove the will; with Lowenstein missing, it's all the more imperative that Drayton return. Find out why he hasn't. While he's here, it's my business and my problem — and I've more than enough of both to contend with already." He passed the corona and matches over to me.

"Thank you." I lit the cigar and drew gently on it. It was a little strong for my taste.

"Here's a thought! If you can't find anything out, put him on the next Royal Mail packet and we'll let the Cape Town police worry about it!"

Melville had an energy and enthusiasm that made one feel as if one were the most important thing in the world to him. I was overwhelmed by his charisma. It seemed — it was — a privilege to work for him. But that wasn't why I agreed to his proposal so quickly. Nor was it my loyalty to the Crown. The real reason was Miss Paterson. The young, brazen, ravishing Miss Paterson had sown a seed of doubt in my mind and I wanted to find out more about the circumstances of Ellen's death.

As a police agent, I'd be in the most practical position to do that.

3. Henry Marshall, Esquire

Five hours later I was sitting in Granges in Piccadilly, enjoying my first pipe of the day. The straight-stemmed meerschaum had survived the war and I was smoking an aromatic mix of blended, spicy Turkish tobacco from Astleys in Jermyn Street, milder and smoother than Melville's cigar. The tobacconist had been recommended to me by a young lieutenant from the Queen's Bays called Forsythe, five months ago. It was the last thing he said to me before a Boer sniper blew the back of his skull off. We didn't know one another very well, but I haven't forgotten him or his tobacconist. There are a lot of things about the war I haven't forgotten. Thinking about Forsythe and the bouquet of pink roses and lilies I'd placed on Ellen's grave recalled a host of distressing memories I'd rather have avoided, but I had little else to occupy my mind.

The day had been eminently unsuccessful.

My maiden use of the telephone had proved inauspicious, and I'd had to be content with speaking to Carey's valet. I'd left a message requesting Carey contact me as a matter of urgency, and then returned to the reading room of the London Library in St James' Square. All that my further researches into the shikari had revealed was his most recent addition to the Zoological Society's Gardens: a pair of young giraffes.

Melville's dossier on Drayton yielded the intelligence that my former colleague was residing at Devonshire House as the guest of His Grace, the Duke of Devonshire. Spencer Cavendish was the recently-appointed Leader of the House of Lords, and the not-so-recently appointed Lord President of the Council and President of the British Empire League — amongst numerous lesser titles. An extremely influential individual. I'd wanted to surprise Drayton so I'd risked calling without an appointment. He was out and I'd not even managed to gain entry into the grounds, let alone the house. I left my card, and thus immediately lost the initiative. In a vain attempt to regain it, I'd tried the Savoy and the National Liberal Club, his regular haunts according to Melville.

The sum total of my investigations lay on the table in the form of two newspapers, each containing a single item of interest. I'd decided on *The*

News of the World, recalling it as a prohibited publication at Westminster. I believe my English master had referred to it as 'the worst example of the gutter press'. He may have had a point, but Sunday's issue revealed that Lieutenant Francis Carey was engaged in a torrid affair with the only daughter of Baron de Staal, the Russian ambassador in London. Apparently the baron wasn't known for his tolerance, and it was speculated that despite the likelihood of Carey having worked in their employ in Afghanistan, the Okhrana — the Tsar's dreaded secret police — might terminate his courtship permanently. It was also alleged that Carey was a former lover of Lady Curzon, wife of the Viceroy of India. Probably nine-tenths humbug, but there was certain to be a kernel of truth.

The Times made somewhat more factual reading. A paragraph dated yesterday, Tuesday August the fifth, read:

Mr Rhodes' will has been proved at the Master's Office in Cape Town. Letters of administration have been granted to Mr L.I. Mitchel, right being reserved to the absent executors to prove later on. The delay has been due to legal complications consequent on the fact that all the executors are not domiciled here.

Melville had been explicit that the will couldn't be proved until both Drayton and Lowenstein had returned to Cape Town. I wondered if there was some sort of cover-up in progress, but eight years of police work had taught me the value of Occam's razor: the simplest solution to a problem is usually the correct one. Given that the late Mr Rhodes was one of the wealthiest men in the world, it was hardly surprising that there were complications and that the execution of his will was taking some time.

I finished my pipe, dropped some coins on the newspapers and strolled down Piccadilly. As I approached the corner of Green Park, I turned up Berkeley Street, alongside the curtain wall of Devonshire House. There were fewer pedestrians here and the road was much quieter. The estate continued for several hundred yards until Bolton Row, where I passed the gardens of Lansdowne House before entering a residential square. The middle of the square comprised an elliptical green, which sported a Pre-Raphaelite sculpture, and was lined with dozens of plane trees stretching high into the heavens. The road ran around the green, a prosaic barrier between the unpretentious grace of nature and the ostentatious stone of the great dwellings. I found 40 Berkeley Square, a Georgian townhouse with a massive frontage.

I took a deep breath and pressed the electric bell.

A few seconds later it was opened by an immaculate butler, complete with spotless white gloves. "Good afternoon, sir, how may I be of assistance?"

Determined to succeed where I'd failed at Devonshire House, I snapped an air of command into my voice. "Good afternoon. I'm here to see Mr Marshall."

"Do you have an appointment, sir?"

"Mr Marshall will see me." I reached inside my coat.

"I'm afraid Mr Marshall doesn't receive visitors without prior — "

I thrust my card at him. "Present this to Mr Marshall." As he took it, I strode inside. "And be quick about it. I shall wait in the hall."

He moved deftly out my way, closed the door behind me, and hesitated. He watched me place my hat on the stand, examined the card, and made up his mind. "One moment, please, Inspector Marshall." He disappeared up the stairs.

The only visiting cards I had were old ones identifying me as an inspector in the Durban Borough Police, in which I'd served until the war began. I looked around as I waited, noting the tasteful luxury. The house, like my father's new wife, had been acquired since my departure. I'd been born in Singapore, but we'd lived in the west end of Glasgow for most of my childhood. I attended Westminster as a boarder, and it was thus from London that I'd left for Bechuanaland. Four years later, Henry Marshall moved to London to look after his business interests, which had progressed from entrepôt trading and shipping to investment banking. I'd always known he was well-heeled, but it seemed he had prospered unreservedly in my absence.

The butler trotted down the stairs, requested that I follow him, and led me back up. He stopped at a heavy oak door on the first floor, and announced me. I entered my father's study and saw him for the first time in eleven years. He was standing next to the fireplace, hands clasped behind his back, contemplating a photograph of him shaking hands with the captain of the *Thermopylae*, one of the fastest tea clippers of its time.

My father was fifty-seven and he had not aged well. He'd abandoned his mutton-chop whiskers for a more fashionable moustache, twirled at each end. Like his hair, it had been dyed dark brown. The lines in his face were much deeper than at our last meeting, and his waistline much expanded, giving him a corpulent aspect.

I walked over to him.

He kept his hands behind his back and scowled. "The Devil take you, what do you mean by coming here unannounced!" He had been taller than me, but middle age had shrunk him, and he squinted up at my five feet and ten inches. I noticed his accent had changed; there was no trace of Scotland left.

I didn't answer.

He lashed out with his left hand, waving my card under my nose. "An inspector! Pah! An inspector in some godforsaken colonial police force that no one gives a damn about? Pathetic." He cast it into the empty grate. "I had a commission arranged for you in the Scots Greys. The Royal Scots Greys! But you threw that in my face, like everything else. Now what the hell has caused you to darken my door after a decade? State your business, or get out and don't return."

"What happened to Ellen?"

"How would that be any of your concern? When you decided to go to Africa you severed all ties with this household. You turned your back on your family. You ceased to be my son."

"No, I turned my back on you. Mother was already dead and Ellen and I corresponded regularly. You prevented her from visiting me, but as soon as she had means of her own, she did."

"Means? Means!" he spat. "Yes, like you she also turned her back on me. Took her inheritance and squandered it on that bloody monstrosity in Sussex Place and a year's travel. A woman — on her own — opprobrious conduct. But she'd already showed her true colours when she decided to become a veterinary surgeon. The shame of it!"

"The shame; to earn her own wages in an honoured profession rather than eke out a meagre existence as some," I regarded the room around us, "cut-throat plutocrat's wife." He started forward. I thought he was going to strike me, but I held my ground. "I ask you again, what happened to Ellen?"

His anger vanished. "When she moved into her house, I had little to do with her. She'd visit here each month out of courtesy, but that was all. I was informed by a grubby policeman that she had fallen off her horse while riding in Regent's Park. She broke her neck." He shrugged. "She left money for her own funeral arrangements, and appointed you as her executor. You weren't here, as usual, so I arranged for her burial in St James' Church. Her solicitors are seeing to the rest. That is all." His eyes were focused on some point in the distance, or perhaps nowhere at all.

"Was there an inquest?" I asked.

"An inquest? Yes, there was."

"Why?"

"Why? Why!" The vehemence returned as quickly as it had abated. "What the devil has it got to do with you! Do you think you can barge in here, some trumped up police official from the back of beyond, and question my actions? I treat my children properly, even if they don't return the compliment."

"What about me?"

"You are no longer my son! You call me a cut-throat plutocrat as if it were something to be ashamed of. I am a plutocrat, and I am proud of it. *You* should be proud of it. Thirty years ago I cut loose of the civil service and risked everything I had as an entrepreneur. When you were born I was working sixteen hours a day, seven days a week, just to stay in business. I built my company from nothing to one of the most successful on the Clydebank. I built it with my own sweat and toil. I made enough money to send you to one of the foremost schools in England, and your sister to the University of Glasgow, even if it was against my wishes.

"Now — now — " thick spittle formed at the corner of his mouth, "do you know who my last visitor was? The Earl of Rosebery. Yes, that's right, the former Prime Minister. He is a neighbour of mine and I am honoured to receive him as my guest from time to time. This house! Do you know who lived here? Baron Clive of Plassey. Clive of India, one of the Empire's greatest heroes. All of this I made on my own. And when I give you a firm foundation, what do you do with it? What have you done with your life? You're a disgrace."

I swallowed my anger and pride, and spoke as evenly as I could. "What about Lieutenant Carey, have you spoken to him?"

"Why the bloody hell would I speak to him? It's the coroner's job to ask damn fool questions, not mine. I don't pay taxes so I can do some idle functionary's job for him! Now get out." He walked over to his desk, limping and stooped, and pressed a buzzer.

I stared at him for three seconds, turned, and left. The butler was on his way up the stairs with two footmen. I cut through them, grabbed my hat, and slammed the door behind me.

I marched out into Berkeley Square as thunder rumbled overhead, but it was silent tears — not the rain — that wet my face. As much as I despised him, there was still a small part of me that wanted to please my father and win his approval. In the moments he'd spoken of Ellen's death, I'd had a vague memory of some happier time, before the indifference and the spite. I thought of Ellen, my dear sister, and how I hadn't seen her until she'd come out to Natal in 'ninety-nine. It was the second time I'd been called a disgrace today, and my father and Miss Paterson were right. I could've returned to visit Ellen, even if I'd been determined never to set foot in my father's house again. If only I'd known our future together was to be so short…

Now Ellen was gone and I was too late.

I tried not to think about my father, or my failings, as I walked back to Piccadilly. The only thing I could do for Ellen now was find out what had really happened. Even though I reckoned Miss Paterson was seeking some sort of natural justice or emotional closure that didn't exist, I owed it to her and Ellen to discover the truth. I was soaked through by the time I reached the Windsor.

There were no messages for me, so I bathed, dressed, and fixed upon a plan of action for the evening. I took a table as soon as the hotel restaurant opened at six-thirty, and decided to restrict myself to three courses. The waiter had just placed the first in front of me when a big, muscular man burst into the dining-room. He was clean-shaven with a long, thin scar that began above his left eye, and cut diagonally through the eyebrow to the bridge of his nose. It was clearly from a knife. He hadn't bothered to remove his brown bowler hat. His eyes scoured the room until they settled on me. At that instant one of the attendants accosted him, but he shrugged the man off and made directly for my table. As he came closer I noticed a piece of his right ear was missing, bitten off by the look of the jagged outline.

I put down my knife and fork, dabbed my moustache with my napkin, and pushed my chair back a little. "May I help you, sir?"

"Major Marshall?"

"I am."

"Come with me." It was an order, not a request.

"You're from Scotland Yard?"

He nodded. "Yeah. We just found Lowenstein. He's dead. Someone bashed his head in."

4. Murder in Bohemia

"Don't spare the horse this time," the detective snarled at the driver as we climbed aboard the cab.

We set off.

"You have me at a disadvantage, sir."

"Name's Truegood. Let's cut the chaff, Major. I don't care if you are a war hero, I don't want you getting in my way any more than I want a case of Cupid's. Mr M told me you're on the payroll and said to take you, so that's what I'm doing."

Offensive as he was, I had little to gain from aggravating him. "You're one of Superintendent Melville's inspectors?"

"That's what I said."

"Where was Lowenstein found?"

"A lodging-house in Tottenham Street."

"Where's that?" I asked.

"I thought you were supposed to have lived in London? Near Fitzroy Square. The area is full of Chartists, anarchists, a few harmless socialists — our very own Bohemia."

"When was his body found?"

"Five o'clock. You going to ask questions all the way?"

I was not. I took out my watch and calculated that we had less than two hours of daylight left. Even if the premises had electric lighting, natural light is always preferable when conducting a minute examination. The traffic thinned out after we left Leicester Square, we made good progress up Charing Cross, and then drove along soot-stained Tottenham Court Road. The driver took the next left after Goodge Street, and pulled up outside 18 Tottenham Street, a third-rate Georgian terraced house next to a tobacconist's. A uniformed police constable was standing sentry, and the front door was open.

Truegood alighted from the cab with a Gladstone bag, dismissed the driver, and acknowledged the constable's salute with a grunt. He led the way into a cramped entrance hall which had barely enough space for a narrow flight of stairs and a passage between two interior doors. He halted and bellowed, "Sergeant Aitken!"

"Inspector Truegood, sir? Up here, sir; upstairs, right to the top." A face appeared briefly over the banister above.

We ascended the three flights of stairs to the third floor, where Aitken, a clean-shaven man with a scarred chin, waited with another uniformed constable. "Evening, sir. I'm Sergeant Aitken, D Division CID. The deceased were lodging under the name Otto Isaacs, but I found these documents indicating otherwise." He pulled a sheaf of folded papers from his coat pocket. "They was — "

Truegood snatched them from him. "I suppose you and your constables have been tramping all over the scene like a herd of bloody great elephants!"

"No, sir! Constable Smith secured the room as soon as he established Lowenstein were dead. I had a quick look, but as soon as I found those documents and saw the name, I sent for the Yard — and the police surgeon."

"Who else lives here?" Truegood asked as he leafed through the papers. I noted he touched each one in exactly the same place.

"The landlady and her daughter, and a Russian couple. They're all in their rooms waiting for you, and I've got a constable at the front and back to make sure no one comes or goes."

Truegood knelt and opened the Gladstone. One of the compartments held envelopes and folded paper bags of various sizes; he placed the documents in another, which was empty. "Where were these?"

"In the bedroom, sir. Under the lifted floorboard. You can't miss it."

Truegood closed the bag, and stood. "You just told me you hadn't disturbed the scene of the offence."

"I haven't, sir, the floorboard were like that when I found it."

"The body was discovered at five o'clock?"

"Just after, sir."

"Right. Go keep an eye on these witnesses for me. This is Major Marshall, a private agent. Collins should be here shortly. Show him up as soon as he arrives."

"Yes, sir." Aitken and the constable left us.

"Don't touch anything," growled Truegood as we entered the sitting-room.

The chamber was about fifteen feet square, sparsely furnished and ill-maintained. A man lay prone on the floor between a sofa and an upended kneehole table. His right temple had been smashed with a heavy, blunt object. The grey clay of his brain was visible where it had been pierced with bloody splinters from his skull. Thick, cranial blood was mixed with clear cerebrospinal fluid in his hair, down his right cheek, and had formed a dried pool on the rug beneath him.

Truegood put his bag and hat on the sideboard and glanced around the room, as if fixing the co-ordinates of a map in his mind. Then he walked over to the body and knelt down next to it, careful to avoid the blood. "Right, we're going to turn him over — that way, away from the claret. Hold on a minute!" He produced a piece of chalk and carefully marked four places on the floor: the top of Lowenstein's head, Lowenstein's left shoulder, and the two points where the table touched the ground. When he'd finished, he moved the table away.

We rolled Lowenstein onto his back. His body was cold to the touch and he was as rigid as the floorboards. As we set him down his right eyeball swung free from its socket. It appeared he had been struck at least twice, and one of the blows had dislodged his eye. The eyeball hung on his right cheek, an inch of optic nerve connecting the bulb to the bloody hole. It looked as if a parasite had thrust its way out from his brain to feed on the blood covering his face. Lowenstein was a tall, emaciated young man in his late twenties. He was dressed in his shirtsleeves, without a collar attached. His clothes and shoes were of the finest quality, but worn and dirty.

Truegood began searching his pockets. Without looking up at me he asked, "What do you think you're doing?"

"Sketching the scene of the offence," I replied, pencil and notebook in hand. "Don't be prancing about yet, there's been enough of that already."

"I won't. I'll estimate."

He grunted, withdrew a magnifying glass from inside his coat, and began a minute examination of the corpse. I was impressed. The quality of detection still varied greatly throughout the Empire police forces, and I hadn't been sure what to expect. In Pitsani I'd been largely left to my own devices, but with the assistance of Drayton, had read as widely as possible in the field of medical jurisprudence. When I'd moved to Durban, I'd found Superintendent Alexander a thorough and meticulous detective who'd refined the lessons I'd learned from Dr Gross' *Criminal Investigation*. I'd lost touch with developments during the war, although I'd heard that Francis Galton's *Finger Prints* was being regarded with new respect.

While Truegood scrutinised Lowenstein's mortal remains, I continued my sketch and reflected on what I knew of the deceased. Eric Lowenstein was a confidential clerk with Wernher, Beit & Co, in Cape Town. He was a trusted employee of the director, Alfred Beit, one of the South African 'goldbugs'. Beit had been a business partner of Rhodes, a joint director of the British South Africa Company, De Beers, Rand Mines and various other enterprises. Like Rhodes, he had suffered a temporary setback in his fortunes when he was implicated in the Jameson Raid, but was still a powerful and influential individual; even more so, now that Rhodes was dead. Lowenstein was one of the two witnesses to the last amendment Rhodes had made to his will in March. He had returned to London in April, and was reported missing several weeks later.

Truegood finished examining the body, and began moving around it in an ever-increasing radius.

"Do you want me to start searching?" I asked.

"Yeah."

I removed my hat and coat, and rolled up my sleeves. Beginning with the bedroom door, I moved around the walls and furniture in an anti-clockwise direction. A wing chair with arms rubbed smooth sat in a corner. There was only one other chair in the room, under a scratched old dining table which obviously doubled as a writing desk. It wasn't difficult to deduce that Lowenstein hadn't received many — or any — callers. I looked back at the body. For someone who'd just spent several years in the Cape Colony, his skin was very pale. I wondered how often he'd left his rooms. I found eight cigarette butts in the fireplace, all of the same type. I continued around to the tortoise stove and the windows. The drapes were pulled open, but the windows fastened down with hasps. I scrutinised the table, chair, and gas-lamp. Underneath the table there was a large stack of old newspapers. They were all halfpenny *Daily Mails*, every issue from yesterday right back to the sixth of May.

Truegood was at the sideboard.

"Anything?" I asked.

"Some hairs, fibres. Probably belong to Lowenstein." He jerked his head towards the other room.

I retrieved my notebook and pencil, and followed.

The bedchamber was just over half the size of the sitting-room, and also without a carpet. Other than the bed there was a single chest of drawers, a wardrobe and a washstand. All four items were in a state of disrepair. In between the bed and the wardrobe part of a floorboard had been lifted, and in the cavity beneath was a large quantity of coins and notes. Lowenstein's pocket-watch, gold-plated, lay on top of the chest of drawers. Truegood knelt to examine the money, but didn't touch it. He pulled an empty chamber pot from under the bed. Then he opened the wardrobe to reveal a brown morning coat and waistcoat that matched the trousers Lowenstein was wearing, a creased white shirt and an empty portmanteau. The chest of drawers contained two night-shirts, a few toiletries and a half-full carton of cigarettes. They were ready-made, but cheap, the same as those in the grate.

"Likes to travel light, our friend," Truegood muttered to himself. He turned to me. "Finished?"

"Yes."

"Then let's see if you're worth whatever Mr M's paying you." He pushed past me into the sitting-room. "Tell me what happened."

I dressed without hurrying and then positioned myself behind the sofa. "Lowenstein was sitting here. He was struck in the temple from behind," I made a chopping motion with my right hand, "by a man who was right-handed. He toppled forward, knocking the table over. He would have been stunned, or perhaps even unconscious. His assailant then walked around," I moved towards the window, "probably this way, and administered the *coup de grace*. One — no, two — more strikes to the same area. The weapon was small, blunt, and heavy. Perhaps a hammer, or the grip of a very heavy stick. Lowenstein must have known the murderer because — "

"They usually do," Truegood interrupted. There was a noise from the stairs, and he left, returning a few seconds later with an elderly gentleman wearing a top hat and frock coat. His long, jowly face was framed by untidy wisps of white hair. His deep-set eyes were doleful and my impression was of a basset hound in human shape. "This is Major Marshall, Doc. He's working for Mr M."

"Is he?" The doctor raised his eyebrows.

I extended my hand. "Alec Marshall, pleased to meet you, Doctor."

"John Maycock, how do you do?"

"I've turned the body over, but I'd appreciate it if you didn't move anything until Collins has finished," Truegood cut in.

"You've called Collins, have you?"

"Yeah. I'll send Aitken up to lend you a hand, if need be."

"Will you be requiring a post-mortem examination on this one?" Maycock asked.

"Yeah, I will."

"I'll see to it first thing tomorrow if you like."

"Much appreciated, Doc."

"You'll be attending?"

"No. We aren't half busy at the moment, I haven't got time. I'll leave you to it." Truegood picked up his hat and bag, and we left the doctor.

Aitken was ascending the stairs with another detective. Aitken carried a bulky portable camera, while the other chap struggled with a tripod-mounted model.

"The doc's just arrived, Collins," rapped out Truegood. "Let him finish and then photograph everything. Everything. Both rooms, all angles. Got it?"

"Evening, sir," Collins replied, slightly out of breath from the climb. "Are there any fingerprints?"

"No, but I still want the photographs. And I want it photographed exactly as I found it. I'll show you." He led Collins into the sitting-room, leaving Aitken and me on the landing.

"The constable who found the body is to be commended," I said. "He did well not to disturb the scene of the offence."

"I'll be sure to pass that on, sir."

Truegood returned, tossing his bag to Aitken. "Give the doc and Collins whatever help they need. When Collins is finished, put the money under the floorboard in one of the evidence bags. Make sure you seal and label it. Got it?"

"Yes, sir."

"Then arrange for the removal of the body. Got it?"

"Yes, sir."

"Once the dearly departed is gone, I want you to tear the place apart."

"Sir?"

"You heard me. Tear the place to pieces. Lowenstein hid his money and his personal papers. Maybe he hid something else as well. Check the floorboards, the walls, everything. Got it?"

"Yes, sir."

"Right. Who lives here?"

"Mrs Curran and her daughter downstairs. The Russians are on the floor below, a Mr and Mrs Ilyin."

Truegood turned to me. "Come on."

I followed him down the stairs. "If you were going to have the offence-scene photographed, why did you let me make a sketch?"

"You never know with the photographs. They don't always come out too clear."

"Do you photograph all offence-scenes?" I asked, impressed once again.

"No. Collins works for the Fingerprint Branch. Always use them if they're available. Our chief's mad about it. You haven't heard of the Galton-Henry classification?"

"No, but I've read Galton's book."

Truegood looked at me as if I was a complete fool. "That's fifteen years old. Mr Henry's refined his system, but I'm not giving lessons."

One of the constables was waiting on the landing below us. Truegood shot me another look. "Don't ask any questions — that's my job." He knocked once on the door and flung it open.

5. The Penang Lawyer

Mrs Curran was up and at him immediately. "This is an absolute outrage, Inspector! Here my young child and I are, victims of violence, and we're being treated like prisoners in my own home. I must protest — "

"Sit down and shut up. You're both suspects and if you don't tell me what I want to know sharpish, you'll find yourselves in quod proper."

She was a slovenly, bulky woman, and she sat on the divan instantly — joining her daughter, who was about fifteen years old and unwashed. The room was much better furnished than the one above, and boasted a carpet, although there were still damp patches on the walls. I took out my notebook and repaired to a wing chair to record the conversation.

Truegood nodded his approval and remained standing. "Start at the beginning. Tell us everything you know about your lodger. Don't leave anything out because my colleague is writing down every single word. If you lie to me — or forget to tell me anything — it'll be a night in quod for you. Got it?"

She nodded, and began. "Mr Isaacs came to me on Monday the fifth of May. He'd seen my advertisement in the newspaper and wanted to rent the rooms. Only he wanted them on his own terms — which they were peculiar — but he was prepared to pay a fair price for them."

"What were his terms?"

"He didn't want the first floor rooms. He only wanted the top floor, even though it's a bit smaller. I told him the Ilyins was already there, but he offered me sixty pounds for three months' rent. I moved the Ilyins downstairs. What else could a poor woman in reduced circumstances do? I should have charged them more for the extra space. Too generous by far, that's me, Inspector, I can tell you —"

"Get on with it."

"That wasn't all. He told me he liked his privacy. He wanted all his meals served in his room, and didn't want me giving his name to anyone what came asking. I offered him a key to the front door, but he didn't want none. And do you know what? He never left the house did Mr Isaacs, so he didn't. Not once since he's been here. He hardly even left his rooms except to make use of the... facilities... downstairs. I told him that if he thought he was going to lock himself away, he couldn't expect to keep me out, so Lizzie went in every other day to sweep and clean.

"Mr Isaacs stopped taking breakfast after a while, but he didn't ask for any money back, so I didn't mind none. I work my fingers to the bone running this household, Inspector; I have to take every chance I can get to make a few pennies. Lizzie took him up his dinner at midday, with a cup of coffee. I'm sure he only left his bedroom then. Sometimes, late at night, we could hear him pacing around above us. But I could never be sure because *my* house is in a good state of repair — not like some — and *my* floorboards don't creak very much. Also, the neighbours," she pointed towards the fireplace, "aren't gentlefolk like I take in here. They're forever shouting and screaming into the night. Foxed half the time... now, where was I?"

"You said Mr Isaacs paid you three months' rent in advance on the fifth of May. Is that right?" I asked.

Truegood glared at me — opened his mouth — then changed his mind.

"Yes, sir, that's what he did."

"He was due to pay you again, yesterday?"

"No, sir, he paid me two weeks ago. He paid twenty-two pounds for another month on top of the three. He said the extra two was for keeping a quiet about his being here, and that if I carried on keeping a quiet, there'd be plenty more where that came from."

"Did anything else out of the ordinary happen between May and last night?" asked Truegood.

"Not at all. He had his queer ways, but it weren't for me to say nothing."

"Did anyone ask about him?"

"Not until yesterday, they didn't."

"Who was it?"

"He didn't leave his name. He was dressed like a gent, but I know a wrong 'un when I see one, and he were a wrong 'un. He asked if a Mr Lowenstein was living here. When I said no, he said the gentleman might be using another name, and gave a description of Mr Isaacs. But I didn't tell him nothing. Mr Isaacs paid me good money to keep my mouth shut and I'm not one to tell a tale or gossip with strangers."

"What did he look like, this wrong 'un?"

"Smart dressed. Short, with one of them horseshoe moustaches in brown. Oh, and he had a gold tooth," she grimaced to reveal a gap in her own teeth, and jabbed at it, "right there."

"What time was that?"

"I'm not sure. Before dinner. Late morning, I think."

"What happened next?"

"What do you mean what happened next? Nothing. I told him to be on his way, and he went."

"I saw the gent with the gold tooth," Lizzie piped up for the first time.

"Lizzie, you didn't tell me about that!"

"Let her talk. Tell us what happened, Lizzie."

"It were after lunch. I was hanging out the washing and I saw the gentleman walking in the street behind. He tipped his hat and said good afternoon. I said good afternoon back and went inside. But I remember him because when he smiled I could see the gold in his tooth."

"Lizzie, I really wish you wouldn't flirt with gentlemen so, you're not nearly old enough. No good will come of it — "

"Did you speak to this man?" Truegood asked the girl.

"I said good afternoon, that was all."

"He didn't ask you anything?"

"No, sir."

"Did anything else out of the ordinary happen yesterday?" Truegood resumed questioning the landlady.

"No, Inspector, it didn't. I s'pose you wants to know about last night and I came to find the… body?"

"Go on."

"Some time after Lizzie and I was asleep — unfortunately I'm forced to share with my daughter and rent both of the other floors — a time after midnight and before dawn, I woke up with the noise of talking and footsteps. I couldn't be sure because like I said the neighbours is wont to make all sorts of racket at ungodly hours. Then I must have just dropped off again, when I heard a noise. I don't know what it were, but it were loud. After that there was some more footsteps and I were thinking about getting up to find out what was going on, when I fell back to sleep. And thank the Lord. I might have been murdered just like Mr Isaacs!"

"When did you discover he was dead?"

"Lizzie took up his dinner and coffee and knocked on his door. He quite often doesn't open up right away, in which case she just sits it on the floor. She came back later and saw it hadn't been touched. I thought it were strange: because he doesn't have breakfast, he almost always eats his dinner. Then, when I found out about the back door, I wanted to know who was responsible, so I came up myself. That was —"

"The back door?" Truegood interrupted.

"Yes. When I got up this morning, I found the back door — the kitchen door — unlocked. Obviously I thought Lizzie had unlocked it before me, so I didn't say nothing. But later, in the afternoon, Lizzie asked me if I were tired from being up so early, and we realised someone had left it unlocked last night. The key was in the door, but it was unlocked. All night! I can't have that sort of thing going on in my house, so I went up to ask Mr Isaacs if he were responsible. I would've asked the Russians first, but they was both out at work. When I knocked on Mr Isaacs' door, there were no answer. I weren't going to be put off that easily, so I told him I were coming in and opened the door, and — oh, the shock to my poor heart — a murder under my own roof!"

"You went inside?" asked Truegood.

"I didn't dare. As soon as I saw him lying there with all the blood, I screamed. I nearly swooned, but Lizzie took me away — didn't you, girl?"

"You called for the police and no one went in until the constable arrived?"

"That's right."

"Lizzie, did you go in?"

"No, sir, it was awful. I didn't want to go into a room with no dead person."

I guessed that they were both telling the truth. Even the most cursory search of Lowenstein's rooms would have revealed the small fortune buried in the floor, and I couldn't imagine much of it being left by the time the constable arrived had these two been in the room.

"That was about four o'clock, was it?"

"No, later than that; about five o'clock."

"Was his door locked?"

"No." Mrs Curran shook her head.

"When was the last time either of you saw Mr Isaacs alive?"

"I told you I heard him pacing about last night, he — "

"*Saw*, Mrs Curran. When was the last time you or Lizzie saw him alive?"

"That was me," said Lizzie, pleased to be the centre of attention again. "I saw him when I took him his tea yesterday evening."

"What time was that?"

"Six o'clock."

"Did he eat it?"

"Why yes, sir," she replied, looking confused.

"The other lodgers — the Ilyins — how long have they been living here?" Truegood asked Mrs Curran.

"Since the beginning of the year, the end of January."

"Did Mr Isaacs talk to them?"

"No. Only just so as to say good morning — or good evening, or the like — if he passed them on the stairs and such."

"No one else asked for Mr Isaacs or a Mr Lowenstein while he was here?"

"No one."

"And nothing out of the ordinary happened since Mr Isaacs rented your rooms? Think before you answer. You too, Lizzie."

They both shook their heads. Truegood looked at me. I was surprised by the courtesy. "You said that Mr Isaacs never left the premises, Mrs Curran. Is that right?"

"Yes, sir. Not since he walked in here at the beginning of May with just that little travelling case."

I looked at Lizzie. "You didn't see him leave, either?" She shook her head, more emphatically this time. "Mr Isaacs smoked cigarettes. Surely he must have stepped out to the tobacconist's to replenish his supply?"

"He never left the house, sir. His tobacco and all his sundries and etceteras he sent the boy for."

"The boy?"

"Harry. A young lad from across the road. He helps me and Lizzie out during the week."

"Go and fetch him for me, Lizzie," said Truegood. "We'll speak to him downstairs. We'll talk again later, Mrs Curran. Don't leave the house in the mean time." She muttered a protest as we left.

We escorted Lizzie out, and Truegood spoke the constable on guard. Dr Maycock met us on his way down. "Right, Doc, what can you tell me?"

"As I've said before, this is not yet an exact science, but given the temperature of the body and the fact that rigor mortis is still present, my estimate is that he was killed twelve to thirty-six hours ago. Yes, yes, Truegood, I know what you're like, so I'll make an educated guess before you badger me... twelve to eighteen hours... but I'll not commit to that. He was struck from behind with a heavy, blunt object. It appears that he fell in the same position you marked with the chalk. He was probably insensible. He was then struck either two or three more times — I can't be certain at present. One of the blows cracked the zygomatic bone, forcing the bulb from the orbital cavity. I should be able to tell you more after the post-mortem."

"Thanks, Doc."

"Good evening, gentlemen." Dr Maycock continued his egress.

"Are you going to question the Russians next?" I asked Truegood.

"Yeah, why?"

"I'll join you shortly. I'm going to have a look outside while it's still light."

Truegood grunted again and I left him on the first floor landing as I followed the doctor out of the front door. There were three steps down to the pavement, with no front garden, and no external access to the cellar or coal hole. Mrs Curran's establishment was a mid-terrace, with a dingy tobacconist's — White & Son — at number twenty and another private residence at number sixteen. I greeted the constable as I crossed the road for a better look. Most of the houses on the street were residential, with the exception of the tobacconist's, a public house called the Three Compasses, and a tiny bookshop on the corner of Whitfield Street. I looked up at the three pairs of windows above the ground floor: Mr and Mrs Ilyin, Mrs Curran and Lizzie, and Lowenstein.

As I re-entered the house, the mortuary wagon arrived with two attendants. I examined the front door lock, and found no signs of tampering. I ignored the stairs to the cellar and explored the three rooms on the ground floor, a kitchen, a bathroom and a water closet. The key was in the back door, in the kitchen. I turned it a couple of times. It was well oiled and made very little noise. Once again, there was no sign that the lock had been forced. The garden was a small rectangle with the same air of neglect as the inside of the house. Three low brick walls of just over waist height marked the boundaries. The rear of White & Son was piled high with packing crates. The garden on the other side was overgrown, with two trees obscuring much of the view. I crouched next to the dustbin and examined the ground for traces of footprints. Another constable was talking to a woman in the narrow lane behind. The row of houses opposite were all of a similar type, also backing onto the alleyway. All those I could see appeared residential.

There was a very faint impression where the grass had been trodden recently.

The constable saw me. "Good evening, sir. Would you be with the inspector?"

"I am indeed, Constable. Major Marshall."

"Very good, sir." He threw up a salute.

"Did you pass this way?"

"Yes, sir. Sergeant Aitken sent me to secure the rear of the premises."

"What size boot do you take?"

He blinked his incomprehension, and then discipline took over. "Size eight, sir."

"Thank you." As I'd suspected, the footprints were his. The ground was too hard to retain impressions visible to the naked eye, and the blades of grass would have resumed their positions had the track not been very recent. I kept my eyes low as I made my way to the far wall, but found nothing else. I observed the premises from the rear, but there was nothing of immediate significance, except that I realised an intruder would have to have entered through either the front or the back door. A climb was out of the question. The kitchen door would be the obvious choice, and had been used according to Mrs Curran's evidence. I looked over the rear wall into the alley, also without result.

I retraced my steps and stopped next to the dustbin. It was a large metal receptacle fastened with a catch, but unlocked. I opened the catch and lifted the lid. Inside, on top of the ash, was a heavy, black stick of the kind known as a penang lawyer.

The rounded silver grip was covered with dried blood.

6. What the Boy Said

I took out my handkerchief and used it in lifting the stick, holding it at a point about three inches from the grip. It was heavy, with a flattened silver knob for a handle, and an iron ferrule at the bottom. The wood was from the stem of a miniature palm, hardened by fire and polished smooth. I blew some of the ash from the upper part. The silver had an 'A' embossed on it, and the ferrule was worn. I twisted my hand to and fro and examined the wood immediately under the head. There were two fine black hairs stuck in the blood. There was also evidence that the head had been removed — probably to hollow and weight the stick with melted lead — and replaced. I estimated the total length at just over thirty inches.

I closed the dustbin and took the penang lawyer upstairs to Aitken, requesting he look after it until Truegood was ready. Then I went back down to the first floor and entered the Ilyins' sitting-room, which was just like Lowenstein's. The Russians were in their late thirties, both grim-faced and haggard; Mr Ilyin wore a black beard and thick spectacles, and the extreme pallor of Mrs Ilyin's skin was heightened by her pitch-black hair. Truegood was standing in front of the fireplace, while they sat huddled together on the sofa.

"That's what I said. I'm not interested in the Autonomie Club, or your leaflets, or any of that. I want to know what happened here last night."

"But we know nothing of this," said Mr Ilyin.

"You don't seem to understand, Lischinsky. I'm not interested in you and your anarchist friends at the moment — but that could all change if you don't cooperate. I'll make life very difficult for you and your mates — you know I don't make idle threats. I might start with that printer's in Little Goodge Street, or maybe even the grocers in Charlotte Street. The one where your sister works."

Mrs Ilyin — or Miss Lischinsky, or whoever she was — turned to Lischinsky and rattled off a short tirade in Russian. The only word I recognised was 'Melville'.

"On the other hand, I might just speak to a pal of mine in the Okhrana. We all know they have men in London, and how difficult it is to protect those enclaves that refuse to co-operate with the police..."

The Lischinskys looked at one another in fear, and the brother said to Truegood: "We live here because we know we are safe from the Tsarist oppressors, Chief Investigator. We have no wish to bring trouble upon ourselves. Both my sister and I slept soundly last night. We did not hear anything. We did not know anything of the murder until this evening."

"What about you?" Truegood pointed at the woman. "What have you got to say?"

She shook her head, and when she spoke her accent was much thicker than her brother's. "Nothing, sir. I know nothing of what happened."

"You never spoke to Mr Isaacs?" Truegood stabbed at Lischinsky.

"No, sir, I did not. He was a private individual. My sister and I respected his privacy, and did not encourage any conversation beyond common courtesy."

"Right, make sure neither of you leaves here without a forwarding address. Got it?"

"Yes, I have got it."

Truegood jerked his head towards the door and I left. He joined me on the landing. "I found the murder weapon in the dustbin. A penang lawyer, weighted with lead. It's upstairs with Aitken."

"Just like that, in the dustbin?"

"Take a look for yourself. The silver head is covered in blood, and there are hairs stuck in it. Black hairs, which I'm sure analysis will show to be Lowenstein's."

Truegood was unimpressed.

At that moment Lizzie came running up the stairs. "Harry's here. He's waiting in the kitchen."

"We'll get back to the stick." Truegood followed the girl. A scruffy lad of about twelve was waiting in the kitchen with his cap held in both hands.

Truegood smiled for the first time since I'd met him. "Young Harold?"

"Yessir. Good evenin', sirs, Lizzie said youse wanted a word with me."

Truegood took a shilling from his pocket and began rolling it over the back of his thick fingers. Harry's head moved forward, his eyes transfixed by the progress of the coin. Truegood suddenly closed his fist over it. "Harry!"

"Yessir!"

"You did for Mr Isaacs, the gentleman who lived on the top floor, didn't you?"

"Yessir. 'e sent me out to get 'is things for 'im twice a week. Mostly twice a week, but sometimes only once."

"Where did he send you?"

"The tobacconist's, the chemist, and the post office, sir. I got 'im whatever 'e asked for, sir."

"How often did you go to the post office?" I asked before Truegood could say anything.

"Er… five times, sir. I thinks."

"What did you do there?"

"I posted 'is letters for 'im, sir. Is it true 'e were murdered, sir? It's a right shame, cos 'e were a real gennelman — always gave me a good tip, 'e did." He was talking to me, but looking at Truegood's fist.

I removed a shilling from my own pocket. "Harry!"

"Yessir!"

"You said Mr Isaacs sent you to the post office five times?"

"Yessir."

I kept the coin visible between thumb and forefinger. "Can you remember when he sent you, and what you posted for him?"

"Nossir. Yessir. I can't remember when, except that the last time were about three weeks ago. But I know what I posted."

"And what was that?"

"Just one letter, sir."

"One letter on each occasion?"

"Yessir."

"Can you remember any of the names or addresses on the letters?" Unlikely, but worth a try.

"Yessir. Nossir. I can't remember the addresses, but I can remember the names on all of them."

"All of them?" Perhaps my second shilling hadn't been such a good idea.

"Yessir. It were the same name on all of them, and I remembered it cos it were funny."

I tossed him my coin. "And what was it?"

"*Road*, sir. It were road, just like the road what we walks on. But it 'ad lots of letters before and after it, what I didn't understand. I don't read so good since I left school…"

Truegood was weaving the shilling through his fingers again, but didn't appear to have reacted to the boy's statement. I took out my notebook and pencil, found a blank page, and wrote: *Col. F.W. Rhodes, D.S.O.* "Did it look anything like that?"

"Yessir. That were it exactly."

"Colonel Frank Rhodes," I said to Truegood. Rhodes' oldest brother, Francis William, was also a celebrity. I'd met him in Ladysmith, during the siege, at the beginning of the war.

Truegood nodded and tossed Harry the second shilling. "We might want to ask you some more questions later, Harry. Where do you live?"

"Across the street, sir. Number twenty-one."

"Off you go then, son."

"Thank you, sir. Thank you, sir." He dashed from the room, banging the front door closed as he left the house.

"Time to get back to the Yard," Truegood said, "so you better show me this stick."

We went up to the top floor, passing Collins en route. He was heaving his equipment down the stairs on his own. "All done, sir. Do you want them sent to your office when they're ready?"

"No, you'd better send them direct to Mr M."

"Right you are, sir."

Aitken and the constable had begun their search. Truegood took only a quick look at the weapon before placing it inside one of his paper bags. He secured it with a piece of string and attached a label to it. He gave Aitken several more instructions, confirmed that Lowenstein's money was in the Gladstone, and took the bag and the covered stick with him. The two attendants from the mortuary entered the house as we walked out into the night. A short walk brought us to Tottenham Court Road, where I hailed a cab. Truegood was silent throughout the journey. The driver stopped on the Embankment; we alighted, and I paid and dismissed him.

Truegood said, "We need to talk," and stomped off into police headquarters. It was after ten o'clock and, except for two guards, the building was deserted. Truegood had to unlock several doors and switch on electric lights as we went. Our destination was an office about the same size as Melville's, but apparently shared by at least four detectives.

I pulled out a chair as Truegood made space on his desk, set down his bag, and removed the penang lawyer from its covering. Then he took an unlabelled bottle of whisky and two dusty glasses from a cabinet. He poured us each a generous measure, resumed his seat, and took a long swallow.

"Mr M obviously trusts you, Marshall, and you seem to know what you're doing, so I'll agree to pool our resources at the moment." He raised a cautionary finger. "Only because I haven't got the men I need to investigate this…and because of Mr M."

I took a sip of the whisky. It wasn't bad.

"Tell me what you deduced from the crime scene," he asked.

"Lowenstein was obviously in fear for his life, very possibly in connection with Rhodes' will. Three months ago he went into hiding. He adopted the name Isaacs and never left the house — not even to go to the tobacconist's, even though it was only next door. His murder shows his fear was justified. He took three months lodging in Mrs Curran's anonymous establishment, and sent letters to Colonel Rhodes — perhaps for assistance of some sort. Whatever his plan was — if he had one — it obviously didn't work, because he found himself there for longer than the three months."

I paused to take another sip of whisky.

"Yesterday, someone caught up with him. Perhaps the murderer or a private detective making inquiries. Somehow the man discovered where Lowenstein was. The girl could have given it away, or he could have seen him at the window from the back — it doesn't matter. Early this morning, the murderer gained access to the premises. Again, I'm not quite sure how, but he entered and went up to Lowenstein's room without disturbing the household. Not only was he known to Lowenstein, but the clerk didn't consider his visitor a physical threat — he would have tried to raise the alarm in either case. At some point the murderer hit him in the temple with that." I pointed to the stick. "He must have made a search of the rooms to find Lowenstein's papers and money, although he was apparently not interested in the latter. You haven't told me what those documents were, or how much money there was."

"Thirty-seven pounds, eight shillings, and four and a half pence. I haven't examined them in any great detail, but the documents appear to be a letter of appointment from a manager at Wernher, Beit and Company dated 1896, and correspondence with a Miss Crawford beginning two years ago. The most recent was a letter from his parents, who live in Kimberley, wherever that is. It was dated the end of March, and mentioned Rhodes' death."

"Kimberley is a diamond mining town in the Cape Colony. It's where Rhodes made his first fortune. Were the letters all addressed to Lowenstein in Cape Town?"

"Yeah."

"I know he went into hiding in the first week of May, but remind me when he arrived in England," I asked.

"The end of April. Hold on." Truegood rummaged through the folders and papers on his desk until he found the right one. "Yeah, the twenty-sixth of April."

"He wasn't here very long before he went into hiding. To return to the crime: the murderer found the money and documents, and possibly removed one or more of the latter. Then he left the house by the back door, decided he didn't want to walk the streets with a bloodied stick, and deposited the weapon in the dustbin. He probably hopped over the wall into the back-alley, and made good his escape on foot. Unless that's what we're meant to believe, and it was in fact the Ilyins — the Russians — who manufactured the scene of the offence to lead us astray."

"Don't concern yourself with Grigor and Varya Lischinsky."

"Why not?"

"They're anarchists, on our watch list."

I shrugged. "Lowenstein could have taken a liking to the lady, and the brother might have been jealous. Most murders are committed by friends or family of the victim —"

"I'm well aware of criminal procedure and theory, thank you," Truegood cut me off, "but it's bloody unlikely. We suspect them of being Okhrana agents, planted to infiltrate the expatriate anarchist community. I doubt they would draw attention to themselves like this. Not unless they wanted to end up the same way, either at the hands of the nihilists or their colleagues."

"But when you mentioned the Okhrana — "

"It's called double bluff, Marshall. The purpose of the part of the interrogation you heard was to reassure them that I didn't know they were Okhrana agents."

He obviously wasn't as stupid as he looked. "Is there anything else I should know before we continue?" I asked.

"I'm not going to tell you any more than necessary. Right now, that's it. Where would you start looking for the murderer?"

"Two places. Drayton and the weapon; Drayton has been looking for Lowenstein. Perhaps he — or an agent in his employ — found him. And the stick is a good place to start."

"Is it?" Truegood was sceptical.

"Yes. The stick tells us several things about the murderer: he is shorter than you and I, he received it as a gift some time ago from someone he was attached to and he leads a dangerous lifestyle."

"Even if you're right, it hardly narrows it down, does it? You and I are both tall, so all you've identified is a man of average height. The stick is worn, so he's had it a while. He had it weighted rather than change it for another one, so it has sentimental value to him and he needs a weapon he can carry unobtrusively. Obviously he needs a weapon, he's a bloody murderer, isn't he? What about the letter engraved on the head?"

"Either his own initial or that of the person who gave it to him."

"You're doing a great job, Marshall. Come on, drink up, let's go and feel the killer's collar now!"

I wondered how long I was going to have to put up with this. "So you don't think that finding the murder weapon is any use?"

"It's only use is in court, once we've already got hold of our villain. It won't lead us to him."

I was starting to get angry. "What will? What do you intend to do?"

"I've three leads to follow. Drayton first, then the fella that was nosing about. It sounds to me like he might be a Family man."

"A family man?"

"Local criminal fraternity. Could be Hoxton, Westminster, or the East End. I'll send Lamb round first thing tomorrow to see if he can get any more from the Currans. We'll go and see Drayton together, so you can renew your acquaintance. But before we do that, I've a job for you."

"And what's that?"

"The third lead, Colonel Rhodes."

"Do you want me to wire him?"

"No, I want you to visit him."

"I'm not going back to the Cape on some wild goose chase."

"No, you're going to the Langham Hotel."

"What for?"

"Colonel Rhodes is there. He arrived with Viscount Kitchener last month. He's in the Prince of Wales' procession on Saturday."

7. Colonel Frank Rhodes

I breakfasted even earlier on Thursday morning, in the hope of finding Colonel Rhodes before he left his hotel. Truegood had arranged an appointment with Drayton at Devonshire House for noon, and Carey had invited me to dinner at the Travellers Club for eight. I'd not intended to do anything so cordial as dine with Carey, but it seemed the most expeditious method of securing an audience. Before I left, I telephoned Miss Paterson, who very kindly agreed to meet me at Ellen's house tomorrow. I took the first cab in the queue, instructed the driver to take me to the Langham, and flicked through the morning's *Times*. I read of the King's return from Cowes, and the restoration of his health on the Isle of Wight following his emergency operation at the end of June. After waiting so long to ascend the throne, Albert — or Edward, as he chose to be crowned — had been required to delay his coronation while he convalesced.

There was no further mention of Rhodes' will.

Our progress was slow, a phenomenon I was quickly coming to expect of any horse-drawn journey through London, and my thoughts turned to Colonel Rhodes.

He'd been commissioned in the First Royal Dragoons and served with distinction in several campaigns in India and Africa. He'd also invested in diamonds and gold with his brother, and conspired in the illegal invasion of the South African Republic — more commonly known as the Jameson Raid — in the last week of 1895. Dr Jameson and Sir John Willoughby had led a column of five hundred British South Africa Company Police — which included the recently incorporated Bechuanaland Police contingent — and eight Maxim guns into the SAR. Meanwhile Colonel Rhodes had led an uprising against Paul Kruger's Boer government in Johannesburg. Four days later, after a small skirmish, Jameson surrendered. Colonel Rhodes hung on for a few more days then also capitulated, completing the farce.

Although it was never proved, it was obvious that Joseph Chamberlain — the Colonial Secretary then as now — had known about the raid, and done nothing to stop it. It had been planned by Rhodes and Beit, and was typical of the methods Rhodes employed to satisfy his lust for power and conquest. Colonel Rhodes had been released after his brother paid Kruger a heavy fine, and discharged from the army in disgrace. His bravery at Omdurman, where he had been wounded while serving as a war correspondent with Kitchener's army, had resulted in his restoration to the army list. It was rumoured that Rhodes and Kitchener had become friends, which may also have accounted for the reinstatement.

Colonel Rhodes was one of the celebrities amongst the ten thousand besieged soldiers in Ladysmith, where he was serving as a war correspondent again. He, Jameson, Sir John Willoughby, and Lord Ava had been specifically targeted by the big Boer guns. Lord Ava was killed at the Battle of Waggon Hill. He was rescued by Colonel Rhodes, but died from his wounds later. I was also wounded at Waggon Hill. I subsequently contracted enteric fever, with the result that I shared a hospital tent with Jameson, who was similarly afflicted. Although we were never formally introduced, we spent the remainder of the siege together.

Colonel Rhodes had acquitted himself well throughout the war and was very popular with the troops. I knew that his Distinguished Service Order — in contrast to those of so many aristocratic or celebrity officers — had been hard won, but I didn't approve of his family's unscrupulous pursuit of expanding their private empire. I'd joined the Bechuanaland police to keep the Queen's peace, not extend the already vast territories of a man whose ambition and greed seemed to know no bounds.

At length, I caught sight of the grandiose edifice of the Langham looming above us. Like so many of Westminster's prominent buildings, it was Georgian and constructed of light-coloured stone imported from the west country. The hotel had been styled Europe's first deluxe establishment when it was opened, and was the height of luxury with England's first hydraulic lifts. My father had always made a point of staying there before he moved to London, and I had a vague recollection of dining in one of the restaurants while I was a schoolboy. Forty years on, the Langham still held a justifiable reputation as the most sumptuous pile in London.

The driver stopped outside the imposing portico. I paid my fare, returned the doorman's greeting, and walked into an elegant foyer where the stately sense of space was magnified by a high ceiling and arched doorways. I announced myself at reception, parted with another of my cards, and was directed to wait in the equally lavish parlour. Ten minutes later an attendant arrived to tell me that Colonel Rhodes was still breakfasting and had an imminent appointment at Buckingham Palace, but could spare me a few minutes in between if I was prepared to wait. It sounded like humbug, but I acquiesced, resuming my perusal of *The Times*.

I studied the roll of officers in South Africa returning to their units from the sick list for familiar names. Half-past nine came and went and I turned my attention to the international news. By ten o'clock I knew all about the meeting of the Kaiser and the Tsar, and the German support of the Boers through the Pan-German League, amongst other organisations. I'd just started on the mail and shipping intelligence when the attendant reappeared and asked me to follow him.

I was taken to a splendid suite of rooms on the second floor. I couldn't be sure if there was a drawing room in addition to the sitting-room, but I could see a balcony overlooking Portland Place. Colonel Rhodes had changed little since I last saw him two years ago. He was hawk-faced, with a bristling moustache, close-cropped grey hair and a haughty bearing. He was shorter than me, slim and energetic for a man in his early fifties. He was wearing the dress uniform of a colonel in the Royal Dragoons: a scarlet tunic with gold shoulder cord and braid, a gold sash and waist belt and close cut blue overalls with a thick gold stripe. His throat was adorned with the Companion of the Most Honourable Order of the Bath and his chest covered with decorations. In addition to the white cross of the DSO, there were four campaign medals, with half a dozen clasps representing specific actions.

He looked me up and down, and advanced towards me.

"Good morning, Colonel Rhodes."

"The moral major," he replied. "I don't believe we've met since Ladysmith."

"No, sir, we have not."

He was standing close to me now, his mouth tight and disapproving under a moustache which was still dark. "In that case," he remarked, "allow me to congratulate you on your VC. As one of the officers present, I know you deserved the honour." He offered his hand, and we shook. "Not just for your rescue of Trooper Millar, but also your conduct during the earlier part of the battle — particularly your attempts to reach Lieutenant Hall with the Highlanders."

I was taken aback by his generosity, and mumbled, "Thank you, sir."

He turned and walked away, his manner suddenly changing. "Now, Major, it is only out of respect for your courage that I have allowed you to intrude upon my timetable today." He faced me from across the room. "As you can see I am due at the Palace to rehearse for Saturday. We both know there's no love lost between us, so state your business."

"I'm here to inform you that Mr Eric Lowenstein is dead."

"You say the name as if it should mean something to me, or refer to a gentleman of my acquaintance. It does neither."

"Mr Lowenstein was an employee of Wernher, Beit & Co, a confidential clerk. He was also one of the witnesses to your late brother's will."

"You seem to be poorly informed on all counts, Marshall. I have made my own way in the world and have nothing to do with my late brother's estate — though I naturally approve of his intentions. His desire to leave the fruits of his labour to the greater good of the British Empire is typical of the self-sacrifice he displayed throughout his regrettably short life."

"Mr Lowenstein was murdered."

Colonel Rhodes snapped, "What has that to do with me? I asked you to be succinct, but if you insist on wasting my — "

"Mr Lowenstein corresponded with you before his death. In fact, sir, you were his only correspondent. He wrote to you five times between May and July."

"You have these letters in your possession?" The corner of his mouth lifted in a sardonic smile.

"No, sir, I do not."

"The gentleman in question had a reply from me?"

"If he did, I am not aware of it."

"That is because I did not receive any letters from the gentleman — small surprise in view of the fact that we never met, and now obviously never will."

"Mr Lowenstein was in hiding at the time of his murder," I prompted.

"What of it? I had no communication from this Lowenstein, and I am unable to assist you any further with this matter, even if I were inclined to do so. And I assure you I am not."

"May I ask when you arrived in London?"

"You really are trying my patience, Marshall, but I have a sense that if I humour you for a few moments now, it might save me hours of tiresome pestering later. The matter is one of public record. I arrived with Viscount Kitchener on Saturday the twelfth of July. Now I think I've submitted myself to your meddlesome questions far beyond the extent of common decency. I bid — "

"Just one more question, please." He nodded, once. "Where were you on Wednesday morning between the hours of midnight and six o'clock?"

Colonel Rhodes flashed a malicious smile under his moustache, licking his lips like a beast about to feed. "I hope for your sake that you're in the employ of either an official body or an influential patron — otherwise you're going to find yourself in a pickle. I was a guest at the Travellers Club. I returned here at about one o'clock in the morning and retired shortly thereafter."

"With whom did you dine, sir?"

He snarled, "I expected better from an officer and a gentleman. If you wish to question me in an official capacity I suggest you return with your credentials, present them to my solicitor, and arrange a formal interview next week. Is that clear?"

"It is."

"You know, Dr Jameson could've used you in Johannesburg in 'ninety-six. Your friend was an asset, of course, but had you ridden with the doctor... Don't preach piety to me!" He waved his fist at me. "For a man who was too much of a pacifist to join our South African adventure, you took to war like a duck to water, didn't you? Don't try to deny it. I saw you the day Lord Ava was killed. I saw the hatred in your face. You weren't so fussy about killing Dutchmen then, were you?"

"Good day, Colonel," I made for the door.

"Marshall." I stopped, but didn't turn round. "Be careful, London can be just as dangerous as the veldt."

I left the Langham greatly disturbed by Colonel Rhodes' reminder of Waggon Hill. I didn't know how many Boers I'd shot during the battle, but I remembered the faces of the three I'd killed at close quarters very well. They came to me some nights when I couldn't sleep, and other nights when I could. Two men and a beardless boy. I fought to keep the images of that day, the Siege of Ladysmith, the whole war, from flooding my mind completely. I tried to concentrate on the task at hand, and I found one thing that helped me to focus on the present.

Colonel Rhodes had lied.

He'd hidden it very well, but I knew he'd received at least one of Lowenstein's letters. That was why he'd asked what proof I had. The steamers usually took twenty days from Cape Town to Southampton, which meant that Colonel Rhodes hadn't left the Cape until the last week in June. I could check the newspapers, but the exact date wasn't important. If Lowenstein had sent letters to Colonel Rhodes early in May, he would've received one or more by the time he left. Furthermore, he had no alibi, and he was the right height for the penang lawyer.

My next appointment was of far greater concern. For four years Dr Morgan Drayton and I had been as close as brothers in the Bechuanaland Protectorate. Then there'd been a parting of ways. I'd refused to work for the British South Africa Company, resigned my commission, and left for Durban. He'd thrown in his lot with Rhodes and Jameson, taken part in the Raid, fought for Rhodes in the Second Matabele War, and become Jameson's right hand man. Perhaps because we had been so close and shared so much, our parting had been anything but cordial.

It would be an interesting reunion.

8. Doctor Morgan Drayton

Truegood met me at Granges, and I gave him a summary of my interview with Colonel Rhodes as we walked along Piccadilly. When I finished, I asked if he had made any progress.

"No. Lamb and I spent the morning following up the Family man. No joy yet. Sergeant Aitken and his men are pursuing house-to-house inquiries in Tottenham Street and surrounds. Probably a waste of time, but you never know with Fitzroy. Nothing new from the post-mortem, either. Doc just confirmed what he told us yesterday."

"What about Drayton, was he happy to co-operate?"

He scowled. "I dunno if he was happy, do I? I couldn't read his expression over the bloody telephone. But he didn't give any chaff about it. And I didn't mention you, either."

"Probably a good idea."

For the second time in two days I approached the gates in the high brick wall surrounding Devonshire House. Truegood knocked on the pedestrian door. If the footman recognised me, he didn't show it. Truegood presented his card. We were escorted across the courtyard to the main entrance of the Palladian mansion, a pillared veranda underneath a balcony, which in turn was directly under an undecorated pediment. The butler admitted us and took our hats. He led us through a magnificent hall into a palatial parlour with a chandelier hanging from an ornamented rosette in the richly decorated ceiling. A landscape hung on the wall above the fireplace. I knew enough about art to identify it as the work of one of the old masters, and enough about the Duke of Devonshire to be certain it was an original.

Morgan Drayton awaited us; he seemed very much at home in the refined ostentation of his surroundings. His Savile Row morning dress was augmented with an emerald cravat, secured with a diamond pin that matched his cufflinks. He held a Russian cigarette in his long, delicate surgeon's fingers. He didn't look a day over the thirty-one years of age he'd been in 'ninety-five, when I'd last seen him. Drayton took his colouring from his Portuguese mother, his hair so black it was almost blue, and his skin pale and freckled. His waxed moustache and chin puff matched the elegance of his movements. My appearance caused only a second's hesitation before he was in front of me, hand outstretched.

"Alec, what an unexpected pleasure."

I shook his hand, and was immediately reminded of the strength in his lithe figure. "Good day, Morgan, how are you keeping?"

"Very well, thank you. Please accept my sincere condolences on the passing of Miss Marshall." He placed his left hand on my forearm.

I responded somewhat abruptly. "You knew my sister?"

"No, unfortunately not," he answered, "but I read of her terrible accident in the papers. I realised at once that the article referred to your sister, of course, a most admirable young lady. I received your card yesterday; I'm so sorry to have missed you."

I should have realised from what Miss Paterson had told me that many people who hadn't met Ellen, knew of her. "Thank you."

"And of course my congratulations on your decoration. Well done, indeed." I nodded and he shook hands with Truegood. "Good day, Inspector Truegood, I had no idea you were bringing Major Marshall along. He and I were friends in Pitsani, some years ago. May I offer either of you gentlemen a drink? Cigarette? Cigar? Then do sit down, make yourselves comfortable, and tell me what brings you to Devonshire House."

We all sat and Truegood said, "Major Marshall is assisting me with my inquiries. You don't have any objection?"

"Not at all. You've done me a great service by bringing him here."

"Have you been looking for a confidential clerk by the name of Eric Lowenstein?"

"It is no secret, Inspector. In the last week of May I employed two private inquiry agents for the purpose, Messrs Littlechild and Slater."

"Mr John Littlechild?"

"The very same. I thought you'd be familiar with Mr Littlechild, if not Mr Slater. Mr Henry Slater is a private detective with offices in Basinghall Street, in the City."

"Why do you want to find Mr Lowenstein?"

"Because he is missing, Inspector, why on earth else?" Drayton smiled affably.

Truegood stumbled; he was like a great bull that suddenly grasps that neither muleta nor matador are in front of him. "What I meant was why you as opposed to his family or friends."

"I believe his family are in the Cape Colony and I am here," Drayton smiled again and drew on his black cigarette.

"Then you're a friend of his?" Truegood persisted.

"'Colleague' would be a more accurate description. We both have associations with the late Mr Rhodes. I am private secretary to Dr Jameson, and Mr Lowenstein is a confidential clerk of Mr Beit's."

"So who asked you to look for Lowenstein?" said Truegood.

"My employer, Dr Jim."

"Why Dr Jameson and not Mr Beit?"

"As I've been in London since April, Mr Beit left the matter in Dr Jim's hands. It concerns the execution of the late Mr Rhodes' last will and testament. Due to the considerable legacy involved, there have been several delays in proving the will. Dr Jim instructed me to send Mr Lowenstein back to Cape Town. I suspect that will no longer be possible, will it?"

Truegood faltered again and Drayton rose, walked over to the fireplace, and threw his cigarette in the grate. "Come now, Inspector. When a senior member of the official detective force arrives with a highly decorated officer as his agent, it can only mean one thing: Mr Lowenstein is dead. Not only dead, but murdered. Is that not so?" He leant against the marble mantelpiece.

"How did you know he was murdered?" Truegood demanded.

"Because you just told me, my dear sir. I'll have to wire Dr Jim with the news before I leave."

"Before you leave?" Truegood repeated.

"For Cape Town. The situation regarding the will has become quite urgent, and I booked passage on a steamer on Tuesday. I leave the day after the coronation. How did it happen?" asked Drayton.

Truegood had been about to ask another question and Drayton's enquiry caught the detective off balance. "He… he was beaten to death with a penang lawyer, some time between midnight and dawn yesterday morning," came the answer.

"Upon my word! A random attack or a calculated murder?"

"Impossible to tell at the moment." Truegood recovered before he gave away everything we had.

"Before you ask, I'll tell you that I dined here on Tuesday night, and didn't leave the house until… about nine o'clock on Wednesday morning. His Grace and several of his family were at dinner and there's a horde of staff who can vouch for my movements — or lack thereof — during the night. But if you think I know anything that may be of assistance to you, ask away." He waved in a magnanimous gesture.

"Firstly, I wonder why you've given me an alibi before I asked for one," said Truegood.

"Major Marshall will tell you that I have some small experience of police work, Inspector. Mr Lowenstein goes missing; I spend two months looking for him; he is discovered murdered; it requires no great stretch of the imagination… May I ask where you found his body?"

"In a house near Fitzroy Square."

"Really? My choice of private detectives was obviously poor. Not only did they fail to find Mr Lowenstein, but neither of them appear to have learned of his death yet."

"Mr Lowenstein was living under an assumed name," I said.

"Is that so? Should I infer he was in hiding?" Drayton sat down again, withdrew a gold-plated case from his coat pocket, and lit another cigarette.

"It looks that way. Can you think of any reason?" I asked.

Drayton considered my question, blew a cloud of smoke at the chandelier, and shook his head slowly from side to side. "I've no idea what game the fellow was playing, except that it was evidently a deadly one. He absented himself from Cape Town without Mr Beit's permission shortly after Mr Rhodes' passing. I believe he arrived in London at the end of April and took lodgings at Sam's in the Strand — under his own name. At the time his whereabouts were none of my concern; I found this out after he disappeared. In May Dr Jim informed me that either Mr Lowenstein or I were required in Cape Town in connection with Mr Rhodes' will. We had both been witnesses to one of Mr Rhodes' several amendments and either of us was required to give confirmation of his signature. I was unable to go myself, so I attempted to make contact with Mr Lowenstein. I couldn't find him, feared for his safety, and hired Messrs Littlechild and Slater for the purpose."

"You feared for his safety — why?" Truegood interrupted.

"No particular reason, I'm sure, but he left his employer without notice and then disappeared, so it seemed likely that something untoward was afoot. I don't think you've been honest with me, have you, Inspector? If Mr Lowenstein was hiding from someone, then it's most unlikely his death was the result of a random attack, isn't it?"

"Yeah, well it's my job to consider all the possibilities," he mumbled.

"Quite, quite. And not to give civilians and suspects information they aren't required to know. My apologies, no reproof was intended. I'm just trying to understand what happened as best I can. I don't want to come across as trying to tell you your job, but I wonder if you're aware that I wasn't the only one looking for Mr Lowenstein."

"You weren't?" said Truegood.

"No. I was informed by Mr Littlechild that a Mr Hugh Armstrong, private secretary to Viscount Milner, has been making his own inquiries into Mr Lowenstein's whereabouts for the last two weeks."

Sir Alfred Milner was the former high commissioner in Cape Town, currently responsible for the reconstruction of the defeated Boer republics. He had been elevated to the peerage by the King last year, and had negotiated the Boer surrender with Kitchener at the end of May.

Truegood withdrew his pocketbook and asked, "Mr Armstrong? Do you know where I can find him, Doctor?"

"I do. He is a resident at the Arundel, off the Strand. Other than his employment, and the fact that he is a lawyer by profession, I know nothing about him."

"You haven't met him before, in the Cape?" asked Truegood.

"No."

"You said that you and Mr Lowenstein were witnesses to one of the amendments to Mr Rhodes' will; is that right?"

"Indeed."

"What was the particular amendment, Doctor?"

Drayton smiled apologetically. "I'm afraid it would be indiscreet of me to disclose the precise details before the will has been proved, Inspector."

"You're refusing to assist me with a murder investigation?"

"Come now, that's hardly the case. You must understand that the details of Mr Rhodes' will are entirely confidential. There are numerous individuals and organisations that stand to benefit a great deal from his generosity. There has already been much speculation — "

Truegood held up his hand, and for the first time I felt he was in control. "Are you going to tell me, or not?"

"I'm afraid not, Inspector. I'm sworn to secrecy on the matter, and I can hardly see how it bears any relevance to Mr Lowenstein's demise."

"That's for me to decide."

"It certainly is, and I very much regret not being able to assist you. However, I can direct you to Chief Inspector Maquire, head of the Cape Town CID. I've no doubt he'll be able to solicit any relevant information from Mr B.F. Hawkesley, who was Mr Rhodes' legal advisor."

Truegood scribbled away. "This Mr Hawkesley, does he live in Cape Town?"

"He does. He and Chief Inspector Maguire worked in close cooperation in the matter of the scandalous behaviour of Princess Radziwill last year." Drayton's eyebrows danced and his eyes gleamed. I could tell his tongue was firmly in his cheek as he led the bull Truegood by the ring in his nose.

Truegood continued to write, then hesitated, and chewed on his pencil.

Drayton took the opportunity to address me. "Dr Jim spoke extremely highly of your conduct during the siege."

"Did he? By the time we fell back to Ladysmith, I was expecting to see you. I'd heard the two of you had become inseparable."

Drayton laughed, blowing out another cloud of smoke. "No, I had the honour to spend the first few months of the war with Mr Rhodes in Kimberley."

Kimberley had been besieged at the same time as Ladysmith. "Yes, I heard he'd flown to protect the source of his wealth."

"Whatever you may feel about Mr Rhodes, he was no coward. I know you admire courage in all men, Alec, as much as you hate senseless slaughter."

He was right on both counts, but while I admired courage I also knew that many courageous men were ruthless, and that one of the most ruthless men I'd ever met was right in front of me. "I still wish your employer hadn't been at Ladysmith," I said.

"You do?"

"Yes. I'm sure it was only because of him, Colonel Rhodes, and Sir John that the Boers were so persistent." I smiled for the first time, hoping to convince him of my goodwill.

"Yes, all three of the conspirators in a single town, and you with them. It looks like you ended up defending Dr Jim after all. You should have joined us, Alec, you should have joined us."

Truegood interrupted my angry retort. For once, his rudeness was welcome.

"I've one more question, Doctor. Will you be staying here until you leave on Sunday?"

"I shall indeed."

"Right. You've got my card. If you can think of anything else regarding Mr Lowenstein, I'd appreciate it if you'd let me know."

Drayton stood, placed his cigarette in an ash-receiver, and offered his hand to Truegood again. "Of course, Inspector." They shook, and he turned to me. "It's such a pleasure to see you again, Alec. Perhaps when I return to London we might renew our acquaintance? If you intend to remain in England, that is."

I suspected that my mission for Melville had become redundant with the news of Drayton's imminent departure, but I took his hand anyway. "I'm done with Africa. I'm at the Windsor Hotel. They'll have my forwarding address."

"Good. My very best wishes until such time as our paths meet."

As soon as we were shown out onto Piccadilly Truegood said, "I'm off back to the Yard, to find Mr M and this Armstrong fella. What do you think?"

"I don't think anything, but I know Drayton. Did he kill Lowenstein, or have him killed? Impossible to say. All he will have told us was exactly what he wanted us to know — no more and no less."

"Bit like you, then."

"What?"

"You've just told me bugger-all as well. I could see he was a clever nob all on my own, thanks. If you want to be in on Armstrong, wait at your hotel."

"Hold on," I said.

"What?"

"Some people might take offence at your abruptness, Inspector, but luckily for you I don't stand on ceremony. Who is this Mr Littlechild that Drayton was talking about?"

"John Littlechild. He was a detective at the Yard."

"You mean Chief Inspector Littlechild, head of the Special Irish Branch?"

"The same, he went into private practice in 'ninety-three. He was in the news for working on the Oscar Wilde case in 'ninety-five."

"Drayton obviously spared no expense. What about Slater, do you know him?"

"Yeah, not quite as sought after as Mr Littlechild, but he also commands a hefty fee. He has a very reputable private agency, handles a lot of financial matters. Be at your hotel." He marched off up Piccadilly.

I waited for a gap in the traffic, entered the melee, and almost tripped over an orderly boy scooping up a pile of steaming horse droppings. I crossed Green Park for the Windsor, resuming what was already a well-trod route since my recent return to the metropolis.

The penang lawyer was — as far as I was concerned — the only real clue we had to the killer's identity. The walking stick belonged to a man of average height. Drayton was slightly above average, but I knew it didn't belong to him anyway. He carried a heavy ebony cane with a twenty-seven inch Wilkinson sword blade concealed inside. Or at least he had when we'd shared rooms in Pitsani. I thought that there was more chance that the engraved 'A' on the head of the penang lawyer referred to the person who had given rather than received the gift, but either was possible.

In that case, did the 'A' stand for Armstrong?

9. Lieutenant Francis Carey

My cab stopped outside 106 Pall Mall at a few minutes to eight, and I alighted in the only top hat, white gloves, and tailcoat in my possession. My limited wardrobe did not stretch to an opera cape and I displayed a colonial lack of sophistication by using a cane made from a jackalberry tree, more cudgel than gentleman's stick. I paid the driver and walked up the stairs into the Florentine palazzo of the Travellers Club. I deposited my hat, stick, and gloves with an attendant, and was directed to the Inner Hall, where I was approached by a lean man a couple of inches shorter than me. He was swarthy, with dark brown hair, a thin moustache, and piercing blue eyes. He would have been handsome were it not for the thick, sensual lips which seemed at odds with the economy of the rest of his features. I knew he was only in his mid-thirties, but his lifestyle seemed to have aged him prematurely.

"Major Marshall?"

"Lieutenant Carey?"

"How do you do, sir? Francis Carey at your service."

I shook his hand. "Pleased to meet you, sir. Alec Marshall."

"Allow me to extend my deepest condolences with regards to your loss, Major. I had the honour of occasional meetings with Dr Marshall at the Zoological Gardens and I know she is sorely missed by all who had the pleasure of her acquaintance." He shook his head. "Damned shame it was, such a damn shame."

"Thank you, Lieutenant."

"And allow me to congratulate you on your Victoria Cross, Major. Dr Marshall was very proud. She told everyone about it. Mafeking, wasn't it?"

"Ladysmith. Thank you again, but we're both out the army, so please don't feel the need to address me by my rank."

"No, there doesn't seem much point, what," he snorted. "D'ye mind if we forage immediately? I'm so hungry I could eat a horse. Well, I have eaten horse and so have you, no doubt. Tastes like Bovril! That's sporting of you. It's upstairs to the Coffee Room."

He was right, I'd eaten horse at Ladysmith.

'Coffee Room' was a misnomer, as it was actually a vast dining hall with dozens of tables arranged in neat rows, dominated by a huge chandelier which hung all the way down to within six feet from the floor. We were shown to a table in the corner furthest from the entrance. I let Carey choose the wine, never having made any pretence of expertise in the matter myself. He ordered a bottle of French white, gave his approval to the bouquet and taste, and let the waiter pour. I took a sip and congratulated him on his selection, though I thought it awful. We made polite conversation through the first course, a delicious serving of whitebait.

When we'd finished the creamed venison, I decided it was time to come to the point of our meeting. "I've read all the newspaper reports on Dr Marshall's accident," I said, "but as I wasn't able to attend the inquest, I was hoping you'd be kind enough to give me a personal account."

"It's the least I could do for you, old boy. What would you like to know?"

"Everything, from the beginning."

He pursed his thick lips, which he had a habit of twitching from side to side. "You don't say? Well, Dr Marshall and I were both Fellows of the Zoological Society, so we'd met prior to her employment at the Gardens last year. Dr Marshall was the best thing that ever happened to the animals. That Gibbs is a damned fool — and a drunkard."

"Gibbs? Is that the other veterinary surgeon?"

"Yes. By George, do excuse me, I almost forgot you've been fighting Johnny Boer for the last couple of years. You'll know that the Royal College of Veterinary Surgeons refused to admit Dr Marshall to the register, despite the testimonial she brought from her principal at the university?"

"Yes."

"Because those old fools at the College can't bear the thought of working with a lady, Dr Marshall's official title was *assistant to* the veterinary surgeon. Complete and utter tosh, I assure you, because Dr Marshall quickly established herself as the real surgeon at the zoo. Everybody knew it." His smile was warm, but it did not reach his eyes. The braised celery arrived, and there was a pause before Carey resumed his narrative. "Dr Marshall attended a lecture I gave shortly after my return from East Africa in April, and seemed rather enthusiastic about my work for the Society. That — and her status — were why I decided to try and enlist her support for the safari I'm planning."

I'd only intended to pick at the celery, especially seeing as there were three more courses to come, but I finished it. Like the previous dishes, it was too tasty to resist. I took a sip of both the wine and water, and waited for Carey to continue.

"This is still very hush-hush at the moment — so I'd rather you didn't let on — but I'm trying to arrange an expedition into the Karakoram Range. That's next to the Himalayas, between Kashmir and China. The mountains are largely unexplored, although I'm a shikari rather than a cartographer, and it's the indigenous species I'm after. There are Snow Leopards and Marco Polo Sheep, and there's even talk of a sub-species of Ibex. Thing is, I've got two problems. One is good old currency." He grinned as he rubbed his thumb and forefinger together. "The Zoological Society leadership isn't convinced it's going to be worth the expense. They think it's a job for the Royal or the Royal Geographical, and they're probably right, too."

Our next course was roast goose, which we both devoured. I wondered when Carey would eventually reach the evening of the twenty-second of May, but he seemed at pains to establish honourable motives for having been alone with Ellen. "You were saying, about the Karakoram expedition?" I prompted.

"Not so loud, old boy." He put a finger to his lips. "I think I've managed to secure a sponsor, but it's not confirmed yet. But yes, finance is the first problem — always is. The second is that blasted Baron Curzon."

"The Viceroy of India?"

"The very same. I'm afraid he's taken a damned awkward dislike to me — spread a lot of bunkum about me working for the Russians in Afghanistan — and does his best to make life difficult for me whenever he can. And it's all over the baroness. I had the good fortune make the acquaintance of Miss Mary Leiter before their marriage and the rotter can't get over it. That was why I sought Dr Marshall's assistance — bloody wish I hadn't, of course — but it's too late now."

"Did Dr Marshall know why you wanted to talk to her?"

"Not exactly. I asked if I might accompany her on her evening ride in order to discuss the acquisition of new exhibits. It was Dr Marshall's habit to exercise the horses from the zoo stables in Regent's Park after work. I met her at the stables at half-past seven. Dr Marshall enjoyed full use of the park, except for Hertford Villa, so it was while we were in The Holme that the dreadful accident happened. I hadn't even broached the subject yet."

"What time was it?" I asked, my appetite suddenly gone.

"About ten minutes to nine, just before dusk. The Holme is one of the few places where there's enough of a clear run for the horses to enjoy a gallop. Dr Marshall suggested a race, and we were going hell for leather between the house and the boating lake when I glanced behind and couldn't see her. I was surprised, because of her reputation for competence in the saddle. I turned back at once. As soon as I rounded the trees I saw the horse and then — by George, I've seen enough death, but the sight of Dr Marshall lying on the ground was appalling. I'm afraid she expired before I reached her."

"What did you do?"

"What did I do, you say? I probably stood and gawped for a minute. I couldn't believe my eyes. When I came to my senses, I rode off to the house to summon help. Then I went back and waited with... Dr Marshall's body." He shook his head again. "Such a waste; she was such an intelligent, spirited lady."

The waiter placed our potato scallops in front of us. I couldn't touch mine. Carey's regret seemed genuine, but his appetite was still hearty. "Do you have any explanation that would account for Dr Marshall's fall?"

"It's plain and simple, what. I blame the lady's injury."

The newspapers had mentioned this. "Do you mean the scratches on her arm?"

"Yes, that's it, from a lion cub she'd been treating earlier in the week. Three scratches, all very deep. They must have weakened her grip. At the speed we were riding it doesn't take much to fall off. A slight loss of balance in the saddle — well, I don't need to tell you, do I? I forgot I'm talking to a cavalry officer."

"Mounted infantry, actually," I said.

"All the same, surely?"

"I suppose you're right, given the nature of modern warfare, but I'm no great expert on horses, or riding them — unlike my sister. I've always regarded them as a means to an end, rather than an end in themselves."

"I enjoy a good gallop, but I'm much the same. My new passion is automobiles. I completed The Trial in 1900. The transport of the future, says I. All the rage in America and just a matter of time before they really take off over here. I've got one of my own, a Panhard-Levassar, very same one I used in The Trial."

Two years ago, sixty-five automobiles had left Hyde Park Corner on a thousand and ten mile round trip through Great Britain. Much to the pleasure of the Automobile Club — and the surprise of the general public — all the vehicles had completed the route successfully.

"Do you think Dr Marshall's wound was enough to cause the accident?"

He thought for a moment or two. "Not to cause the accident, but certainly to prevent her from recovering from a jolt if her mount had shied or stumbled. I assume it was the former because the horse itself was uninjured. It's vexing, but it's the only way I can make any sense of the tragedy. I hope I've been clear enough, I do have a habit of going off and on a tangent at times."

"You've been most candid, sir, which is exactly what I sought."

"I'm glad to have been of some small assistance. I must beg your pardon for taking so long to get back to you, but I was out of town on Tuesday night and only returned late yesterday. Do those scallops not agree with you?"

Our conversation returned to our earlier inconsequential talk, with Carey quizzing me on which parts of Africa I'd lived in. After the final course, a vanilla soufflé, I accepted his offer of a glass of port. He led me back down to the Smoking Room, where I declined a cigar, and lit my pipe. It was difficult to conceive of Carey as a cold-blooded murderer in the oak-panelled luxury of our surroundings. Although it was Ellen's murder I was investigating, I couldn't help but note that Carey was exactly the right height for the penang lawyer. I also had no doubt that there were any number of wealthy ladies who could have given the stick to him — Lady Curzon for a start.

I had every reason to dislike Carey, yet I found myself enjoying his company. I hadn't intended to stay any longer than necessary, but accepted a second post-prandial drink. We talked about our respective military service and then Carey's safaris. He soon brought the conversation back to his forthcoming expedition, which seemed to be something of an obsession with him. He confessed that he had high hopes the Duke of Bedford would sponsor him after his visit to the Duke's estate in Woburn — which was where he spent Tuesday night.

I mentally crossed him off my list of potential penang lawyer owners.

When he offered me a third glass of port, I thanked him for his hospitality and excused myself. I recovered my accoutrements from the attendant, and stepped out onto a warm, breezy Pall Mall. As I reached for my watch I heard: "Evenin', Major."

"Good evening, Lamb."

He touched his hat. "Superintendent Melville apologizes for the hour, but he'd like to see you at the Yard, sir."

I looked at my watch: it was just before eleven. "Doesn't he ever sleep?" I asked with a smile.

"I can't see the guvnor goin' home until that crown is safely on His Majesty's noggin, if you'll pardon the liberty, sir."

10. Confession of Faith

Perhaps Lamb wasn't exaggerating because the second thing I noticed on entering Melville's office was the camp-bed in a corner. The first was Truegood, who took one look at my full dress and rolled his eyes skyward. Melville was sitting at his desk, wreathed in cigar smoke; the window behind him was open.

"Hello, Marshall, good of you to drop by!"

"Good evening, gentlemen."

"Sit down, sit down, please. Lamb, if you'd be kind enough to bring us in a fresh pot of coffee, that'll be all."

I withdrew an envelope from my coat, and placed it on the desk. "A report on my interview with Colonel Rhodes."

"Good fellow." He offered me a cigar as he took a fresh one for himself.

"I prefer my pipe, thank you." I said as I took a seat in the empty chair. "There's also something I want to ask you about when we've finished."

"While Truegood brings you up-to-date with his investigation, I'll take the opportunity to have a quick look at this." He put on a pair of spectacles.

I removed my pipe and prepared it.

"First, we got a witness from Aitken's house-to-house inquiries. One of the neighbours — the daughter of the drunken tobacconist the harridan was talking about — saw our man. Miss Pullman said she couldn't sleep and happened to be looking out her window when she saw a fella walk from the Curran house to the bottom of the garden, and hop over the wall into the alley. She said it was just after half-three on Wednesday morning, which fits in with the rest of the evidence. Unfortunately all she can tell us is that the suspect was wearing a wideawake hat, did not have a beard, and was of average height. Much like your stick, all it gives us is most of the male population of London."

"If she said that he didn't have a beard, does that mean she didn't see much of his face? If that is so then he could either have worn a moustache or been clean-shaven."

"Yeah," answered Truegood.

"I suppose the wide-brimmed hat would be an excellent way to keep one's face concealed, particularly from people on the upper floors of the surrounding houses."

"Hmm, I'm not sure about the hat… "

"What do you mean?" I asked.

"Never mind. Second, Lamb thinks he knows who was nosing about on Tuesday. His name is Rose, and he's one of Murgatroyd's men."

"Who's Murgatroyd?"

"One of the Family fathers in Devil's Acre. Runs a number of fences, and keeps a retinue of villains for enforcement purposes. We'll find Rose, but it might take some time. Third, I've been in touch with both Littlechild and Slater. They confirmed Drayton's story to the letter, and if there was any foul play on his part, it won't have been through either of them. Last, I contacted Armstrong. Drayton was right, he arrived in Southampton on the twenty-sixth of July, and he's staying at the Arundel. We're meeting him there tomorrow at nine."

Lamb returned with a fresh pot of coffee, milk and a cup and saucer for me.

Melville looked up from my report. "Thank you, Lamb, you can knock off now."

"I'll see you first thing, as arranged," said Truegood.

"Yes, sir. Goodnight gentlemen." Lamb left us again.

I lit my pipe, puffed until I was satisfied it was alight, then eased back into the soft leather of the chair.

Melville removed his spectacles and poured three cups of coffee. "You think Rhodes is lying?"

"I'm sure of it."

"He wants to stand clear of the whole thing. Either he killed Lowenstein or he just doesn't want to have his name connected with the murder," said Truegood.

"Very good, Truegood, very good. He's recently been made a Companion of the Order of the Bath for his war service, and he's taking part in the coronation as an aide-de-camp. The war has brought something of a renaissance to his career and reputation, and he won't want it tarnished in any way."

"Who'd have thought it, only six years after the Jameson Raid," I muttered.

"I've read Truegood's report on Drayton. Do you have any observations you'd like to add?"

"As I said to Truegood, he will only have let us see and hear what he wanted. He also gave us Armstrong, which means that either he thinks Milner's involved, and he wants to help us; or he's involved himself, and he wants to put us on a false scent."

"It sounds as if you don't trust him at all, but you've successfully renewed your acquaintance nonetheless." Melville drew on his cigar and released another cloud of smoke into the blue-grey atmosphere.

"Yes," I said, "although I don't expect it'll do you much good because he's returning to Cape Town on Sunday. We need to know more about Rhodes' will and what's going on in the Cape. I know we can't be certain, but it seems likely that Lowenstein's murder is related to the will in some way, perhaps even directly connected to the complications."

"Well done, Marshall, well done. That's exactly why I've brought you here at this hour: I want you and Truegood together, so I don't have to repeat myself. Make yourselves comfortable, gentlemen, and help yourselves to another cup of coffee." He took a sip of his own. "The late Mr Rhodes suffered from congenital ill health, and was convinced he wouldn't live long. In that respect he was right. It is unusual for a man of his means to die at forty-eight, but he'd already had several heart attacks, and was actually originally sent out to the Cape Colony as a cure for his ailments. The combination of Rhodes' desire for immortality through his legacy and his physical frailty meant that he kept his affairs in a constant state of readiness for the execution of his will.

"There were seven wills, as I've mentioned before, and several dozen amendments and codicils. We don't need to know the details of each, but the seventh and most important was drafted three years ago. The bulk of his fortune was to go to the formation of an Imperial Party in Britain. The party would be led by his six executors: W.T. Stead, the journalist; Hawkesley, his solicitor; Alfred Beit, the financier; the Earl Grey, Director of the BSAC; the Earl of Rosebery, the former Prime Minister and Mr Lewis Mitchell, his banker.

"Rhodes made six amendments to that last will. The first was to remove Stead as a trustee for his betrayal in opposing the South African

War; the second was the inclusion of five German students in his colonial scholarships to Oxford; the third was the addition of Sir Alfred Milner as a sixth executor, and the fourth bequeathed Dalham Hall in Suffolk to his family. The fifth amendment was made on the twelfth of March this year, when Rhodes was living in a tin-roofed cottage in a place called Muizenberg. He was, quite literally, on his death-bed, and he appointed Jameson as a seventh executor. Jameson and his private secretary were in constant attendance. Four days before he died, Rhodes made his final amendment. It was witnessed by Drayton and Lowenstein. The will remained the same, but the executors had changed." Melville paused, and beamed at the moment of suspense he'd created. "Any guesses, gentlemen?"

Truegood and I both shook our heads.

"The seven executors were reduced to one. The entire fortune of Cecil John Rhodes, the BSAC, De Beers, and all the rest — the greatest legacy of the largest empire in the world — was to be administered by a single gentleman."

"Jameson," I said

Melville's smile lifted even higher, wrinkling his cheeks and eyes. "Marshall, I knew I'd chosen well when I recruited your assistance in this little matter."

"How the hell did you know that?" asked Truegood.

I shrugged. "I know Drayton and his master."

"The six executors who were excluded are naturally contesting the will and that's the real reason for the delay. Drayton left for England the day after the final amendment and Lowenstein a week or so after Rhodes' death. Unfortunately for Jameson that put them both out of the Colony when they were required to prove the will. He wired Drayton to send Lowenstein back and that's exactly when Mr Beit's clerk disappeared. Drayton spent the next three months looking for Lowenstein, but we found him first. Marshall, you appear confused."

I realised my pipe had gone out, and removed it from my mouth. "I am. I know Jameson is arrogant, but he must have known the amendment would be contested. So why allow both the witnesses to leave the Cape? And why, when the will was contested, did he instruct Drayton to hunt for Lowenstein? He should have recalled him immediately and got someone else to do the job."

"Unfortunately, I have very few answers at the minute. It does appear, however, that Jameson — and thus Drayton — had every reason for wanting Lowenstein alive. As for Drayton, if he fails to return to Cape Town to authenticate Rhodes' signature by the end of this month, the codicil will be considered invalid."

I made a quick mental calculation.

"There must be thousands of examples of Rhodes' signature, and hundreds who can validate it," said Truegood.

"There are, and the signature is not an exact match. But you'll remember that the amendment was made only four days before his death, when he'd been terminally ill for nearly two months. Jameson claims the slight difference is due to Rhodes' health. Handwriting experts were brought in to compare the signature with the one in the previous codicil and to some other documents he signed in March. Their evidence was inconclusive, and the matter now rests upon the two witnesses affirming that they saw Rhodes sign his name to the document. Or rather one witness, as of Wednesday."

"And if that one witness doesn't get on his steamer on Sunday, Jameson will have been thwarted," I said. "If there are no delays he should arrive in Cape Town on the thirtieth of the month, with a single day to spare."

"Yes, he's cutting it a bit fine, isn't he?" said Melville. I've no idea where the allegiances of Hawkesley and Mitchell lie, but the other four executors are all extremely powerful men who are very unhappy with Jameson and his friends. If I had to choose one of them as the most likely to take direct action against Jameson, it would be Milner."

"Armstrong," said Truegood.

"Yes. Lord Milner is a current favourite of His Majesty; nevertheless, some of the leaders of our great nation have expressed certain doubts about him. Milner knew Rhodes during his early career in journalism, but he first came to prominence after the Jameson Raid. Lord Rosmead, the High Commissioner for Southern Africa, was forced to resign over the debacle, and Mr Chamberlain chose Milner to replace him. Both Chamberlain and Milner are aggressive imperialists, and they both believed that the only solution to the South African problem was the complete domination of the Dutch by the British.

"Since Milner's appointment as high commissioner he began to gather a group of young men about him known as his 'kindergarten', some of whom are likely to be future leaders in the Empire. Armstrong, his private secretary for the last year, is one of these men. I want you both to keep this intelligence in mind when you meet him this morning. I know little of the man except that he's twenty-six, Scots, and a lawyer by profession. Find the evidence, follow it, and I'll support you all the way. Any questions?"

"I'd like to ask you about the other matter I mentioned," I said.

"Of course. Perhaps this is a good time for you to get a few hours of sleep, Truegood. I know you're going to Devil's Acre before you interview Armstrong."

"Thank you, sir." He stood. "I'll pick you up at your hotel," he said to me. "Goodnight, gentlemen."

"One of my best detectives," Melville said when he'd left. "Honest, hard-working, and tough as old boots, but not the most tactful of men, which is why I want to talk to you alone. If you can delay the other matter for a little while longer, I have something I'd like you to read."

"Let me get my pipe going again." I knocked the loose tobacco and ashes out in the fireplace, resumed my seat, and packed my pipe once more. That's why I prefer a meerschaum to a briar: it doesn't require drying out between pipes. Sometimes several days would go by without my taking a pull on it; other days it seemed I hardly stopped.

Melville cut another cigar. As soon as I had the pipe lit, he removed a leather file from one of his drawers, selected four sheets of paper, and handed them to me. "This is an exact duplicate of the master copy, with the exception of the handwriting. The original was written in Kimberley in 'seventy-seven, and signed by Rhodes. It is, in fact, his second will."

With that introduction I read the most extraordinary document I've ever seen in my life.

It was entitled *Confession of Faith*, and began with Rhodes expressing his regret that Britain had lost America in the War of Independence in 1783. He commented on the superiority of the Anglo-Saxon race, and the desirability of maintaining its dominance of international affairs. The second paragraph concerned Rhodes' induction into a Masonic Lodge, whose ceremonies he regarded as ridiculous. Then there followed:

The idea gleaming and dancing before one's eyes like a will-of-the-wisp at last frames itself into a plan. Why should we not form a secret society with but one object, the furtherance of the British Empire and the bringing of the whole uncivilised world under British rule, for the recovery of the United States, for the making of the Anglo-Saxon race, for but one Empire. What a dream, but yet it is probable, it is possible.

Rhodes waxed lyrical on the loss of America again, made scathing reference to the inferior Irish and German immigrants who had filled the country, and asserted the value of a secret society with the aim of increasing British territory and populating as many countries as possible with Anglo-Saxons. Rhodes then suggested the Romish Church as a model for the extension of the Empire, and provided examples of three different types of young men whose patriotism could be harnessed by the society he wished to establish. This paragraph was in parenthesis.

In every colonial legislature the Society should attempt to have its members prepared at all times to vote or speak and advocate the closer union of England and the colonies, to crush all disloyalty and every movement for the severance of our Empire. The Society should inspire and even own portions of the press; for the press rules the mind of the people. The Society should always be searching for members who might by their position in the world, by their energies or character, forward the object — but the ballot and test for admittance should be severe.

There was a further comment on the proposed exclusivity of the society, and the final paragraph left all of Rhodes' worldly goods to Mr S. G. Shippard and Lord Carnarvon to 'try to form such a Society with such an object'.

I digested what I'd just read before asking, "Is this genuine?"

"It is."

"So Rhodes was a Freemason?"

"He was initiated at Oriel College, Oxford, on the 2nd June 1877, which is when he wrote the first draft of that, but he didn't take his membership very seriously. The Masons were his inspiration, but the Society of Jesus — better known as the Jesuits — was the organisation he wished to imitate."

I didn't know very much about the Jesuits, other than that they were a group of missionaries within the Roman Catholic Church who had a strong focus on education — which tied in with Rhodes' colonial scholarships. "That was twenty-five years ago; did Rhodes still feel the same way when he died?"

"Exactly, but he used the euphemism 'Imperial Party' instead. Once his final bid to return to the premiership of the Cape Colony failed in ninety-eight, he devoted the rest of his life to what he called 'the Idea', and selecting the right men to rule the Empire."

"An Empire that he wanted to cover the whole world?"

"Yes. Rhodes literally wanted the entire world to be ruled by one great, big British Empire administered as a federation. He went into more detail than that," Melville indicated the *Confession* with his cigar, "even suggesting that Germany and America were too powerful to conquer by force, and should be infiltrated by Empire loyalists using the scholarship system. He envisaged it would take the society two hundred years before the British Empire and the world were one and the same."

That was what disturbed me most about the *Confession* and the secret society. It was not the raving of a madman. The Idea was real. It had been logically constructed, carefully considered, and meticulously planned. "Does that mean all six of the 1899 executors supported the idea of a secret society?"

"At the time, yes. I know Milner approves of the Idea and Jameson's support goes without saying. I'm not sure how Beit, Grey, and Rosebery stand, but until I have evidence to the contrary, I regard them as sympathisers."

"Knowing what I do about Drayton, Jameson, and Rhodes, I'm not shocked by any of this. I assume the next thing you're going to tell me is that the society was actually formed some time in the last twenty-five years?"

"As you'll have gathered my intelligence comes from several very highly-placed sources. This is strictly between you and me: I have been told that the Society of the Elect was established by Mr Rhodes and Lord Milner during a meeting at one of the university colleges in Oxford early in 1891. Both Mr Rhodes and Lord Milner are of course graduates of the university. I have no confirmation of the identities of any other members."

"Lowenstein's murder is probably concerned with the money rather than the society." I tossed the four sheets onto Melville's desk.

"Good fellow. I recruited you to bring me intelligence on Drayton. That won't be possible for a while, but in the mean time I should like you to solve Lowenstein's murder. Use Truegood and his resources, and your own skills. Superintendent Alexander seemed to think you made an excellent detective, so I want you to prove him right and give Truegood his arrest."

"I'll do my best."

"I know you will. Now, it's extremely late and you still have to get back to your hotel. You mentioned another matter?"

"I'm not going to beat about the bush: you're aware of the circumstances of my sister's death at the end of May; I'd like to have a look at the police and coroner's reports."

"You suspect foul play and you wish to make your own investigation?"

"I'm not sure of my answer to either of those questions. Let me put it this way, I'd like to reassure myself that no one was to blame."

Melville placed his cigar in the ash-receiver. "Very good, I'll have the files sent here first thing tomorrow." I stood and he came over to shake my hand again. "Thank you again for your assistance, and good luck."

"Goodnight, Melville."

11. Hugh Armstrong, Esquire

I rose at six-thirty, only four hours after falling asleep. The staff at the hotel were prepared for my early breakfasts, so I was sitting in the parlour with the *Times* when Truegood appeared just after half-past eight. I followed him to a waiting cab, remembering to take my stick today, as befitted a gentleman stepping out in town. He said nothing for the first few minutes of our journey to the Arundel, so I occupied myself with observing the final preparations for the coronation procession. All of the stands, most with canvas roofs, had been erected, but decorations were still being added. In Whitehall we passed under an arch which had been especially put up, apparently by a Canadian concern as the large letters read: *Canada: Kitchener: Hero in War and Peace*. There was a huge portrait of Queen Alexandra on the left and King Edward on the right.

Colonel Rhodes had served under Kitchener at Omdurman, which was the latter's great victory in the Anglo-Egyptian Sudan, directly after which he'd been created Baron Kitchener of Khartoum and Aspall. I remembered that Rhodes and Kitchener had both been awarded honorary degrees by Oxford University before the war started, and apparently become friends in the last years of Rhodes' life. I'd met Kitchener once, when he'd pinned the VC on my chest at a parade in Bloemfontein. He'd been aloof and emotionless, much as I'd expected. Like Milner, he'd also collected a group of younger men around him, called his 'band of boys'. Kitchener and Milner had negotiated the terms of the peace treaty with the Boers together. Milner not only wanted unconditional capitulation, but the complete eradication of the Boer cultural identity, something like the English tried in the Highlands after Bonnie Prince Charlie's rebellion in 1745. It was Kitchener who was the more conciliatory of the two, which said a lot about Milner.

"There's something I want to tell you." Truegood broke in on my thoughts.

"Yes?"

He leant out the cab to make sure the driver was where he was supposed to be — behind and above us — and then glanced at the trapdoor to make sure it was shut. When Truegood was satisfied, he continued. "It's probably nothing, but if we're working together — if you're working for me — then I believe in sharing everything that's relevant. But this is confidential, got it?"

"Yes."

"It's about the wideawake hat."

"The one the murderer was wearing?"

"I don't bloody know, do I, or I'd be feeling his collar. *Someone's* wideawake hat and there aren't many people who wear them. Not many Englishmen anyway. On the seventh of July Mr Chamberlain, the Colonial Secretary — "

"I know who Chamberlain is."

"Mr Chamberlain, who was chairing the Colonial Conference at the time, was involved in an accident, just here."

"Where?"

"The Canadian Arch, the one we just passed through... You know, big sign saying 'Canada' on it?"

"Got it."

"Christ, you're not too quick on the uptake are you? Chamberlain was in a hansom and the horse slipped and fell. He was shaken up and the window shattered, the result being he received a bad scalp wound and had to be taken straight to hospital. It was two weeks before he got back to his conference with the colonial premiers — who were all here for the coronation, by the way. At the beginning of this year we received intelligence that Chamberlain was a target for anarchist groups, because of his involvement in the war, so Mr M sent me to investigate.

"There were surprisingly few witnesses given the location of the incident, but it all seemed above board. I spoke to the driver, an American called Thomas Stringer, who lived in Blackfriars Road. He'd only been working for the company for a fortnight, but there was nothing suspicious — until I went back a couple of days later."

"Why did you go back?" I asked.

"Just a routine visit. Something I always do, you never know what you'll find. And what do you think I found?"

His unpleasant personality aside, Truegood was indeed thorough. "No Stringer," I suggested.

"Exactly, no Stringer. So I checked the referees he'd given the Improved Cab Company and neither of them existed either. I couldn't find any other record of the fella. He'd rented the rooms a month in advance, but only moved in shortly before taking work as a driver. Nobody knew anything about him and I was inclined to think he'd never existed. Mr M said to leave it at the time, and file it away for future reference. There was bugger all to go on, anyway, but this Stringer, he wore a wideawake hat. Had it on when the accident happened. I know, probably nothing, but there it is." Truegood looked belligerent, as if daring me to contradict him.

"What did he look like?"

"Average height, average build, tanned skin — early forties according to his papers. Brown hair with a big set of mutton-chop whiskers like some old Crimea veteran. Seemed co-operative enough and there was no reason to bother him again, aside from it being my habit."

"Did you notice his ears?"

"His *ears*, what are you on about?"

"The ears are the most difficult part of the face to disguise."

"No, I didn't notice his bloody ears. Does anyone?"

"Not usually, no. If Stringer was an agent in someone's employ, then I suppose it's possible that the same man could have been used to kill Lowenstein. There are many ties between Rhodes and Chamberlain. I'll keep Stringer in mind."

Truegood grunted a reply and we lapsed into silence.

If someone adopted a disguise, one wouldn't expect them to wear such a striking form of headgear, unless they were deliberately trying to draw attention to themselves. On the other hand, many agents and spies used the same disguises and ruses over and over again, such as keeping the same initials or first name. Stringer, or whoever he really was, probably had nothing to do with Lowenstein, but I was glad Truegood had told me about him.

The Strand was absolutely packed, heaving and surging with horse-drawn and pedestrian traffic like a great asthmatic chest straining to draw breath. As I spent more time travelling about London, I began to notice something else that bothered me far more than the pollution in the air:

the signs of widespread poverty. It wasn't something I recalled from my youth, but then I'd not been brought up to consider the poor as anything other than too lazy or stupid to be anything else. Now, I noticed the men whose knees showed through worn trousers, and the children who went barefoot, and would continue to do so in the winter. If only Rhodes had turned his energy and ability to improving the lot of those within the Empire, rather than conquering those without; unfortunately, men like him never did.

Eventually, we passed Somerset House. Just before we entered the territory of the Inns of Court, we turned off down Arundel Street, towards the river. The driver halted outside the hotel, and waited for us. Like the Windsor, the Arundel was a family, rather than a grand, establishment, which made a refreshing change after the Langham, Devonshire House and the Travellers Club. It was well-appointed in terms of furnishings, and the maintenance and service left nothing to be desired. A smart attendant escorted us to Armstrong's sitting-room without delay.

He was waiting impatiently, despite the fact that we were a minute before time. "Yes, yes, I know who they are." He dismissed our escort. "Now what the hell do you want with me, Inspector, Major — whoever's in charge?"

Truegood said nothing.

Armstrong was a short, thin young man, with fiery red hair and a long, skinny neck. He approached Truegood, changed his mind, and turned to me. "Are you deaf, man?"

I stared down at him. "No."

"What the bloody hell do you want? If I've the courtesy to spare a vulgar policeman and an unemployed soldier my time, I expect them not to waste it."

"Then perhaps you should address Inspector Truegood; he's in charge of the investigation," I said.

"Well?" he turned on Truegood.

Truegood's bulk seemed even greater, in such close proximity to the little man. He waited three seconds before saying, "I've some questions to ask you in relation to a murder investigation."

"I'll charge you to keep a civil tongue in your head!" Armstrong poked Truegood's massive chest. "Do you know who I am? Viscount Milner's private secretary and Baron Rothschild's guest, and I'll have you walking the beat in Whitechapel if you don't hurry up about it."

"I don't care who you are. If you touch me again I'll rip your fucking head off your pencil neck and use it for football practice."

"That'll cost you dearly, Truegood, mark my words!" Armstrong was fuming, but he lowered his hands and edged backwards.

Wisely, in my opinion.

"That's better. Where were you on Wednesday morning, between midnight and dawn?"

"This is — "

"Mr Armstrong!" I snapped, "Just answer the inspector's questions. Then we can be on our way and you can make your complaints."

He cursed under his breath and stormed off to the other side of the room, where he kept his back to us and looked out the window. "Is this about Lowenstein?"

"Yeah," said Truegood.

I made myself comfortable in a chair.

Armstrong turned theatrically, glowered at me, and said, "I was at a banquet in the Middle Temple until half-past twelve. Then I returned here alone and went to bed, as is customary in the early hours of the morning. What else?"

"Have you been looking for Lowenstein?"

"Yes."

"Why?"

"It is no business of yours because it has absolutely nothing to do with his death. I know much more about your job and powers than you do, Inspector, and I know what questions I do and do not have to answer."

"Don't bother, Armstrong," I said. "We know why you were sent to London and we know why you wanted to find Lowenstein. Milner and his cronies aren't very happy about Rhodes' will, are they? They've contested the final amendment and Lowenstein and Drayton were required to authenticate the signature. Lowenstein disappeared and Drayton has been trying to find him ever since. Milner sent you to find out what had caused the delay — or perhaps in sending you he had a more permanent obstruction in mind?"

"What do you think you are insinuating?"

"It's very much in Milner's interest that neither Lowenstein nor Drayton returns to Cape Town," I answered coolly.

"This is libel, Major! I shall ensure that you never again hold the King's commission."

"How did you know Lowenstein was dead?" Truegood asked.

"Because I read the newspapers. Are you capable of reading, I wonder?"

"I'm impressed, Armstrong. You must be a spiritualist, or how else did you know Otto Isaacs was Eric Lowenstein?"

"Because I have a private agent in my employ assisting me in my search. A former police inspector himself, your superior in all sorts of ways."

"Name?"

"Mr Maurice Moser, of Southampton Street, Covent Garden."

"Just the one?"

"What?"

"Is Moser the only private agent in your employ, or have you recruited others. It's not difficult, is it?"

"I'm going to enjoy tearing your career to shreds, strip by bloody strip. No, I did not employ any other agents. Mr Moser was conducting inquiries on the lowest levels of society — the ones with which you are familiar — I was conducting those among the respectable classes myself."

"When did Moser find Lowenstein?"

"After his death."

"Are you sure about that?"

"Yes, why don't you ask him yourself?"

"I will."

"Why do you think Lowenstein was in hiding?" I asked.

"Contrary to your Neanderthal colleague's opinion, I am unable to contact the dead, and have none of the intimate knowledge of Lowenstein's character that would entitle me to an opinion."

"Perhaps he was hiding from you?" I offered.

"Perhaps he was hiding from the Devil, and the Devil found him." His smile was full of malice.

"How long are you going to be in London?" Truegood asked.

"What business is it of yours?"

"I'll need to know when you leave, unless you want to be considered a suspect. A suspect with an alibi that's a cock and bull story."

He didn't deign to reply. "Does that conclude our interview?"

"One more thing," I said, "do you possess a cane?"

"Of course I have a cane — in fact two of them!"

"I'd like to see both."

He cursed again, threw the door open, and charged into his bedroom. A few seconds later he emerged and hurled a slim rosewood cane at me.

I leapt to my feet and caught it. The stick was thin and light, with a silver fluted cross-head, and a horn ferrule. I raised it level with both hands and then placed it on the ground. "Where's the other one?"

"I've no bloody idea! Satisfied?"

I flicked the cane over to him. He reached, fumbled, and it fell to the floor with a clatter. Truegood and I both turned to go.

"When I see Baron Rothschild tomorrow, this little meeting will make a charming anecdote at the dinner table. I'll be sure to mention both your names."

Truegood opened the door for me. As soon as I'd stepped out he addressed Armstrong. "If I return to my old beat in Whitechapel, you'd better make sure I never see you there. I know some people who enjoy a grim taste in footballs." He closed the door behind him.

"That went well," I said as we returned to the hansom.

"I don't need any of your lip on top of that uppity cove."

"No, I'm being serious."

"I'm off to see Moser. Coming?"

"Could you drop me off at the Yard?"

He barked at the driver and the cab lurched forward. "Moser is another one who used to work with Mr M. Only, contrary to Mr-Carrot-Top-back-there's opinion, he's not as respectable as Littlechild or Slater. Not by bloody half."

"You think he's capable of killing Lowenstein?"

"Doubt he'd do it himself, but I'm sure he knows plenty who would. What you so pleased about?"

"The stick. It was exactly the same length as the murder weapon."

"I thought you said the stick belonged to a man of average height, not a runt like him?"

"The size of a walking stick is a function of arm and leg length. They're proportional on most people, but I thought you might have noticed his short arms when he was poking your chest."

"I did."

"On top of which he seems just the sort that would go about with a big, heavy stick emblazoned with his own initial. I know he's shorter than the witness said, and a weakling, but I don't think either of those points rules him out. Armstrong is the first person we've encountered who matches the only physical evidence retrieved at the offence scene."

"Sometimes I wonder about you, Marshall."

"What?"

"Haven't you considered that cursed penang lawyer might have been put there for us to find?"

"Planted? It's possible, but I doubt it."

"Then why didn't our murderer just wipe the gore off on his hanky or coat-tails if he was bothered about walking the streets with a bloody stick?"

Fifteen minutes later the cab dropped me outside the Yard, somewhat less chipper.

12. Death by Misadventure

Melville had already left for Buckingham Palace, to make the final arrangements for tomorrow, but Constable Dawson was expecting me. It appeared the detective was the only one of Melville's men at the Yard. He handed me a single cardboard folder with Melville's compliments, informed me that the superintendent had asked to see me first thing on Monday morning, and showed me to Truegood's office. I sat at the inspector's desk, took out my pencil and notebook, and opened it to a fresh page. With a trembling hand, I unfastened the ribbon on the folder, and removed the papers that constituted the official response to Ellen's death.

There were half a dozen statements taken by the detective who'd investigated, and a similar number of depositions from the inquest. The detective, Sergeant Davies, was from the Marylebone Lane Station in D Division. No post-mortem examination had been conducted, but the divisional police surgeon had been asked for a second opinion as to the cause of death by the coroner, Mr Ernest Gregory, who was not himself medically qualified. This display of professionalism on his part was no doubt due to my father's influence and Ellen's celebrity. The inquest had been held on Monday the twenty-sixth of May in the London County Council offices at the Paddington Street Burial Ground, which was also the site of the local mortuary. Other than Carey's, I didn't recognise any names.

I arranged the papers in chronological order, which meant starting with the stable hand at the zoo, who confirmed it was Dr Marshall's custom to exercise the horses on most evenings. At seven-thirty on Thursday the twenty-second of May, Dr Marshall left the Zoological Gardens on horseback in the company of Lieutenant Carey. According to Josiah Brown, the groom of the chambers at The Holme, Lieutenant Carey arrived at nine o'clock in a state of agitation. He explained that Dr Marshall had fallen from her horse and broken her neck. He instructed Brown to call the police, and immediately returned to the scene of the accident. The police were contacted by telephone, and two footmen were sent out with lanterns to assist the lieutenant.

At twenty minutes to ten, Davies arrived with two constables and the police ambulance. He found Dr Marshall's corpse undisturbed, with Carey and the footmen in attendance. One of the constables had returned to the stables with Carey, where he took a statement from the stable hand. There being no witnesses to the incident, Davies and the other constable made inquiries at The Holme, where Brown's affidavit was recorded. The corpse was removed to the mortuary. Davies took a statement from Carey the following day and spoke to Dr Hall, Ellen's own doctor, after the latter had examined her corpse. Dr Hall's opinion was that the injuries were consistent with the circumstances described by Carey, and the cause of death accidental. He supported Davies' recommendation that no inquest be held.

At the request of the deceased's father, however, the next available date was set for an inquest and a police surgeon, Dr Maycock, was dispatched to examine the body. His examination had been external only, and he'd confirmed the cause of death, but suggested a full post-mortem examination. The coroner had decided it wasn't necessary, and the body was removed from the mortuary by the undertakers. Carey and Brown had both given evidence at the inquest. Carey's evidence was identical to the statement he'd given Davies, which was in turn identical to the account I'd heard at the Travellers Club.

I have no formal medical training, but during the time Drayton and I cohabited, he taught me something of medical jurisprudence and the emergency treatment of life-threatening injuries. Ellen's fifth, sixth, and seventh cervical vertebrae were broken, which meant that death could either have resulted from asphyxiation, or from shock if her spinal cord had been severed by the broken vertebrae. There were contusions on her neck, but no other bones were broken or fractured. There were also contusions on both of Ellen's arms, consistent with an attempt by her to protect herself as she fell from the horse. Damage to the hands and arms are particularly useful to the detective, because the natural human instinct is to throw up one's hands for protection.

The only other wounds recorded were three symmetrical lacerations on her left arm, extending from the brachialis, across the cubital fossa, to the medial group of antibrachial muscles. As I understood it, the lacerations were deep at the upper arm and forearm, but superficial in the crook of the elbow, with no arterial damage. The wound was recent, but not fresh, and had been treated and bandaged. This must have been the scratch from the lion cub Carey had mentioned. If it had damaged Ellen's forearm muscles, then it may well have affected her ability to control a horse.

I thought it curious that she hadn't had any other bones broken, and wondered why Hall hadn't mentioned this. I turned to Dr Maycock's report; he confirmed Hall's details concerning muscular and skeletal damage, but noted that while Ellen's arms were bruised, there were no abrasions. The absence of abrasions was curious given the circumstances of her death: the forward momentum of the horse would've caused Ellen to be propelled in the same direction when she fell off, and when she made contact with the ground she would've rolled or slid forwards. Even though there were no tears to her jacket and gloves, there would still have been abrasions to the skin underneath her clothing were the injury consistent with a fall from a galloping horse.

Gregory hadn't thought it necessary to call either doctor to the inquest, he merely reported that their examinations concurred — which they had, as both stated the cause of death to be a broken neck, consistent with a fall from horseback. The coroner's courts were notorious for their inefficiency and the majority of men appointed as coroners had no medical training at all, which left them entirely at the mercy of the doctor in attendance. When I was growing up, most inquests were conducted in public houses, and the jurors — unpaid, uncomfortable, and mostly unwilling — were usually in a rush to get back to their homes or places of work. There'd been reforms in the intervening years, but the system was still flawed.

Gregory had been unusually thorough in requesting Maycock's opinion in the first instance, so it was to be expected that he'd only used the part of Maycock's evidence that suited his purpose. The majority of Maycock's report was in complete accordance with Hall, so why would Gregory make more work for himself? He'd already gone above and beyond the call of duty. Furthermore, while my father had brought his influence to bear in holding the inquest, he would want the matter closed as quickly as possible and without any hint of scandal. Gregory had recorded the verdict as death by misadventure, and his handling of the inquest was beyond reproach — officially, at least.

I wanted to speak to Dr Maycock and question him further, however. His evidence showed it was possible that Miss Paterson was right, and that Ellen hadn't died by accident. Carey had been riding alone with Ellen, in a private part of Regent's Park, close to dusk. It was difficult to imagine a more perfect scenario for a murder. He was a man of action, a soldier, a hunter, an adventurer — even an assassin according to some. He had the physical and mental resources to commit the crime. Carey could've either engineered the accident, or broken Ellen's neck himself. But opportunity and ability alone don't establish guilt beyond a reasonable doubt. He was a rational man, I'd established as much during our prolonged conversation, and he would need a reason to risk his liberty. Why would he want Ellen dead?

It was the first thing I'd said to Miss Paterson on Wednesday, and I still had no answer. If Miss Paterson was correct and there'd been no relationship between Ellen and Carey, then the only possibility remaining was that he'd been employed by someone else. I couldn't really see Carey as a gun for hire, but perhaps I was wrong. In that case, the more pertinent question was: why would anyone want to kill Ellen? I could only answer that by finding out more about my dear, departed sister. The sister I knew was the one I'd seen in 'ninety-eight. Since then she'd graduated from university and become London's most famous vet. She was a woman making her way in a man's world — a New Woman, at that — and she was bound to have made enemies. I needed to know more about Dr Marshall, which was exactly what I was going to do when I met Miss Paterson in Sussex Place.

I had another look at each one of the pages to make sure I hadn't missed anything, as I wasn't sure I'd be granted access again. When I was satisfied with my notes, I put the documents back in order, returned them to the folder, and re-tied the ribbon. It was already after two o'clock, and my appointment with Miss Paterson was for three. Melville's domain was something of a maze inside, but I eventually found the constables' office, which was much like the one I'd just left, except smaller and more cramped. Dawson was in his shirtsleeves, prodding a typewriter. His tongue protruded from his lips as he made occasional stabs at the machine with his right index finger. He was the very picture of concentration and hadn't heard me come in.

"Excuse me, Dawson," I said, concealing my amusement.

He was startled, then squinted at me before recognition seemed to dawn. "Major Marshall, sir? The superintendent asked me to check up on you, but I'm afraid I've been trying to master this infernal machine. How may I help?" He stood and took his coat from the back of his chair.

I handed him the folder. "Could you see this is returned to Mr Melville? Thank you. Now, I need to speak to one of your surgeons, a Dr Maycock, as soon as possible. It's a matter of urgency, and I don't want to leave it until tomorrow. Where can I find him?"

"I'm not sure, sir, are you staying awhile?"

"I have to be in Regent's Park for three o'clock."

"It may take me a bit, sir, but I'll do my best. Is there a telephone number where I can reach you?"

"I'll try and telephone you, but you can leave a message for me at the Windsor Hotel. Just one more thing, is there a stall nearby that sells hot food? I've not got time to sit down."

"I'm afraid you're too late for the pie man, sir, but there's a dealer who sells hot eels and pickled whelks next to the bridge."

"Thank you."

I strode out onto the Embankment, pleased with the results of my morning's work, but distressed at reading about the death of one I loved. My thoughts returned to the war — as they so often did — and I started humming as I made for the bridge, the words running through my head:

I have come to say good-bye, Dolly Gray
It's no use to ask me why, Dolly Gray,
There's a murmur in the air, you can hear it everywhere,
It's the time to do and dare, Dolly Gray.

Goodbye, Dolly Gray had become the anthem of the Boer War, a merry tune that belied the death and destruction…

"Major Marshall, Major Marshall!"

I turned to see Dawson running towards me. "Yes, what is it?"

"It's Inspector Truegood, sir. He just telephoned for you. He asked if you could meet him at Piccadilly and Down Street. He said to make it quick cos he might not be able to wait."

"Where's Down Street?"

"Right at the bottom, by Hyde Park Corner."
The eels would have to wait.

13. Agent Provocateur

The cab dropped me off outside the Junior Athenaeum Club, a modern French mansion opposite Green Park. Truegood was leaning against the wall, reading *Tit-Bits*. As I approached he looked up. "Took your time."

"I take it from the urgency of your summons that you have someone under observation?"

"*Now* I see why Mr M employed you — and I thought he was just desperate. Come on."

We crossed Piccadilly to a line of trees marking the edge of the park. I noticed the Wellington Statue, opposite Apsley House, two hundred yards or so away at the entrance to Hyde Park. It was warmer today, though still overcast, and a number of people were enjoying a late picnic luncheon. The preparations for the coronation had given the metropolis a festive air, and we would probably have had more company were it not for the increased attraction of the larger park, which had been turned into a temporary military encampment. Troops from all over the Empire were bivouacked there, including the artillery batteries which would initiate the royal salutes tomorrow. Truegood continued towards Hyde Park Corner for a few more paces, then stopped next to two lime trees, in a slight depression. I looked through the trees back across the road, trying to work out why Truegood had sent for me.

"The Cavalry Club! Colonel Rhodes is inside?"

"Colonel Rhodes is having lunch with his guest, Dr Drayton."

"What did Moser have to say?" I asked.

"Not much — at first. Tried to hocus me with a lot of chaff until I turned the screw on him. Then he told me that Armstrong hired him to find Lowenstein on the twenty-eighth of July."

"He didn't waste any time."

"Obviously. Moser employed an agent provocateur to find him, fella called Anthony Patrick O'Donnell, who goes by several other names as well. Said that O'Donnell didn't find him, but found out about the murder first thing yesterday."

"Could O'Donnell have been the man asking questions on Tuesday?"

Truegood looked at me and sneered. "Don't you follow *anything*? That's Rose, and I've got Lamb and Aitken tracking him down."

"I know that, but we could do with having a quiet word with O'Donnell too."

"Just keep an eye on the club. They went in at one, should be out soon." Truegood removed *Tit-Bits* from his coat, indicating that the conversation was over.

I turned my attention from the Cavalry Club to Piccadilly, which was part of the route along which the royal procession would pass tomorrow. There were Venetian masts with pennants aflutter, stands erected at every conceivable vantage point and electric lights hung for the evening illuminations. Omnibuses, hansoms and four-wheelers bounced along, as well as less frequent carts, wagons and bicycles. I took out my watch, quite literally passing the time. Half-past two. I was going to be late for my appointment with Miss Paterson.

"Here we go," said Truegood, stuffing his magazine into his pocket.

Colonel Rhodes and Drayton appeared on the pavement outside the club. They shook hands.

"Which one do you want me to follow?" I asked.

Truegood gave me another scowl. "Don't be bloody stupid, have you ever tailed someone in London before?"

"No," I confessed.

"Then you wouldn't be much good, would you? Just watch."

Colonel Rhodes hailed a cab. I was expecting Drayton to walk up to Devonshire House, but he made for Hyde Park Corner instead. Truegood waited a few seconds before following. The trees were a clever ruse, for there was no way he could see us even if he turned around. Once past Hyde Park Corner, however, we would have to leave cover.

"He's more likely to notice us if we're together," I said.

"Who?"

"Drayton, of course!"

"Christ, all that fresh air in the colonies must've gone to your head," he said as we walked up a gentle slope.

"If we're not following Drayton then what the hell *are* we doing?" I'd really had enough of the big bruiser by now.

"We're following *him*," Truegood pointed to a man walking about thirty yards ahead of us, "and lower your damned voice! When I approach him he'll probably bolt, so I want you to cut across to Constitution Hill, and grab him when he comes your way. Got it?"

"Who is he?"

Truegood shook his head at my stupidity. "Who'd you fucking think? O'Donnell of course. Now move it!"

I held back the reply on my lips, and marched off briskly towards Buckingham Palace Gardens. I made a note of O'Donnell's dress as I departed: bowler, light brown jacket, dark brown trousers. He'd probably make a run for the front of the Palace, from which he'd have half a dozen options — including St James' Park — for escape. I glanced over my shoulder to make sure he couldn't see me and then set off at a trot. As soon as I neared Constitution Hill, I changed direction to follow a path parallel to the road. I maintained my pace for a couple of hundred yards more, until I could see the Palace. Then I stopped, calmed my breathing, and stepped out onto the leafy avenue. There were dozens of people walking in both directions, so I was inconspicuous as I slowly ambled back towards Piccadilly.

I didn't have long to wait.

"Police, stop!" I heard a bellow from up ahead.

O'Donnell came flying towards me, his feet beating a tattoo on the pavement as he sprinted for Buckingham Palace. Truegood emerged from the trees fifty yards or so behind. I pretended not to notice O'Donnell as he bore down to my right. Without interrupting my stroll, I reversed my jackalberry stick, gripping the narrow end and letting the gnarled knot of a handle hang low. O'Donnell's path would bring him less than two feet from my right shoulder. Just before he drew level, I swung the stick hard across my body.

I felt the thump as I clipped him, and turned to follow as he passed.

Nothing happened.

Half a second later he let out an almighty cry, stumbled, cursed, and ploughed headlong into the paving stones. He tumbled, rolled, and rolled again. I pounced, straddling his prone form as he struggled to his feet. In an instant I had the stick under his chin, and tugged him backwards, pulling him off balance.

O'Donnell — on his knees — gripped the stick and tried to pull it away. I was too strong for him.

Truegood arrived a second later, grabbed one of O'Donnell's wrists, and twisted it. O'Donnell flipped around like a child's rag doll and before he could cry out again, Truegood had both his hands handcuffed behind his back.

"I'm glad you used that bloody stick for something," he said to me as he pulled O'Donnell up without effort. "Come on, son, let's go." He crooked his arm under O'Donnell's and steered him towards the Palace.

"Where to?" I asked.

"Grab the first growler you see. We'll go to Rochester Row nick. Now, what was that all about?"

"I don't want any trouble, Truegood," O'Donnell said in a smooth Irish brogue.

"I think you mean 'Mr Truegood', don't you, O'Donnell — or Donnelly — which one is it today?" He raised O'Donnell's arm further up his back, resulting in a canine yelp.

"Sorry, that's what I meant, boss."

"If you didn't want any trouble what did you leg it for?"

"Because every time you and me have a chat, it means trouble."

This piece of irrefutable logic coincided with the appearance of a four-wheeler and after a brief explanation to the driver we were all seated inside. I'd not been in one for years and had forgotten what an uncomfortable, bumpy journey they afforded. Truegood and I sat opposite O'Donnell, who had to lean forward because of the restraints.

"Tell me about your current employment," said Truegood.

"I can't do that, Mr Truegood. If I told everyone what I was up to, I wouldn't be a very good private agent, would I?"

"You aren't." Truegood leant forward so his nose was only a couple of inches from O'Donnell's face. "I do the jokes around here. It wouldn't do for a private agent to get banged up and tell the traps everything he knows, would it? So either you spend a few days being interrogated and I put the word out that you told us everything about the Russians and the French and the whole lot; or, you sing here — now — and I'll drop you off in Covent Garden so you can report to Moser. And I nearly forgot: if you choose the first option, I'll break your fucking legs."

O'Donnell's pale face blanched and he swallowed loudly. "I think I'll choose the second option, Mr Truegood. Was it my current job for Mr Moser you were interested in?"

"How many current jobs have you got?" Truegood answered.

"Four."

"Stick to Moser."

"Mr Moser has me following Dr Drayton until he leaves for Cape Town on Sunday. I report his comings and goings and everything in between."

"Before that."

"Yer, two weeks ago Mr Moser had me looking for a feller called Lowenstein. Eric Lowenstein. He turned up dead yesterday. He was living in a room off the Tottenham Court Road, calling himself Isaacs."

"Where?"

"Tottenham Street, number eighteen."

"How did you find out about it?"

"Come on, Mr Truegood, I can't tell you that."

"I already know how you found out, O'Donnell, but you're going to tell me anyway. If you don't, I'll lock you up as a suspect because I happen to be investigating Lowenstein's murder, and you haven't convinced me that you didn't do it. Convince me you didn't find Lowenstein on Tuesday and then go back late that night and do him in. You or Moser."

"That's not my style, Mr Truegood, you know that. Sure, if I'd found Lowenstein, I would've gone straight to Mr Moser and told him, because he said he'd pay a bounty. But I didn't. I spent most of my time looking for Lowenstein in the East End, but I happened to be at the Autonomie Club yesterday morning when I overheard…people…talking about what had happened in the Tottenham Street house."

Truegood stuck his head out of the carriage and told the driver to take us to Covent Garden. Then he turned back to O'Donnell. "They were asking Grigor Lischinsky what had happened?"

"I don't know what you're talking about," said O'Donnell, extremely agitated.

"Yeah, you do. Seeing as O'Donnell seems to have developed a temporary case of amnesia, allow me to explain for him, Major. Moser, O'Donnell's employer, works for the French police, keeping track of our anarchist community here. The Russian anarchists, and their nihilist pals, are an especially difficult group to infiltrate, but of particular concern to our French colleagues. O'Donnell is the only one of Moser's agents provocateurs that brings him reliable intelligence on the Russians, because he speaks Russian fluently. He also speaks French like a native and the bloody Russians think he's a Frog, don't they?"

"I have some small talent for languages, but I don't know any Lischinsky," said O'Donnell.

"You know just as well as I do that Ilyin is really Lischinsky, and you also know he's an Okhrana agent."

"Are there actually any anarchists in these subversive groups?" I asked.

Truegood grinned. "Not many, despite what the Frogs think. But I bet that's because you and Moser are feeding them plenty of bollocks about the place swarming with mad bombers so you keep getting paid. Yeah, O'Donnell, we know all about it. Now, if you don't want me to turn this growler around, you really need to convince me it wasn't you who got rid of Lowenstein."

"But I don't do the rough stuff, I've got too much upstairs for that. I'm a sneak, you know I am, Mr Truegood. I ask questions, I keep my ear to the ground, and that's all. Everybody knows that."

"How do I know you didn't find Lowenstein and pass it on to Moser?"

"You don't, but I didn't."

"You're not filling me with confidence, O'Donnell. I think it's time we changed direction." He put his head out the window again.

"Mr Truegood!" squeaked O'Donnell. "Look, Mr Moser hired me to find this Lowenstein feller. He didn't tell me why, and he didn't tell me who he was working for. He never does, although I know the Paris traps pay him good coin. All he said was that Lowenstein was probably in hiding and probably using a false name. I've never been to Tottenham Street, and I had no idea Lowenstein was there. As soon as I found out I told Mr Moser, and as soon as I told him, he put me onto this Drayton feller, staying at Devonshire House."

"What are your orders regarding Drayton?" I asked.

"Just like I said. I'm to follow him until he leaves London and take note of where he goes — nothing else. I told you I don't do rough stuff, it's not worth the worries."

Truegood caught my eye, and I wasn't sure what he was getting at until he asked, "Does the name Armstrong mean anything to you?"

"Yer, I know two gents by that name. A Jock feller that works at the docks in Little Barbary, and an Irish ponce in Lambeth. What about them?"

"Never mind." Truegood turned back to me and I shook my head. I didn't think O'Donnell was lying. "You're still not much good to me," said Truegood, addressing O'Donnell.

Truegood moved to call the driver again, but O'Donnell lurched forward, "Wait, Mr Truegood, wait!"

"What?"

"I'll give you something useful, so I will. I'll tell you who did it."

"Who did what?" Truegood said.

"I'll tell you who killed Lowenstein, who the feller in the wideawake hat was."

Truegood and I exchanged glances again before he said, "Get on with it."

"It was the Russians."

"Grigor Lischinsky?" Truegood laughed. "Now you really are wasting my time."

"Hold on, Mr Truegood, hold on. I don't know if it was Ilyin that actually beat Lowenstein to death, but he set it up. I know he's involved, because he was very nervous at the club when they asked him about it. And it makes perfect sense. Have you heard of a feller called Carey?"

"Yeah, is that — "

"Lieutenant Francis Carey, the big game hunter?" I interrupted.

"And not just big game, but the ladies too. Do you know about that, sir?" O'Donnell asked me.

"A little, but I better know more before this journey ends, or it won't just be the inspector you have to contend with."

"I'll tell you, sir, I'll tell you. Carey has a bad reputation with the ladies, but it doesn't keep them away from him. Lord Curzon hates his guts because he had an affair with Curzon's missis before they were married. He even spread rumours that Carey was working for the Russians in Afghanistan, but that's nonsense. The Russians hate Carey even more than Curzon does, because he's supposed to have been involved with their empress. I know, I speak the lingo, remember? Carey had to leave Russia pretty damn quick a couple of years ago. But he's got a thing for the Russian ladies because he's been courting Countess Thécla —"

"Sadly, O'Donnell, I've read *News of the World*. You're not telling me anything new," I said.

"No, I am, just hear me out. The countess is Baron de Staal's daughter — his only daughter — and whatever his feelings about Carey and the empress, he's determined to make sure old Romeo never lays a finger on his Juliet or ruins her reputation. This baron has a name as a hard man in Russia — and that's saying something. He wants Carey removed from the field of play, so he's put the Okhrana on the job. The Ilyins realised that Lowenstein was someone of means and that he was in hiding, so they knew his murder would set the cat among the pigeons. They probably used another Okhrana agent to do the dirty work, but they set up the murder. They had Lowenstein killed to frame Carey."

"And how did they frame Carey, genius?" asked Truegood.

O'Donnell frowned, confused. "The hat, Mr Truegood, the big hat."

"How the hell does that frame Carey?"

"Because everybody knows he wears one all the time."

14. Intrigue at the Zoological Gardens

We dropped off O'Donnell — sans darbies — in Shaftesbury Avenue. Truegood shouted to the driver to take us to Tottenham Street, then shook his head. "The last time I heard anything that ridiculous was when they put the finger on the Duke of Clarence for the Ripper murders. I should've collared him, shouldn't I? Except there might — just *might* — be a grain of truth in amongst all that claptrap, which is why we're off to pay the Lischinskys another visit. If they're not at home, we'll have another look in their rooms as well."

"*You*, not *we*," I said. "I'm already late for an appointment, and I don't fancy any more time in this bonesetter either. I'll get off in Tottenham Court Road and find a cab."

Truegood grunted an ungracious reply. "I've heard a great deal about this Carey in the last few days. Soldier, hunter, lover, traitor... I've also heard rumours he hires his services as an assassin. Is that true?"

"You mean," asked Truegood, "as in, is he available for hire to kill inconvenient witnesses?"

"Or Colonial Secretaries."

"That's what I was thinking. I've no idea if he kills for money, but I can tell you this: if he was hiring himself out to every Tom, Dick, and Harry to do their dirty work, he wouldn't be wearing his damned trademark hat, would he?"

"You have a point there, but that wouldn't stop the Russians from using it to impersonate him. I didn't mention it before, but I happen to know he's also the right size for the penang lawyer, in addition to Armstrong and Colonel Rhodes. We could do with finding out if he carries one."

Truegood ignored my observation. "It's absolutely bloody ludicrous, but if you were an Okhrana agent and the word was out that Carey had to be kept away from this baron's daughter — "

"And you realised there was a man of substance hiding from persecutors in your very own lodgings, then you might just take advantage of the situation. It's possible, but the main point against it is what you initially said about the Russians: they're trying to keep a low profile, so would they risk blowing their cover?"

"Probably not. Depends how influential this ambassador is. Where are you going?"

"It's a private matter."

"Oh yeah, well make sure you check with your hotel; when I've finished in Fitzroy I'm going looking for Lamb and Aitken, and if they've found Rose I'll need your help. Mr M won't give me any more men with the coronation tomorrow."

I nodded my agreement.

When we reached Tottenham Court Road, I exchanged the four-wheeler for a hansom. It was a quarter past three when the driver turned from Upper Baker Street into Sussex Place. The road was a semi-circle facing the south-western side of Regent's Park, with a terrace in the form of an immense block of white stucco adorned with gourd-shaped cupolas and belvederes. The view of the park and boating lake was awe-inspiring, and I wondered how much Ellen had paid for number twenty-seven. I knew the house and her African odyssey had accounted for most of the inheritance she'd received when she'd turned twenty-one, in 'ninety-eight.

The purchase had been against my father's will, consistent with so many of Ellen's choices in life. He didn't think property a wise investment and wanted her to rent, like most people did. When he'd moved to London in 'ninety-six, she'd stayed in Glasgow, living with our aunt while she attended the university. Thus, although she'd owned the house for four years when she died, Ellen had only made it her permanent residence last year, when she'd graduated and begun work at the Zoological Gardens. The house suited her perfectly, with the zoo in the north of the park and the Royal Botanic Gardens in the south, providing the fauna and flora of which she was so fond on her very doorstep. I dismissed the driver, entered the immaculate front garden, and lifted the knocker on the front door.

It was opened before I could knock.

"Mr Marshall — hello — I saw you from the window."

"Good afternoon, Miss Paterson, I'm sorry I'm late." She was enveloped in a figure-hugging, lacy, cream dress, which would have distracted me from my errand, had it not been so grave.

"That's quite all right, do come in."

She admitted me into the hall, where I was astonished to find six servants lined up. I was introduced to every one: butler, housekeeper, lady's maid, cook, parlour maid and scullery maid. Once I'd met them and accepted their kind condolences, Miss Paterson ordered tea and coffee, and took me to the parlour. My heart seemed to stop beating for a second when I saw my own photograph on the mantelpiece, a hurriedly taken portrait in Bloemfontein showing me having received my award. I picked it up and examined it more closely.

"Ellen was delighted when you sent that," said Miss Paterson. I didn't know what to say, and was relieved when she continued. "I was glad you wanted to meet me today, because I wanted to apologise for my conduct on Wednesday."

"Apologise?"

"Please, do sit down. Yes, apologise. Although we've corresponded before, I realised afterwards that it must have been something of a shock to you when I launched into my ideas about what really happened to Ellen — not that I don't stand by what I said, but I realise I was rather judgemental and regret if I offended you in any way."

I replaced the photograph and we each sat in a high-backed chair. "That's very kind of you, but I didn't take offence, and I have an ulterior motive for meeting you here. I'm afraid I hadn't the courage to come on my own... " I was embarrassed. "I couldn't face the thought of blundering about Ellen's house like a complete stranger, which I am — to her household, I mean. Though we didn't see much of one another after I emigrated, I always believed we were very close. We corresponded monthly, sometimes more often, and of course she spent four months with me before the war... I think what I'm trying to say is that I don't want to feel as if we were strangers, because I fear it was my fault that — to some extent — we were."

"I know how Ellen felt about you, and I'm flattered that you find my presence reassuring."

"I do. Ellen was the brave one in the family. It takes intelligence, moral courage, and devotion to stand up to society — and men like our father — and do what she did. She must have known that at the end of five years of hard work, she had very little chance of being admitted to the register."

"Yes, that's right. There's a lady called Miss Cust who graduated from Edinburgh the year before Ellen finished at Glasgow. The Royal College of Veterinary Surgeons wouldn't allow her to take their examination, so Ellen knew what to expect. She was a remarkable woman. Not only a great friend to me, but an inspiration as well. I loved her dearly."

Williams, the butler, arrived with tea, coffee, and pastries, and I waited for him to leave before I asked, "Six servants, did Ellen employ them all?"

"Yes, why?"

"I just thought it was a bit excessive, that's all."

"What on earth makes you say that? My father has ten, although there *are* three of us living at home. I hope you don't intend to get rid of any of them."

"Excuse me?"

"When you move in. Oh." She raised her hand to her mouth. "I do apologise, I thought you knew."

"Knew what?"

"Ellen left you everything. She... well, I don't wish to be indelicate, but we *were* intimate, and she told me that your father had disinherited you. So she left the house in Sussex Place and everything else to you in case something should happen to her."

My God.

If I'd been blessed with the dearest sister in the world, I was cursed to have had her plucked from me so soon. A single tear rolled down my cheek. I wiped it away, but couldn't think of anything to say.

"I'm sorry, I've over-stepped the bounds," said Miss Paterson.

"No, no you haven't. The solicitors wouldn't see me until Wednesday, so I didn't know. Thank you for telling me. And thank you again for meeting me here. I dined with Carey last night and heard his account of the incident. You may be pleased to know that after reading the coroner's report this morning, I'm inclined to agree with your assessment."

"You agree Ellen was murdered!" She started, nearly spilling her tea.

"I think there are inconsistencies between Carey's account and the evidence, but that's all I'm going to say for now."

"Mr Marshall, I'm so pleased you're back in England! I know you'll bring this dreadful business to its proper conclusion."

After our refreshments, Miss Paterson took me on a tour of the house. She'd very kindly kept an eye on the place since Ellen's death, and had been a regular guest prior to that. We finished in Ellen's study, where Miss Paterson had arranged her private papers in neat order for me.

"I know Ellen was a great correspondent, but did she keep a diary?" I asked.

"Oh, yes. She loved writing. If she hadn't been so interested in medicine, I've no doubt she'd have made a much better journalist than me."

"Do you have her most recent diary?"

"I've arranged them all chronologically for you."

"Thank you, but for the moment I just want the last one. The last letter I received from her was dated Wednesday the fourteenth of May. I want to have a look and see if there was anything out of the ordinary — or anything to do with Carey — mentioned from the fourteenth to the twenty-second."

Miss Paterson took a leather-bound journal from one of the bookcases and handed it to me. "That's the last one. Would you like me to leave you a while?"

"I'm not sure how long I'm going to be. I don't want to keep you."

"You won't be. Maggie and I are going to finish packing Ellen's clothes, unless you'd like me to leave it for you?"

"No, that's most kind. I'd appreciate your doing that."

As soon as Miss Paterson left I sat at the desk and opened the journal.

The first entry was dated the first of February. I felt as if I was intruding, reading Ellen's private thoughts, thoughts which were never intended to be seen by anyone else. My discomfort soon changed to intrigue, however, for Ellen had been such an interesting woman. I found her feelings and ideas perceptive and fascinating, even as I was moved by a sweeping sadness. How little of her I had really ever known, and now never would. When she mentioned me, as she frequently did, my eyes watered, and sometimes overflowed. I tried to put my emotions aside, but it was difficult. I must steel myself to the task and try to read the journal as if it were evidence in a crime, which was exactly what I hoped it would be. Not only did I need to scour her diary for mention of anything that might point to a motive for murder, but also to build up a picture of her day-to-day life, of which I regrettably knew so little.

I would not fail Ellen again.

Many of her entries concerned the zoo superintendent, Mr Clarence Bartlett, and how he was continually trying to reduce his expenditure. Ellen had worked as a volunteer at the zoo when she'd returned from Africa, spending all of her university holidays working gratis. When Bartlett realised he could employ her at an assistant's wage after her graduation, he'd jumped at the chance. Ellen was concerned about her finances, for although she would've been comfortable for another eighteen months, there was little prospect of her remuneration improving thereafter. She remained at the zoo purely for the benefit of the animals, knowing how much they would suffer if left to Gibbs' care. It appeared that Carey's description of the resident veterinary surgeon had been accurate. He was an alcoholic, often did more harm than good to the animals, and frequently failed to attend at all. This seemed to suit Bartlett, who paid him a poor wage as well.

I left the journal and went through some of the other letters and accounts Miss Paterson had placed in order for me, to see what Ellen's exact situation had been. Her wages were indeed execrable at one pound, five shillings a week. Sixty-five pounds a year. She had just under eight hundred and seventy pounds left in savings, which would have been unlikely to last longer than eighteen months when she wasn't earning much over the salary she was paying her butler. I felt particularly wretched when I saw that the last withdrawals from her bank had been by her solicitors, following her instructions to pay for her own funeral and burial.

After a while, I replaced the letters and returned to the journal.

In January, after Gibbs had crippled a zebra, Ellen asked Bartlett to replace him and told the superintendent she couldn't cope with all the work on her own. His response had been to remind her how grateful she should be for the job he'd given her. After more butchery by Gibbs in February, Ellen had attempted to enlist the support of Mr Phillip Sclater, secretary of the Zoological Gardens, and Herbrand Russell, the eleventh Duke of Bedford and President of the Royal Zoological Society. Both of these entreaties had fallen upon deaf ears, and Bartlett had reprimanded her for all the trouble she was causing. She knew he wouldn't dismiss her, however, because of the combination of the poor wages she accepted, and the celebrity which had been attached to her sex since she began working there.

I read of Ellen's increased frustration and her decision, just after she'd written her last letter to me, to involve the Humanitarian League. Miss Paterson had agreed to introduce her to a Mr Henry Salt, of the League, who had already voiced concerns as to the conditions in which the animals were kept on several occasions. She was due to meet Mr Salt on Friday the twenty-third of May.

The day after her death in what I now regarded as suspicious circumstances.

I glanced at the weekend of the seventeenth and eighteenth of May, but found nothing of relevance. Frustrated, I skipped through the Monday — which had begun with a visit to our father — and Tuesday. On Wednesday Ellen had made an entry to the effect that Carey had requested to join her on her ride in the park the next evening. She was curious as to why he wanted to meet her, and appeared to know about his proposed expedition to the Karakoram Mountains. She concluded with the words: 'Regardless, he will be sorely disappointed if he expects the ZSL to sponsor him.'

Those were the last words of the last entry. The diary and Ellen's life both ended there. I rose from the desk and walked out onto the small balcony. It presented a truly magnificent view of the park, and I thought about how happy Ellen must have been living here. I was so deep in my thoughts that I didn't hear Miss Paterson enter, and was startled when she appeared suddenly at my elbow.

"I'm sorry, I did knock, but you didn't answer. It's six o'clock already."

"Is it? You're quite right. I was... elsewhere."

"Did you find anything useful in her papers?"

"Perhaps, I can't be sure yet. Have you had a look at them?"

"No, I haven't," she replied. "I didn't realise that they might throw any light on her death at first. By the time I appreciated their use, you were on your way back. I didn't think it would be right for me to intrude. Ellen was your sister; I was only her friend."

"There's no *only* about it, and you seem to have set a great deal of store by my abilities. Far too much, I fear. I wonder why a woman of your obvious intelligence would do that?"

"Because Ellen always expressed such faith in you, and I'd come to trust her judgement implicitly. Having met you, I now know that you won't disappoint either of us." She leant forward on the iron railing and looked across to the park.

I followed Miss Paterson's gaze. "It's a lovely view, isn't it? You — "

"It most certainly is not!" She drew up and glared at me.

"Er... sorry, why... "

"Because we're looking at the place where Lieutenant Carey murdered Ellen. There," she pointed, "across the lake, behind the row of trees. The house beyond is The Holme. They were riding between the house and the lake. That's where it happened."

"If you could spare me a little more of your time, I'd like to go and have a look."

"It's on private property."

"That is the least of my concerns at the moment."

"Well, come on, let's go!"

15. The Holme

I'd noticed a telephone in Ellen's house, and I used it to check if any messages had been left for me at the Windsor. There was nothing from Truegood, but Dr Maycock had very kindly left details of his plans for the rest of the day, which involved a brief return home followed by the Alhambra and the Cavour. I left Ellen's number with the attendant in case anyone else tried to contact me. Miss Paterson reappeared in a fashionable broad-brimmed hat — a cravat, gloves, and parasol completed her ensemble. I was dressed rather casually by comparison, but she didn't seem to mind as she took my arm. She directed us across Sussex Place, and then left along Hanover Terrace, a sombre Doric block adorned with pediments and statues.

"Are we going to Hanover Gate?" I asked.

"Yes. I assume you don't know the park very well?"

"No, but I've a rough idea from what Carey told me. I imagine that he and Ellen trotted down from the zoo, crossed the Long Bridge, and then broke into a gallop through The Holme's grounds. Is that right?"

"Unfortunately, yes. If we enter at Hanover Gate we can cross the Long Bridge and follow their route — if that's what you'd like to do."

"I would. Do you know exactly where she fell?"

"I think so. As I said, it's private property, but I made as many inquiries as I could after, so I've a good idea. Are you going to examine the ground for clues, like the detectives in the periodicals?"

"Not three months after the crime, no."

"Oh... how foolish of me."

"Who owns The Holme?" I asked as we passed under the leafy arch of Hanover Gate.

"I'm not sure. I think it's still the Burton family."

"As in Decimus Burton, the architect?"

"Yes, but I know it's being leased by Lord Francis Hope. He's the second son of the Duke of Newcastle and quite a colourful character. He's been bankrupt since he divorced his wife, an American actress who ran off with a wealthy gentleman from New York. There's even talk that he's going to sell the famous Hope Diamond." Miss Paterson looked at me expectantly. I raised my eyebrows to show my lack of comprehension. "It's supposed to be worth over twenty-five thousand pounds," she said.

"Is it?" I wasn't thinking about Hope, I was thinking about another colourful character: Carey.

"Yes, and that's a conservative estimate."

We walked along the road towards the lake, lined with weeping willows, with Hertford Villa on our left. There were scores of people about, and I wondered again if London was always this full, and how many were tourists, here for the coronation. I was also considering how I could use the ceremony, which would bring the metropolis to a standstill on another bank holiday, to my advantage. We crossed the bridge on to Hanover Island, where there was a boathouse for renting rowboats. A line of trees on the far bank of the lake marked the boundary of The Holme, with Holme Green further down, to our right.

"What are you thinking — if you don't mind my asking?" queried Miss Paterson.

"I heard some more rumours about Carey today. What do you actually know about him? I mean know for a fact, as opposed to hearsay or rumour."

"That's just the problem, isn't it? There is so much gossip about Lieutenant Carey, one never knows quite what to believe. Nobody seems to know anything about his early life, before he joined the West India Regiment. That was in 1890, if I remember correctly. He left after two years and travelled all over Africa and India, hunting and capturing animals. When he was in India he was supposed to have had an — "

"Just the facts, please," I interrupted.

She sighed. "In that case I've probably told you all I know already."

"I know he has a reputation as a ladies' man — or rake — or whatever you wish to call it. I've heard he's been involved with Lord Curzon's wife, the Empress of Russia, and most recently some countess or other."

"The Russian empress! Surely not — that is quite scurrilous. As for Lady Curzon, Lieutenant Carey was certainly acquainted with her in one capacity or another. She's American, and lived in Washington before marrying Lord Curzon, and Carey is supposed to have travelled to

America in his youth. I told you the rumours that he'd worked on an illegal slaver, but that's hearsay as well, of course."

"And how do you know that Lady Curzon knows him?"

"Rumour again, but some of it must be true! I heard from several of my journalist friends that Lieutenant Carey was on most intimate terms with Lady Curzon, and that this displeased the viceroy greatly."

"So much that he accused Carey of spying for the Russians in Afghanistan?"

"You mean he didn't betray his country?"

"I've no idea."

"When you refer to 'some countess or other' I expect you mean Baron de Staal's daughter, the Countess Thécla Orloff Davidoff?"

"If Baron de Staal is the Russian ambassador."

"He is. Lieutenant Carey was a guest at the embassy on several occasions this year. A couple of months ago he was seen accompanying the countess to the opera and theatre. I seem to recall she was also seen with him in his automobile, but I didn't pay much attention at the time. Then suddenly he wasn't welcome at the embassy anymore. That's from one of my colleagues who runs a society column, so I don't know what you'll make of it. It appears that Baron de Staal has forbidden his daughter any further contact with Lieutenant Carey."

"Or perhaps Carey was using Miss de Staal as cover to pass on information because he really is a Russian spy; or perhaps the Russians don't like him because he really did seduce the Empress. Half-truths, bloody nonsense more like!"

"Mr Marshall!"

"Er, my apologies, please excuse my language. I forgot myself." She was frowning very severely. "I find your company so stimulating that for a moment I thought I was talking to another detective." She warmed at this, as I'd intended.

"Well, that's quite understandable, although I'd rather you didn't do it again."

"I won't." There was one matter which Miss Paterson, with her apparently comprehensive knowledge of society, seemed eminently qualified to resolve. I chose my words carefully, however, so as not to influence her answer. "I've a question which may seem rather strange, but the answer to it could prove significant later. Is there any particular style or article of clothing associated with Carey?"

"Do you mean something you could use to identify him?"

Miss Paterson was rather more perceptive than I'd thought. "Yes."

"His hat. He wears a tatty old wideawake hat to all but the most formal of occasions."

We crossed the island and the other side of the bridge, bringing us to a convergence of roads, paths and people. Miss Paterson and social graces faded from my mind. I shook myself free from her hand, ignored her protest, and quickened my step until I was looking directly south, across a small sward leading to the copse that marked the boundary of The Holme. This was it: the very place where Ellen had galloped to her death. As I approached the trees I saw a sturdy wooden fence, about four feet high. There was a gate, but — measuring the distances in my mind — I imagined Ellen and Carey had probably started their race from the bridge. They would only have had to weave through one or two trees before jumping the fence.

I vaulted the fence myself and saw a strip of open ground running between the line of birch and willow trees that marked the edge of the lake and another copse shielding The Holme's gardens and villa. I turned back to open the gate for Miss Paterson, ignored whatever she said, and picked up my pace along the stretch of grass. At the far end, about a hundred and forty yards away, was yet another copse, between the private grounds and Holme Green, a public area. I reached the middle, where the trees from The Holme formed a slight bend, and could see exactly what Carey had been talking of. I stopped, turned all the way around, and closed my eyes, thinking of how secluded the place would be at dusk and after.

"Mr Marshall! What on earth are you doing?" Miss Paterson was marching towards me.

"Look." I pointed behind her, and then ahead of us. "This open stretch, from the first copse to the second, look at it!"

"Well, what about it?" she said, slightly out of breath.

"It's no more than a hundred and forty yards."

"I'll take your word for it. So?"

"Carey's evidence doesn't make sense. Either Ellen jumped the wall where I did, or Carey must've dismounted to open the gate for her. If they walked through the gate then they had an even shorter distance to gallop!"

Miss Paterson tried to follow me, failed, and shook her head. "I'm sure I'm being most dense, but I'm afraid you'll have to explain."

"Have you ridden before?"

"Yes, occasionally."

"A man is faster than a horse over a hundred yards — the first hundred, anyway."

"Really?"

"Yes. I first heard it from an old Boer in Stellaland and tested it many times on myself and others. So, if Ellen only galloped this distance, she couldn't have been going very fast because she'd have had to rein in for the next copse — there's another fence and gate amongst the trees there. But I think they both jumped the first fence—"

"If she was weakened by her wound, she would have fallen there, not here."

"Miss Paterson, you are not only exceptionally pleasing to the eye, but also most astute — that is exactly what I mean!" She coloured, and I realised that in my excitement I'd probably overstepped the mark of propriety. "Look at the lie of the ground here. Except for boaters who stray close to the bank, no one can see us. No one! At dusk, even the boaters wouldn't be able to see between the willows. I'm not saying it makes this the scene of an offence, but it is a perfect place to commit murder."

Miss Paterson faded from my consciousness again and I marched a dozen steps back in the direction we'd come. "There. Carey reins his horse in and shouts out to Ellen. He affects to know very little about horses, but if he's been exploring and hunting for ten years he'll know at least as much as I do. He pretends there's a problem with the animal, perhaps its hoof or shoe. Ellen, being a vet, will dismount to take a closer look. She bends over — he strikes!" I pounded my fist into my palm and Miss Paterson caught her breath. "He breaks her neck — easily done if you know how — waits a few minutes, and goes for help from the house." I pointed to the right. "That's it, that's all he need do."

"Remarkable, it's just as if I'm watching the tragedy unfold."

I spun on my heels. "But why! Why the hell would Carey want Ellen dead? Or who on earth would pay him to kill her if that was it?"

"I don't know," she said softly.

"People don't kill without a reason, a motive."

"So you've said."

"It won't do. There must be something we're missing. Where there is a motive, there is benefit: either an advantage gained or an ill avoided. Who benefits from Ellen's death? Other than me."

"I don't know. I've thought about it over and over and over again, but I can't conceive of anyone."

I offered Miss Paterson my arm once more and we walked along the remainder of the lawn at a more sedate pace. "In her diaries Ellen mentions problems with Bartlett and the conditions the animals were kept in at the zoo. She wrote that you'd arranged for her to talk to a gentleman from the Humanitarian League. Is that right?"

"You don't think — "

"I don't think anything at the moment," I interrupted, "but would that meeting have harmed Bartlett and the zoo management?"

"Well, Bartlett might have found his questionable practices under public scrutiny."

"Then there's also the duke," I said, opening the gate to Holme Green.

"The duke?"

"The Duke of Bedford. Carey was — is — desperate to secure his patronage."

"You don't think — "

"I don't, but it's a start. Ellen made an enemy of Bartlett, and perhaps this man Sclater and Russell as well. We're looking for someone who benefits, and there's one, perhaps more," I finished.

"Oh! That's dreadful, I feel as if I led her to her death!"

"Of course you didn't. I'm thinking out loud, it's just a scatterbrained notion." A tear ran down her left cheek and I wiped it away with my forefinger before offering my handkerchief.

She took it and dabbed her eyes. "Are you sure it wasn't my fault?"

"That's about the only thing I am sure of. There may be more to this matter or there may be something else entirely that I've missed. Tomorrow — no, tomorrow will be a waste of time when it comes to interviewing people, won't it? On Monday I'll pay a visit to Bartlett and Sclater, and make arrangements to see the Duke of Bedford as well. And this Lord Hope."

"Lord Hope, whatever for?"

We joined a crowded path again, on the south side of the lake. "You've described him as a man similar to Carey in character. Also, he's having financial problems. Financial problems can make a man desperate. He may be involved with Carey, or know something about this."

"About tomorrow," she said before pausing. "I'm sure you've had masses of invitations, but I wondered if you'd like to join me — for luncheon or dinner?"

"Actually, I've had none. Either no one knows about my VC or they're bored with war heroes. Who'd be interested in a retired major when Lords Kitchener and Roberts are here?" I laughed. "So I'm most grateful for your kind invitation; thank you very much. There's just one thing: I've been recruited by Superintendent Melville — "

"The King's Detective!"

"Yes."

"How exciting. Is that how you were able to read the official reports of Ellen's death?"

"Something like that," I answered. "Anyway, I'm at Melville's disposal at present, and he may have some use for me tomorrow. If you can provide me with the details of both parties, then I'll let you know whether or not to expect me as soon as I know whether I'll be needed."

"Oh, don't worry about that, just turn up if you can."

"If you're happy with such an informal arrangement, it would suit me better."

"I am. I'm a guest of Lord Morley for luncheon at the National Liberal Club. I'm sure I'll be able to get you in, just ask for me at the door. It starts at eleven o'clock and we'll probably be there until about three. Then father is hosting a dinner at our house. Nothing extravagant, just about twenty guests. I'd like you to meet him, anyway."

"Yes, of course. Thank you."

I led Miss Paterson across York Bridge, at the narrow end of the lake, and shortly we arrived in York Terrace.

"I have to leave you here," she said, "I'm already late for dinner at father's. I come and go as I please, naturally, but I can't let cook down. She's doing something special in advance of tomorrow's feast. Tomorrow's dinner is for seven o'clock, if you aren't working."

I didn't think she came and went as she pleased at all, despite her apparent worldliness. "Thank you again for spending the afternoon with me. It was… helpful, and very — it was good to see you again so soon."

"My pleasure, Mr Marshall. Would you hail me a cab?"

I called one which was passing, and opened the door for Miss Paterson when it stopped alongside.

"Well, I hope we shall see each other tomorrow, Mr Marshall."

"So do I. Miss Paterson, I wonder if you wouldn't call me Alec?"

"I'm not sure that would be proper." She quickly climbed up on to the seat.

"Good evening, Roberta." I closed the door, smiling to myself. Once the cab had left, I walked back along the south-western edge of the park, into Cornwall Terrace, and then Sussex Place. I knocked on Ellen's door and was admitted by Williams, who asked if I would like dinner prepared. He was surprised when I replied that I'd sup with the staff. There had also been a message while I was out. The Windsor had phoned to pass on an invitation to meet at noon tomorrow — alone — at the Monument, in the City of London.

It was from Hugh Armstrong.

16. The Doctor's Revelation

I'd no idea what to make of Armstrong's invitation, but I was determined to meet him. Whatever he was up to, I wanted to know about it. Noon would be about the time the King was crowned, so the streets would be impassable. I had plans for the morning, and wasn't sure how long they'd take, or how I'd get to the City, but I could leave that until tomorrow. In the half hour before dinner I went up to Ellen's study to continue my researches. I began with her second-to-last journal, skimming through the pages for any mention of Carey or Russell. There were none. I went back to the beginning of last year, with the same result, and then joined the servants in the kitchen. The meal was excellent, and although I enjoyed it as much for the fried fillet of trout and garnished ham as for the informal atmosphere, I had another motive for dining with Ellen's staff: to establish some sort of rapport before I questioned them.

After we'd eaten, I interviewed them one by one, in the parlour, starting with Williams. I began with a lengthy preamble regarding the importance of complete candour, and then asked each of the six the same six questions. Unfortunately, all their answers were identical: nothing out of the ordinary had happened to Ellen, or anyone in the household, in the few weeks before her death; she hadn't done anything out of the ordinary herself; no one unknown or new to Ellen's circle had called or left messages for her; Ellen hadn't seemed preoccupied or upset; she hadn't mentioned Carey, and he hadn't telephoned or visited; finally, Ellen had no known enemies. In short, the interviews were a necessary waste of time with regard to evidence, though they afforded me another welcome glimpse into the character and life of my dear sister.

I told Kate, the parlour maid, that I'd see myself out later, and returned to Ellen's study once again. I continued with the journals, going as far back as her visit to South Africa in ninety-nine. There was nothing obviously relevant to her death, but I soon understood how she'd become so well known so quickly. Ellen had been the only woman studying veterinary science at Glasgow University, the only woman volunteer at the Zoological Gardens, and one of a handful of women who were

Fellows of the Zoological Society of London. When she'd returned from her African travels she'd lectured the ZSL, the Royal Society, and Newnham College, Cambridge. She'd found friends and admirers in all these places.

Most of veterinary science was aimed at treating horses, which were both an important part of the economy and a substantial source of revenue for aristocrats practicing the sport of kings. Ellen's decision to specialise in the exotic creatures exhibited in the zoo was thus both unusual and unlikely ever to provide her with much in the way of remuneration — even if Bartlett hadn't been such a slave driver. Bearing in mind my initial observations to Roberta, I also looked for an indication of a man in her life, someone who might have been more than a friend. Once again, there was no evidence that Ellen was anything other than entirely dedicated to her studies and work.

Later, I found myself back at her final diary entry. There were only two differences between Ellen's last week of life and any other week since she'd begun full-time employment at the zoo. One was Carey, and the other Henry Salt of the Humanitarian League. Would her report to Salt be damaging enough to the zoo for Bartlett or the Duke of Bedford to prevent it by whatever means necessary? Surely not. Had Carey taken it upon himself to remove an obstacle for the duke in order to curry favour with him? The idea was preposterous and yet my sister was lying buried in the graveyard at St James' Church.

It was time to see Dr Maycock.

A cab dropped me on the Whitcombe Street side of Leicester Square at just after ten. The square was heaving with throngs of people of all kinds. Some were walking, some shouting, some begging; others were just milling around, enjoying the atmosphere of the night before a bank holiday and — more importantly — the night before the coronation, our first in sixty-five years. I ambled along slowly, taking in the sights and sounds. Leicester Square held particularly fond memories for me. It was here, in the week before I entered Westminster School, that my father brought me to see a 'patriotic demonstration' entitled *For the Colours*. It was the first time I'd been to a music hall and I absolutely loved it.

It was also probably the last happy memory I had of my father. Once I was boarding at Westminster, I grew my own way, which was very different to his. I thought about Ellen again, and how much he must have hated the fact that she'd become a New Woman. He'd been unable to influence the lives of either of his children for all the money and power he'd accumulated. Ellen had been particularly brave for — where I had in effect run away to make my own life — she'd done it under his disapproving gaze. She'd struggled against overwhelming odds and succeeded.

I was going to make sure that whoever had extinguished such a bright flame paid the piper.

When I'd watched *For the Colours* with my father in 'eighty-six, the Alhambra had recently been rebuilt after a fire. The new building had been added to and altered three times since, until it completely dominated the square. The two tall towers and massive dome were in the Moorish style, with lavish fenestrations all over the hundred-foot-high frontage. Many people didn't like it, and the square was regarded as London's dirtiest and most unpleasant, full of foreign styles and languages. It was certainly dirty and full of foreign influences, but I enjoyed the atmosphere. Here, in amongst the ebb and flow of humanity in all its forms, one felt not only at the centre of the world's greatest empire, but at very centre of the planet.

Leicester Square recalled Rhodes and his Society of the Elect. He may have scoffed at Freemasonry, but his Idea wasn't very different from theirs. Although I'd declined an offer to join a Lodge in Durban, I knew a little about Masonic beliefs and practices. They were neither pro- nor anti-Christian, and acknowledged the supremacy of the Great Architect of the Universe. What or who the Great Architect might be, was for each man to decide on his own, but in order to join, one must consider this power both supreme and beneficial. The character and works of the Supreme Being were understood and explained using the allegory of the craft of stonemasonry.

Rhodes, however, regarded himself as the Supreme Being rather than the Worshipful Master of a Lodge. He had recreated himself in the image of the Great Architect of Empire, with the intention of imposing his own moral values on the entire world. He was the Architect, as he saw it, and men like Milner, Chamberlain, and Jameson were the individual Lodge Masters, continuing his great work to its ultimate conclusion: a world where only England remained, because every other country had been Anglicised. Milner had already begun his work in the SAR and the

Orange Free State. It wasn't enough that they had acknowledged British sovereignty, he wanted them to speak in English, to pray in English, to *be* English. The irony was that should Milner succeed, he would never consider them English — they would always be something lesser.

The Great Architect's work must be dismantled. Perhaps there wouldn't be much to it. Milner and Jameson were obviously at loggerheads and the more the executors of Rhodes' will squabbled amongst themselves, the less likely they were to collude in ruling the Empire. Perhaps the Society and the Idea were already crumbling and wouldn't outlive Rhodes for much longer — or perhaps not. Either way I resolved to place myself at Melville's disposal until Rhodes' work had been undone.

I jostled my way to the front entrance of the Alhambra, where posters advertised tonight's performances. For all its foreign appearance the theatre had always been a bastion of patriotism and support for King, country, and Empire. Tonight was no exception: Dr Maycock was at *Britannia's Realm*. The operetta was about to finish, and would be followed by *In Japan* and then variety shows late into the night. As soon as the mass exodus from the theatre began, I moved over to the entrance of the Cavour. I saw Dr Maycock approaching the restaurant with a group of nearly a dozen men and women. He was deep in conversation with a lady a few years younger than him, and didn't notice my greeting. I tugged at his arm.

He stared blankly, then recognised me. "Marshall, good Lord, it's Major Marshall! How do you do? Come inside and join us for a drink!"

"Thank you, Doctor, but I'd like a private word if it's all the same. I won't take much of your time."

"Let's go inside anyway. You can buy me a drink. It'll be just as noisy inside as out, so no one'll hear us."

He was right; the bustle was even greater inside, with parties of diners coming and going, and waiters weaving expertly in between the tables. Maycock excused himself from his companions and took me past the giant square buffet table to the drinks bar. At his request, I ordered a single malt whisky, which turned out to be Glenmorangie. Not my favourite, but I ordered one for myself as well. He took his without water so I thought I'd better make it a double measure for him and a single for me.

He raised tumbler and voice simultaneously: "Your good health, Major, and my condolences on your loss."

"Thank you." We touched glasses, and drank. I leant close to him, so as not to have to shout above the noise. "You knew Dr Marshall was my sister?"

"I did, but I didn't consider it appropriate to mention it at the time."

"No, of course not. I've read the coroner's summary, and the various reports — including your own — and I noted that you wanted a full post-mortem examination conducted."

"Quite so. Not that I expected my recommendation to be followed; it seldom is, I'm afraid."

"That's a shame. The reason you wanted to investigate further was the absence of abrasions, wasn't it?"

"Yes, old chap, quite." He took a second, healthy swig of his whisky.

"What about the absence of skeletal damage, isn't that also suspicious? In my understanding the only bones broken were in my sister's neck."

"That's correct, but I wouldn't regard that as suspicious in itself."

"No?"

"No. I've seen plenty of deaths from falls. In a case such as this where there was considerable horizontal as well as vertical motion, there aren't always broken bones. You've just come back from the war, haven't you? You must've seen dozens of men fall off horses."

"Yes, but none of them died from it, although one did break his back."

"Poor fellow, how very unlucky. Breaks or fractures do occur, but not always. There are, however, always abrasions. Always." He finished his drink and looked wistfully at the empty glass. I finished mine and ordered a second round, with another double measure for him. He grinned and continued. "Thank you, sir. I said it wasn't suspicious on its own, but of course I didn't take the absence of skeletal or dermatological damage in isolation. No, I looked at all the evidence presented, physical and circumstantial. Tell me, what do you think happened?"

"I think Carey murdered her."

"Your good health… ah, thank God for the Scots! So do I. And that was my opinion before I discovered that Dr Marshall was in the company of a man with so dubious a reputation. Do you know why I thought that, Major?"

"No," I said.

"First and foremost because I'm a suspicious old bastard. That's right. I've spent twenty-five years as a police surgeon and my experience is that when one piece of evidence fails to fit the rest, it's an indication of circumstantial or deliberate duplicity." He tapped his red nose and his jowls shivered. "Not to put too fine a point on it, when I smell a rat, it's because there usually is one. A great, bloody big beast of a rat. I'm not infallible, and sometimes it's impossible to prove anything, but most of the time I'm right. I've been at it too long and too hard for it to be any other way. This time I know I'm right. My experience aside there was another reason why I wanted the full post-mortem examination." He paused for a drink. "You recall the bruises on Dr Marshall's arms?"

"There was something about — "

"There certainly was. I'd stake my life on it that they were inflicted post-mortem."

17. The Maltese Tiger

I stumbled out into Leicester Square in a daze, bumping into people and wandering without any clear purpose or direction in mind. Maycock's observations shouldn't have shocked me, but they had. My head was suddenly pounding with the alcohol and noise, and I had the sickening sensation of an abominable truth waiting to be stripped bare. Maycock said the bruises were inflicted post-mortem; I struggled to keep a ghastly image at bay. Eventually I found my way back to Whitcombe Street, fell into a cab like a drunk, and mumbled the destination to the driver. I closed my eyes tight shut and saw everything — saw exactly what had happened to Ellen in The Holme. Pictures played through my mind in a relentless theatograph, just like the visions of war that wouldn't stop.

Carey had reined in. He had called to Ellen and dismounted. She had dismounted and gone to his assistance. When she was vulnerable he had struck, broken her neck, and watched her expire. He'd waited a short while to make sure she was dead, then he'd remounted, galloped off to The Holme, and raised the alarm. He'd returned to Ellen's corpse long before anyone else had arrived. He'd looked at Ellen, perhaps trying to imagine what the police would see, and realised that there should be more damage to her person to verify his story.

Then he had beaten her dead body.

Not just beaten it, but beaten it hard and repeatedly. Maycock had explained that while molecular life remains in the tissues it is possible to produce a slight degree of blood extravasation, but only if considerable force is applied. Carey couldn't risk using his boots, they would have left scuff marks. So he got down on his knees and punched Ellen's corpse. Punched her arms over and over again until bruises were produced. Bruises that would show some attempt by Ellen to protect herself as she fell from the horse. Once he was satisfied, Carey had stood by the body with the horses and waited for the servants from The Holme and the police.

He hadn't taken the abrasions into consideration — and why should he? He probably had less medical training than me, and I hadn't thought about them. He hadn't taken Roberta's persistence or my return to London into consideration either. He'd committed his murder, performed for the police and the jurors, and then resumed his efforts to find a patron for his accursed expedition. An incompetent or idle coroner had done the rest for him. I was a fool; I'd let him charm me. After our meal at the Travellers Club, Carey must have thought he was finally safe from the law and justice.

He was wrong.

In times of crisis I've always found it useful to do something — anything — because concentrating on the action forces the fear and shock aside. I now knew that Carey had killed Ellen, but I still didn't know why, and I wanted to find out who his employer had been. Carey may have been the instrument of Ellen's death, but I was positive there was someone else behind it. The resolve that followed my realisation sharpened my senses, and when I alighted from the cab the driver probably thought I'd sobered up in the fresh air.

I double-checked the message from Armstrong with the attendant, went straight up to my sitting-room, and removed Ellen's last journal from my coat pocket. I placed it on the desk. It was after eleven, but I wasn't going to allow myself to sleep until I'd found something that gave me a clue as to the motive for her murder. I stripped to my shirtsleeves, poured a glass of water from the carafe, and prepared my pipe. The routine of packing, lighting and smoking a pipe is a form of ritual, something like the Japanese tea ceremony. Like many rituals it serves as a calming interlude, concentrating the mind on a mundane task and sequence. The ritual gave me a temporary respite from the horror and once the meerschaum was drawing well, I found it a little easier to focus.

I opened the journal at the last entry:

Wednesday, May 21st, 1902.

What a week this is turning out to be! After Monday's oddity and my meeting with Mr Salt still to come, Lt Carey has asked to join me on my evening ride tomorrow. We have met thrice before, through the ZSL, but never in private. He has a frightful reputation where ladies are concerned, and I have heard rumours that he has ruined many women of all classes. Despite his rakish exploits, I've always found him interesting, for while he affects an air of insouciance, he is actually a very serious zoologist. Even though I take pride in eschewing the hypocrisy with which our society regards women, I must be careful where Lt Carey is concerned. I wouldn't want anyone to think I was foolish enough to find him attractive, or be thought of as 'one of his women', though I alone knew it to be false. If practicing veterinary medicine and sitting astride a horse is a part of what it means to be a New Woman, then so is keeping men like Lt Carey at a respectable distance.

I've read all three of his publications and attended half of a dozen (I think) of his addresses to the ZSL, and found them all stimulating. He seems to possess a knack for combining scholarship with adventure and I can certainly see why so many women find him alluring. On all three occasions we met, however, he treated me as a fellow scientist rather than a woman, which was as unexpected as it was refreshing. Though I shall guard against it, I am quite sure his interest in me is not amorous. Which leads me to my main reason for agreeing to meet him: I am curious. Why should he suddenly want a private interview?

I know he seeks a patron for an expedition to the Karakoram Mountains, and has sought funding from the ZSL. He tried to secure sponsorship by claiming that he'll bring back several exotic species, including a Snow Leopard, Marco Polo Sheep, and an Ibex. Perhaps he wants my support, although he must realise I've little influence. I know he is an extremely competent hunter, but I'm sure the most the Gardens will ever see of a Snow Leopard is its pelt.

Not that it matters. If he hasn't done so already, Mr Bartlett is sure to raise objections that the expedition will waste valuable resources which could better be directed to the Gardens. Sometimes I feel he must either be bent on the destruction of the Gardens or embezzling vast sums of money. Those are the only two motives I can imagine for his gross mismanagement. Lt Carey may have more luck with the Duke of Bedford, who often seems more keen on increasing his own private collection than looking after the public Gardens.

I won't go on about the unpleasant aspects of work, I'll only depress myself.

After our few conversations and reading 'In Search of the Maltese Tiger', I think Lt Carey has become obsessed with the animal, and it wouldn't surprise me if that was the real aim of his Asian expedition. A blue tiger? It's quite possible, of course. White tigers have been documented in the Bengal subspecies and we call black leopards *'panthers'*, so there's no reason why there shouldn't be a blue tiger, but I expect it will remain his very own chimera. Regardless, he will be sorely disappointed if he expects the ZSL to sponsor him.

That was all for the final entry.

I'd never heard of a Maltese Tiger, but I assumed it was either very rare or extinct, and obviously blue in colour. I puffed on my pipe and considered what I'd just read. Had I missed anything on my first, hurried, reading in Ellen's study? I didn't think so. Ellen knew Carey from their common fellowship of the ZSL and his interest in the zoo. Ellen wasn't sure why he wanted to see her, but guessed it might be something to do with the expedition — which still seemed to be the focus of his energies. There was nothing new here.

The entry for Tuesday was confusing, involving the interaction of three individuals — Jim, Tom, and Bill — with a crowd of onlookers. When I read of Jim and Tom eating a broom, I realised that the former two names referred to Indian Rhinoceroses, and the latter to their keeper. Bill's practice of delighting onlookers by feeding the beasts brooms, shovels, and buckets had brought him a reprimand from Ellen twice before. On this third occasion she had gone to see Bartlett to request the man's dismissal, but had been unable to find him and reported the matter to Sclater instead.

Later in the afternoon, while attending to the cubs at the Lion House, she'd been wounded by 'little Horatio'. After treating the wound herself, she'd gone to see her own doctor, Dr Hall, whose practice in Harley Street was only a short distance away. Hall had cleaned and dressed the wound and told her to rest for the remainder of the day, but she and Roberta had spent the evening at the Women Journalist's Club in Henrietta Street. Ellen had been pleased to meet Miss Flora Shaw, soon to be Mrs Frederick Lugard. Miss Shaw had addressed the ladies on the subject of overcoming the barriers faced by women journalists, one for which she was conspicuously qualified. Afterwards, Ellen and Roberta had enjoyed a discussion with her over a cup of tea.

I knew of Flora Shaw by reputation. She was probably the most famous lady journalist in Britain. She had travelled widely, was an acknowledged expert on colonial affairs throughout the Empire, and had been appointed as the first Colonial Editor of the *Times*. At the age of fifty she'd recently announced her intention to retire from journalism and marry Lugard, who held some official position somewhere in West Africa. Shaw was also a close friend of Rhodes — the only woman in his very masculine circle — and there was much speculation as to her role in the Jameson Raid.

Some said she'd been as complicit as Rhodes and Chamberlain, and others that she'd actually been the driving force behind it, egging Rhodes on until he launched the invasion. I doubted the latter, myself, because I didn't think Rhodes needed any encouragement when it came to annexing new territories; it was his life's work. At the very least, however, Shaw had covered up the official sanction of the raid by destroying a series of telegrams implicating Rhodes, Chamberlain, and Mr G. E. Buckle, *The Times'* editor. Whatever the truth, no one believed her innocent. Shaw had appeared before the same committee of inquiry that investigated Rhodes and Chamberlain. Like them, she'd given evidence and been exonerated, but then most people accepted the committee as a farce, regardless of whether they approved of the raid or not.

In the last two days of her life Ellen had mixed with dangerous people, although there was still no indication as why any of them would want her dead. I turned to Monday's entry:

Monday, May 19th, 1902.

I did not go to work this morning after my exertions at the weekend, and visited Father instead. I know how queer he can be at times, but even so, there was a most peculiar occurrence, after which he brought my call to an abrupt end. I have tried to make sense of what happened and can only think that my words must have triggered some recollection, or that his memory just happened to recover at that particular instant. I have been very concerned over Father's mental health of late, though he will not brook any discussion on the subject. I shall set down what occurred.

Knowing how much Father stands on ceremony, I telephoned after breakfast to see if my visit would be convenient. I didn't speak to him, but Cammidge told me Father would receive me at half-past ten. On arrival I was shown into the parlour by Anderson (a new servant, a footman I think). The door was left open and a few minutes later I heard Father descending the stairs with another gentleman, whose name I didn't hear and whom I didn't see. The gentleman mentioned Alfred Lyttelton, the famous sportsman who's now with Lord Milner in South Africa, and

Father wasn't very pleased with whatever he said. Then the gentleman said something about the chamberlain at the Liberal Club on Saturday, and Father bade him a very curt good day.

I heard the front door close and a moment later Father stuck his head around the parlour door. When he saw me he expressed his surprise at my presence and asked who had let me in. I told him and asked him about Mr Lyttelton (thinking I might be able to secure an interview for Roberta when he returns to England) and the strangest thing happened: Father denied mentioning him. I told him that I knew all about Mr Lyttelton because he was the only man to represent England in both football and cricket, but Father changed the subject to one of his new business enterprises. We had only been speaking for a few minutes (he hadn't even rung for tea), when he suddenly went as white as a sheet, told me he had an urgent matter to attend to, and dismissed me! It was not even twenty minutes to eleven when I left.

Sometimes I wish I'd been like Alec and cut all ties with Father, for his callousness since Mother died hurts me so deeply. I have resolved not to visit him again for at least three months unless he sends an apology (which he won't). I read in the newspapers today that delegates from the Boer army met Lords Milner and Kitchener in Pretoria yesterday. At last it seems as if the war will really be over. I do hope nothing happens to Alec while they are negotiating the peace treaty. It would be so ironic, after his having already been twice wounded and contracting enteric fever. Please be safe, Alec, my thoughts are with you constantly! I shall say an extra prayer for him tonight.

I watched a drop of water splatter on the page and realised I was crying.

I closed the journal and paced up and down the room awhile, thinking about Ellen and I, and our early life together. I didn't feel as if I could face any more of her diary at present, but I must somehow find the strength. The pain was my penance for not making more of our short time together while Ellen was alive. I continued my pacing until after one, when I sat in an armchair, exhausted by the day's events…

I woke to a loud hammering. I was still in my shirtsleeves in the armchair.

"Marshall, open this bloody door!"

"Hold your damned horses!" I bawled back, thinking that they'd wake the whole bloody hotel. I rose from the chair, my joints aching, and staggered to the lamp, which I'd left on. Ellen's journal was on the desk with my watch. I fumbled for it and saw the time: five minutes past four. I stormed to the door and threw it open. "What the hell do you want at this hour!"

Truegood's muscular frame blocked the doorway. "You. Get dressed, we've found Rose. He's in a public house Devil's Acre."

I froze, realised what the news entailed, and rushed into my bedroom.

From the sitting-room I heard Truegood say, "Make sure you're armed."

18. Devil's Acre

Despite the auspicious day ahead, I decided to forgo Sunday best in favour of a brown worsted suit. I took my homburg, but not my stick. Ten minutes after Truegood had rudely awakened me, we marched out of the Windsor together. "No cab?" I asked.

"We're not going far." He strode up Victoria Street at a brisk pace.

Aside from the streetlamps, there was the faint half-light of false dawn, but we were the only people abroad. "Any news about the Russians?" I asked.

"No. Neither of them were in, so I decided to have a little nosy about. With the landlady's permission, of course. I didn't find anything to do with Lowenstein or Carey, but I did find a coded communication. I made a copy and gave it to Chief Inspector Quinn — he's got a fella that can decipher the Russian ones — but that won't be until tomorrow at the earliest. Probably Monday."

"Where are we going?"

"The Otter's Pocket. It's a thieves' den, Murgatroyd uses it as his headquarters. As suspected, Rose is one of his adams. Lamb found him late last night."

"Did you say this Murgatroyd is some sort of criminal boss?"

Truegood gave me one of his characteristic scathing glances. "Yeah. He's the Family man that runs Devil's Acre. All the fences, captains, ponces and bawds pay him a portion of their earnings. Or he makes sure they're no longer fit to practice their trades. He'll have some tough customers at the Pocket, and something tells me he won't come quietly. This way." Truegood steered me right into Strutton Gardens, then left into Old Pye Street.

The change in surroundings was unbelievable, given that we were only yards from Victoria Street, one of London's busiest thoroughfares. All of a sudden we were in a dark, narrow road overflowing with a crowded mass of filthy, ramshackle houses, separated by ginnels and alleys so narrow they looked like tunnels. Many of the low-pitched hovels had rags or newspapers instead of panes of glass, others were almost roofless.

Beggars lay snoring in doorways. Within a few steps, we were approached by two tired and bedraggled prostitutes. Truegood waved them away, and growled at a third who accosted us immediately after. Fifty years ago, we would've been unlikely to return from what Charles Dickens coined 'Devil's Acre' alive on a ramble such as this. By the time of the great writer's death, however, the Metropolitan Board of Works and the American banker George Peabody had begun to clear the slums and build affordable housing. The area had improved dramatically in my lifetime, but it was still best avoided by those who wished to keep a hold of their purses.

"I've spent all morning trying to assemble a squad of constables. I eventually managed to rustle up some of the A Division night shift; let's hope they bloody turn up." We passed a house leaning so far into the road that its collapse seemed imminent. Opposite, a pawnbroker's was chained and locked, with iron bars over broken windows. A dingy courtyard brought us to an intersection with a wider, cleaner road, where we halted. Truegood stood under a streetlamp and turned towards Victoria Street. "New Pye Street; they'd better be here."

He waved at nothing in particular and we were rewarded with the sound of a low whistle. A Black Maria emerged from the shadows, the horse's hooves striking like bells on the street surface. A constable and a sergeant sat atop the police carriage and another six constables trooped along next to it. I noticed that all the policemen wore cutlasses, something I remembered from my schooldays, but hadn't seen since my return.

"Come on," said Truegood, leading me across the intersection into the darkness ahead.

The Black Maria's clattering receded and I looked back to see it continuing down the street we'd just crossed. The six constables, joined by their sergeant, followed us. Ahead, Peabody's Rochester Buildings, a giant block of flats with Dutch gables, sat squat above the surrounding dwellings. To our right an alley opened up — a rough-looking man with a frayed coat and soft cap lurched towards us. I tensed — reached into my coat — and relaxed as I recognised an unwashed and unshaven version of Sergeant Aitken.

"Morning, gents." He grinned.

Truegood turned to the uniformed sergeant. "How many armed?"

"Only myself and one other, it was all — "

"Take three men down there with you, the armed constable comes with me. Station yourselves at the back of The Otter's Pocket, two on each side. Collar anyone who leaves and be careful, because they might be armed. If you hear one blast of the whistle, just the men with pistols come to our assistance. Two blasts, everyone converges on us. Got it?"

The four men nodded and disappeared into the shadows.

"Murgatroyd has spike nails set in the back wall of the public house, so he and his adams can make a rapid exit if necessary. When we go in the front I expect most of the household will leg it out the back." I noticed that of the three remaining constables, two carried sledgehammers, and the other a revolver. "You men with the locksmith's daughters know what you're doing?" They replied in the affirmative. "Stay outside with them unless you hear the single whistle," Truegood said to the third, who nodded.

Aitken led our party forward to another alleyway, parallel to the one from which he'd sprung. "This is St Anne's Lane."

Once we'd left Old Pye Street there were no lamps and we would have required lanterns to navigate were it not for the faint light from the rising sun. Like its neighbours, the lane was narrow and the houses leaned at odd angles, looming in the dimness. A few yards ahead a shadow darker than the rest gradually took human shape and I made out another homeless man slumped on the road, there being no pavement to offer a more suitable bed. As we approached he stirred and rose, and I saw he had an eye patch and a matted black beard. He, too, grinned and I realised that Sergeant Lamb lurked under the theatrical props.

He reported to Truegood, speaking in a whisper. "He's in there. So's Murgatroyd, Bird, and the landlord and his wife. There may be others."

I could just make out where Lamb had pointed, a few dozen yards further down the road. The Otter's Pocket was a Tudor style house with two small gables and a narrow doorway set deep in the middle of the structure. The façade was blackened and peeling, and there were three sets of windows, indicating that the gables had been converted into garrets. There was no sign advertising a public house and no light from any of the windows. The three uniformed men walked past and waited outside the house next door, which was anonymous and tumbledown. All of the buildings in the lane were dark and quiet.

Truegood addressed me. "Rose is a tubby little cove with a goatee." He gave me a pair of handcuffs and a knuckleduster, both of which I dropped into my side pocket.

Lamb removed his eye patch, and drew a snub-nosed Webley. Aitken removed a bullseye lantern from under his coat. When it was alight, he clipped it to the front of his belt, and produced a similar revolver along with a short truncheon.

Truegood took a lantern from Lamb and clipped it to his own belt. "If they're armed, chances are they'll use them, so be prepared. But we need Rose alive, no matter what. The front and back are covered, so we'll go straight in, straight up to the second floor. If we need help, one blast on the whistle for the two armed men, two blasts for the lot. Got it, Aitken?"

"Yes, sir."

"Lamb?"

"Yes, sir."

"Marshall, stick with me." Truegood withdrew his watch and I looked over his shoulder. It was twenty-eight minutes to five. Truegood waved to the uniformed men and replaced his watch. "Let's go," he said. I noticed a life-preserver had appeared in his left hand.

As the two constables with the sledgehammers moved to the front door, we crossed the lane. I drew my Broomhandle Mauser from its shoulder rig. I'd acquired the pistol from a dead Boer at Ladysmith and used it for the rest of the war. I slipped the brass knuckles over my left fist. The four of us crouched down in a neat row in front of one of the windows: Truegood, myself, Lamb, and Aitken. It wasn't an ideal position, but we had little choice, as the doorway was barely big enough for the two constables to wield their universal keys.

It appeared that everyone was waiting for a pre-arranged signal of which I was not aware.

A low growl issued from inside the house.

Then another.

Dogs began barking.

"Now, now!" shouted Truegood.

"Heave!" The constables hefted the hammers into the door, one heavy thump after the other. The dogs went berserk, but there was no crack of wood.

"Again!" Truegood shouted needlessly. "Heave!"

Thump, thump — then a crackle — a crash as the door imploded.

"Get out, get out!" Truegood dragged one of the men from the doorway, flung him into the street, and squeezed into the space created. He booted the remains of the door, burst into the house, and shot the first dog in mid leap. "Police! This is a raid! Police!"

A boom echoed across the city as the guns in Hyde Park fired their first salute. It was dawn on coronation day.

The other two dogs yelped at the noise of the shot and fled. I was at Truegood's shoulder as he entered a vestibule with two doorways and a flight of mouldy stairs. He charged up; I followed.

From above I heard shouts, a scream, and rapid footsteps.

Truegood reached the first floor landing and a door opened in front of him. A skinny, bare-chested man came out — I saw the flash of a shiv. Truegood hit him in the jaw with his elbow and rushed for the next flight of stairs. Bare Chest fell back against the wall, swore, and came forward again, blade raised.

I hit him as hard as I could across the bridge of the nose.

His face exploded in a cloud of blood and he screamed, dropping to the floor.

Truegood surged ahead and I took the stairs three at a time to catch him. Behind me I heard a roar followed by a gunshot. Truegood gained the second floor as three loud bangs came from below. He dropped his life preserver and reached for his whistle. A door to the right opened and a man in a nightshirt, wielding a poker, stepped out. He saw Truegood and I — thought better of it — disappeared back into the room.

Truegood's piercing whistle cut through the noise in the house: one long, loud blast.

I joined Truegood as he reached for a door to the left — it opened — a man in a greatcoat raised a sawn-off shotgun.

Truegood dived left — I dived right — thunder and lightning exploded on the landing.

I looked up and saw Greatcoat run for the stairs. I raised the Mauser and he threw his weapon at me. I squeezed the trigger — the shotgun hit my arm — my shot went wide. Greatcoat hurled himself down the stairs. I scrambled to my feet and gave chase.

"That's Murgatroyd!" Truegood shouted. "Find Rose!" Behind me, I heard him kick in the door Nightshirt had shut.

I jumped down to the first floor, where Aitken lay slumped, a smear of blood on the wall behind him. Lamb was struggling with a huge, bald man in a velveteen coat, the pair fighting for control of an axe handle. The big man threw Lamb down the stairs, saw me, and pulled the weapon back to swing.

I raised the Mauser — someone leapt on my back, knocking me to one side. "Leave 'im alone, you fuckin' bravo!" I heard as my right ear was covered in spittle. A hand reached for my eyes.

Velveteen Coat hacked at me with his weapon — there wasn't time to fire — the axe handle caught the corner — skimmed along the wall.

He bellowed and pulled back for a second blow.

I threw the woman off me.

Velveteen Coat swung.

I shot him — once, twice — two to the chest.

I heard a crash behind me — Truegood — and a muffled curse below.

Truegood kicked in another door and I dashed down to the ground floor — a constable was there, revolver drawn — more curses from below.

"Down to the basement!" I led the way, but it was pitch black. I shoved the constable in front, the light from his lantern bouncing up and down the walls as we ran. A damp cellar was full of dusty barrels, and I was overcome by the smell of raw sewage. I heard more curses, saw there was a door at the back, and ran to it.

I opened the door and stepped in —

"Stop!"

It was Lamb.

I froze, and tottered over a cesspit about four feet square. I lost my balance and pitched forward —"

"Got you!" The constable grabbed a fistful of my coat and hauled me back.

The cesspit was directly in front of the door. On the other side of it, Lamb was flinging filth off him.

"Where'd he go!"

"Through there," Lamb spat.

Above us I heard two more blasts from a whistle.

I leapt over the cesspit. The constable followed and shone the lantern at the side wall. There was a two-foot square hole. I took the lantern from the constable's belt, thrust it out in front of me, and prepared to crawl in.

"Major, leave it!" I turned to Lamb.

"That's Murgatroyd. He's armed, and he might be waitin'. It's not worth it. Aitken's hit." Lamb jumped back over the cesspit and disappeared into the cellar.

My every instinct was to continue the pursuit, but he was right. Not only was it foolhardy, but it was Rose we wanted. I told the constable to wait there, negotiated the cesspit again, and found Lamb assisting two more constables to remove Aitken from the building. Velveteen Coat was gurgling and gasping, from which I gathered I'd hit him in the lungs.

I checked the room Velveteen Coat had come from — empty — and then the one opposite. The woman who'd attacked me was lying naked and insensible. I grabbed hold of one of her arms and dragged her to Bare Chest, who was sitting clutching his face. I handcuffed the two of them together, and pocketed Bare Chest's blade along with my brass knuckles.

I heard a heavy step on the floor above. Truegood marched Nightshirt and another woman — this one clothed — down from the top floor. They were also handcuffed to each other.

"Did you get him?" he asked.

"Rose — no."

"Not Rose — Murgatroyd! He nearly blew my head off, and his adam shot Aitken. Did you get him?"

"No. He escaped through a hole in the cellar wall."

"Just wait till I get my hands on that bastard! Where's Aitken?"

"They've taken him out, but he looks bad."

"Strewth!" he snarled, and looked down at Velveteen Coat. For a second I thought he was going to shoot him. "Wait here with these three villains. I'll send a couple of constables up."

"What about — "

"Just wait here!"

I was fuming. What the hell had happened to Rose? None of the men we'd encountered were tubby, and none had goatees either. If Rose had escaped, or not been here in the first place, Aitken's wound was in vain. We'd even managed to lose Murgatroyd in the bargain. I didn't have long to ponder our dismal performance before I was relieved by the sergeant and another constable. I left them with Velveteen Coat and the handcuffed couple, running out to find Truegood. More policemen had appeared, alerted by the gunfire and whistles, and Truegood was standing over a covered body.

It was Aitken.

"He's gone," Truegood said to me. "That fucking animal Murgatroyd. This is not over. It is *not* over."

"Where the hell is Rose?" I demanded.

"Rose. Rose?" he said absently.

"Yes, Rose. The reason this man died."

"Rose is at Rochester Row station."

"What?"

"Come on, let's go. There's nothing we can do for Aitken now."

"So where did Rose go?" I asked, following him.

"Out the back. They always do."

19. The Colonial Secretary's Accident

"Thank you again for the tobacco, sir. Blowin' a cloud helps to get rid of that horrible stench. Latakia, is it?"

Lamb and I were in the washroom of Rochester Row police station. He was sitting on a bench, wrapped in a towel and smoking his briar pipe — filled with my spiced tobacco. I was stripped to the waist, cleaning the blood from my coat with a soapy cloth.

"My pleasure. It's a Turkish blend from Astley's, not bad at all. I'm sorry about Sergeant Aitken. What happened?"

"I didn't know him very well, but he was a good copper. Murgatroyd's got a lot to answer for. After you cracked Milligan in the face I jumped in to put the darbies on him. Saved my life, it did. Aitken was a step behind me. He was about to go into the room Milligan had come out of when Bird opened the other door and gave him two in the back with a Bulldog. I'd just stuck my pistol in my belt for the darbies; when I turned round there was no time to draw and Bird was on me with the axe handle."

"I saw you dancing with him when I got back. He looked as strong as an ox."

"He was. I think Mr Truegood could've handled him, but he was too much for the rest of us. When he threw me down the stairs I looked up and saw you were copin'," he smiled through a cloud of smoke, "so I decided to go after Murgatroyd — who'd already gone flyin' down like a bat from a belfry. I did think about firin' a shot up the stairs, but I didn't want to hit you, sir."

"I'm rather glad you didn't — fire a shot or hit me, that is."

"I thought you were just goin' to shoot Bird anyway."

"I was, but as I was about to pull the trigger, a naked lady of the night leapt on my back and tried to scratch my eyes out. Luckily Bird was so big; the length of his arms and weapon combined ensured he didn't land his first swing. He was just about to deliver the second when I managed to throw her off."

"Yes, sir, I did notice the harpy on your back. There's some that would pay dear for that… Anyway, like a bloody fool I followed Murgatroyd into the cellar. When I got to the bottom of the stairs all I could see was a patch of black in the darkness. I heard a door swingin' on its hinges, fired two shots at it, charged in, and ran — or fell — straight into his trap. One minute I was runnin' through the door, the next I was up to my ears in human waste. I don't know how deep it was, but I nearly lost my pistol in my fright. I was lucky Murgatroyd didn't hang about to shoot me. He scarpered instead." Lamb looked at the pile of folded rags that had been assembled for him after he'd been hosed down and his clothes burnt. "I'm glad I was in mufti, not my best clobber, but I'm not sure about these."

"We could've done with more men, but Inspector Truegood did well with what he had. No matter how many we'd used someone would've been hit; Murgatroyd and his Family were too well armed."

"The dogs were the main problem, sir."

"The dogs?"

"Yes, sir. The guvnor had us set to go in when the guns went off at dawn — to cover our entry. But then the dogs started and gave Murgatroyd all the warnin' he needed. I should've guessed about the dogs. It was too good to be true, no lads keepin' watch *and* no dogs. When I saw there were no young lads, I should've known there'd be dogs."

"It wasn't your fault, Lamb." I patted him on the shoulder. "These things happen in war — police work, I mean. Bird shot him, and I shot Bird. That's all there is to think about."

"Yes, sir, poor old Aitken. I wouldn't like to be in Murgatroyd's shoes. Even though Aitken wasn't one of us, the guvnor's taken it personal. He won't rest until he finds him. He's like that, is Mr Truegood." Having finished my cleaning as best I could, I began dressing. "What's that cannon you're carrying there, sir, if I you don't mind my askin'?"

"It's a Mauser, a new design by the Germans. Not only is it double-action, but it's self-cocking as well, so it's more accurate." I removed the magazine, cocked opened the slide, and ejected the live round into my palm. Then I closed the slide and passed it over to Lamb. "There you are. The Germans are way ahead of us when it comes to weapons and they supplied the Boers — unofficially, of course."

"Good God, it is a cannon, isn't it? How many rounds does it carry, sir?"

"Ten in that magazine. Ten seven-point-six-three rounds. It is a bit bulky, but I had a shoulder rig made to measure."

He handed the pistol back to me as Truegood joined us. "Christ, Lamb, this isn't a Turkish Bath. Get those clothes on sharpish, I've got work for you."

"Yes, guvnor," he replied without enthusiasm.

"Anything?" I asked.

"Not yet. Rose is scared — as he should be after Aitken — but all he's telling is that Murgatroyd sent him to find Lowenstein. He was given a physical description and told the fella was in hiding, but that's it. Doesn't know who commissioned Murgatroyd for the job — if anyone did — or why he wanted him found. It was the girl that gave Lowenstein away. As soon as she told Rose, he reported to Murgatroyd, and he claims not to know what happened thereafter. Apparently Murgatroyd had at least three others on the job as well, but they're all lower down the Family chain of command than Rose."

"Do you believe him?"

"I'm still going to grill the villain all day just because I bloody well can, but yeah, I do. He's scared enough to tell me everything he knows, and he's clever enough to realise the game's up with Murgatroyd. I'm going to grill the two ponces and harlots as well, but I doubt they'll know anything."

"We've got to find Murgatroyd."

"Yeah, it's a good thing you missed him, because we need the bastard alive. But nothing's going to happen until tomorrow. For today, it's just the three of us left."

I finished dressing, put my shoulder rig on, and reloaded the Mauser.

Lamb was muttering something about his clothes having most probably been taken from dead bodies.

"Stop whimpering. Take yourself back to the Yard, get yourself properly dressed, and get back here before Sunday. Got it?"

"Yes, guvnor."

I replaced the Mauser in the shoulder rig and buttoned my coat, presentable once more. "I've a couple of requests to make."

"Go on."

"Have you got a set of skeleton keys?"

"Of course I have. What do you — never mind, I don't want to know. Lamb, bring back a set of skeleton keys, will you? Come on, we'll go to the inspector's office, we can talk there."

We left Lamb making some final adjustments to his ill-fitting clothes, and found a fresh pot of coffee awaiting us in a small, cluttered office at the back of the building. Truegood poured two cups.

"Thank you. I'd like the use of a telephone as well, please."

"Of course. The station has one, use it whenever you want. Anything else?"

"No — actually, I'd better keep you up to date. Armstrong has asked to meet me at the Monument at noon today. Alone."

"You're not going."

"I am, but I'm telling you in case something should happen to me."

He shook his head vigorously. "Take Lamb, at least."

"Thank you for the offer, but I want to find out what he's after. If I take Lamb, it'll almost certainly scare him off."

"It's your skin, but let me know as soon as you're done."

"I shall. Later, I'm going to ring Woburn and speak to one of the Duke of Bedfordshire's staff."

"What for?"

"To confirm Carey's alibi for Lowenstein's murder."

"He has one?" Truegood was surprised.

"He told me he was a guest of the Duke of Bedford on Tuesday night."

"Waste of time, don't you think?"

I took a sip of the coffee, in desperate need of stimulation. Now that the action was over, I was beginning to tire quickly, and I had a long day ahead of me. I took a second sip before answering. "No, not in Carey's case. You're quite right as far as Colonel Rhodes, Armstrong and Drayton are concerned. Any one of them could've slipped out of their hotels — or Devonshire House — crossed Westminster in the dead of night, and killed Lowenstein. But if Carey was at Woburn on Tuesday night and Wednesday morning, then he wouldn't have been able to get to Tottenham Street and back in time, would he?"

"True. What's this interest in Carey? You taking the Russian thing seriously?"

"Aren't you?"

"Once we've got Mr M back on the case, he'll know what to do in that respect. He's an expert with these foreigners."

"And the coded message?"

"Hmm, we'll see what Mr Q can make of that one."

"I've got one more question for you, about Chamberlain's accident — or whatever it really was." I paused for another drink of the coffee.

"What?"

"I know you went back to speak to the driver, but did you keep an eye on Chamberlain afterwards as well?"

"Yeah, of course. I earn my living, you know."

"Well?"

"Well, what?"

"Did anything change? How did it affect Chamberlain — that sort of thing?"

"It didn't. Mr Balfour formed his new government, but he kept Mr Chamberlain as his Colonial Secretary — you know that. The incident happened a week after the start of his Colonial Conference. All the colonial premiers were here for the coronation and Mr Chamberlain took the opportunity to call the conference for the purposes of 'welding the Empire together'. That was how he put it to the papers, but he was probably just trying to increase his influence after Lord Milner attempted to suspend the Cape Colony constitution behind his back in May. The accident didn't even seem to set him back, because he was only off for ten days before he took the chair up again."

"And no changes to his agenda, or anything like that?"

"Only a minor one."

"Which was?"

"Do we have time for this bollocks?" Truegood scowled.

"It might be important."

"When Chamberlain opened the conference on the first of July, he was trying to secure trade advantages for Britain within the Empire. When he came back, he was pushing for the creation of political institutions that would unify the Empire. That's how I read it, anyway." He shrugged. "Happy?"

"It's a difference, isn't it?" I asked.

"It was all about closer union anyway, he just changed the focus a bit. What's it got to do with our investigation?"

I stood, but the office was too small to pace, so I sat on the edge of the desk and enumerated on my fingers instead. "Chamberlain opens the first ever Colonial Conference in Whitehall for an expressed purpose. Seven days later he has an accident which you — *you*, not me — thought was suspicious because of the disappearing cab driver. Four days later the Prime Minister resigns, and six days after that Chamberlain returns to the conference with an amended agenda. Tell me you honestly don't think something's going on."

He shrugged his huge shoulders. "You know these conspiracy theories have got us in trouble before — even Mr M a few years ago. And they've had us chasing our tails. Why the sudden interest in Mr Chamberlain? We're supposed to be solving Lowenstein's murder."

Truegood was not, of course, privy to Rhodes' *Confession of Faith* and the Society of the Elect. For me, however, Chamberlain's accident fitted perfectly. Milner and Chamberlain had been at odds since the war ended. The ostensible reason was over the Cape constitution, but in the light of Rhodes' real legacy, it was more likely for control of the Empire itself. I didn't want to betray Melville's confidences, so I concluded my discourse abruptly.

"I know, I know. Just an idea of mine. I'm going to go back to my hotel, have breakfast and some more of this good stuff," I indicated the coffee, "then I'll come back and see if you've got anything from Rose or the rest of them, and pick up the keys."

"Right, make sure you speak to me as soon as you're done with Carrot Top."

Though it wasn't yet seven, Victoria Street was already busy. A steady trickle of people walked from the station to Westminster Abbey and beyond to find places along the King's route from the Palace to the Abbey. Early revellers were already singing the joys of the day:

Oh! On coronation day, on coronation day,
We'll have a spree, a jubilee, and shout 'Hip, hip, hooray!'
For we'll all be merry, drinking whisky, wine, and sherry,
We'll all be merry on coronation day.

Horse-drawn traffic had been prohibited in several parts of the city — with the exception of the private carriages of those involved in the ceremony — in order to ease congestion and prevent accidents. There were also a large number of policemen about. These would soon be augmented by the thousands of soldiers and sailors from all over the Empire who were taking part in the procession and lining the route.

Over breakfast I contemplated what Truegood had told me about Chamberlain.

The more I learned about Carey, the more I thought him the perfect agent to employ to give a senior politician — someone who felt that as far as physical danger went, he was untouchable — a scare. Everyone knew Carey wore a wideawake hat, therefore Truegood reckoned he'd be unlikely to wear it in disguise. I begged to differ. Carey was a man who lived and prospered by his reputation as a hunter of beasts and men. He was given a clandestine assignment which was exactly the type of commission that would increase his standing. He couldn't make it obvious he was the driver, or he'd have the attentions of Melville's Gang to contend with. Consequently, he disguised himself with an American accent and a set of whiskers; he'd travelled in America, so faking the accent wouldn't have been a problem. Why keep the hat? Because it was so unusual and would enable him to identify himself to a prospective employer at a later date.

Remember the traffic accident that made Mr Chamberlain change his mind about the Colonial Conference? You thought it was an accident too, did you? What was that cab driver wearing? One of these?

I could see Carey smiling in my mind's eye as he touched the brim of his wideawake hat. Would he wear it to a murder? That seemed less likely. A faked accident might pass unnoticed, but murder wouldn't. Murder meant the law, a trial, possibly the death penalty. So if the hat was used to implicate Carey, then it was very likely that he hadn't killed Lowenstein. It was strange how a single item — the wideawake hat — made me suspect guilt in one crime, but innocence in another. If the penang lawyer was his, it may have been planted to leave a fake trail. I hated to admit it, but Truegood had provided a valid alternative to my explanation for finding the stick in the dustbin. It could have been left so the killer didn't have to carry evidence of his crime on his person; it could also have been left for us to recover.

I'd find out if Carey had the opportunity to kill Lowenstein when I spoke to the staff at Woburn. Then, armed with Truegood's keys, I'd find out more about my sister's murderer...

When I broke into his house.

20. The Shikari's Lair

I didn't hurry breakfast. According to the timetable printed in the dailies, the peers and other dignitaries were due to begin arriving at Westminster Abbey from eight-thirty onwards. As far as I knew, Carey wasn't involved in the ceremony, in which case he'd probably spend the morning at one of his clubs. There also wasn't any point in arriving at Rochester Row until Lamb returned with the skeleton keys. I waited until a quarter to nine, by which time I was somewhat refreshed, before leaving the Windsor. I walked out into a Victoria Street more crowded than I could ever have imagined. Despite the ominous black clouds looming overhead, the road was full to capacity, packed with a heaving mob attempting to hurry from the station to Westminster.

I realised that I'd perhaps been over-ambitious in my plans for the day. Having been in Glasgow for the golden jubilee and Durban for the diamond, I'd really had no conception of what London would be like for the coronation. Looking at the multitude, I didn't know how I was going to reach the Monument for noon. It was essential that I gain entry to Carey's rooms — for Ellen's sake — but it was just as important to meet Armstrong. He had the strongest motive for the murder of Lowenstein and was very possibly a representative or even member of the Society of the Elect.

My first concern upon arrival at the police station was to telephone Woburn. I gave the operator the number I required and waited.

"His Grace the Duke of Bedford's residence. Good morning."

"Good morning. I'm Major Marshall, from Scotland Yard. To whom am I speaking?"

"Redmond, sir."

"And your position, Redmond?"

"First under butler, sir. I'm afraid His — "

"His Grace is in London for the coronation. I'm aware of that, Redmond. I'm telephoning to speak to you."

"To me, sir?"

"Yes. You were at work on Tuesday and Wednesday this week?" Silence. I had to seize the initiative, before he questioned my authority or simply terminated the conversation. "I don't have all day, were you at work or not!"

"Ah, yes, sir, I was."

"The information I require concerns one of His Grace's guests, Lieutenant Carey. Do you recall that gentleman?"

"Yes, sir."

"I require the lieutenant's times of arrival and departure at His Grace's estate."

"Yes, sir. Lieutenant Carey arrived at Woburn Abbey at just after seven o'clock on Tuesday evening. He left at about half-past eleven the next morning."

"Did Lieutenant Carey leave the premises at any time between his arrival on Tuesday evening and his departure on Wednesday morning?"

"The lieutenant spent two hours in the park on Wednesday morning, sir. Other than that, he was in the abbey for the rest of his visit. Sir, may I ask —"

"Thank you, you've been most helpful. Good day," I said and replaced the earpiece.

If Carey had been in Bedfordshire between midnight and dawn on Wednesday morning then he couldn't have killed Lowenstein. It was that simple; the consequences for the case were not, however, for Carey's alibi produced more questions than answers. For example, was the wideawake hat worn by the murderer for the purpose of implicating Carey in the crime? Did the penang lawyer belong to Carey — left for the police to find — or was it the killer's, cast aside at the last minute?

I found Lamb waiting in the inspector's office, looking somewhat more presentable. Truegood was questioning Rose with the CID inspector in charge of Sergeant Aitken's murder. I told Lamb about Carey and he handed over a set of sixteen slim metal rods with protrusions of varying lengths extending from their ends. I'd always intended to learn how to pick locks when I was a policeman, but it was a skill I'd never made time to learn. I'd used skeleton keys on about a dozen occasions and found that they worked two-thirds of the time. I thanked Lamb and pocketed them.

I was just about to return to the charge room, when Lamb coughed politely, and handed me what looked like a black silk handkerchief. "The guvnor thought it might come in handy, sir."

It was a folded mask with holes cut out for the eyes and a string to fasten it. I smiled. "Yes, I think it might. Thank you."

"Good luck, sir."

My second telephone call, this time to Blackburn House, was the more important of the two. The operator told me there was no answer and I asked him to try again.

I was connected a minute later. "Lieutenant Carey's residence, good morning." The speaker was breathing heavily.

"Good morning, I'd like to speak to the lieutenant, please."

"Lieutenant Carey isn't available, sir. May I take a message?"

"No thank you. Good day."

That was a pity. I'd hoped that Carey and his staff — however many he kept — would all be out the house by nine o'clock at the latest. I'd definitely need the mask now, although I didn't want to harm anyone that wasn't involved, and hoped his man would have more sense than to play the hero. I found Lamb again, took a pair of handcuffs and a key from him, and left.

I cut through Carlisle Place, passed Victoria Station — still disgorging visitors — and marched up Grosvenor Place, alongside Buckingham Palace Gardens. Hyde Park Corner was packed with a press of spectators abuzz with excited anticipation. I shuffled my way through until I reached Hyde Park itself, left the crowd behind, and broke into a trot. Time was of the essence and a man hurrying along wouldn't attract attention today. I crossed Park Lane, made haste up Audley Street, and finally turned into Upper Grosvenor Street, where I eased my pace. As I was now several streets to the north of the King's route, I shared the road with only a dozen or so others.

Mindful of Assistant Commissioner Henry's advances in the field of detection, I slipped on a pair of thin leather gloves. Carey's rooms were in King Street, between Upper Grosvenor Street and Grosvenor Square, and I found Blackburn House with ease. It was a five storey red brick building with three entrances, the middle one a set of coach doors. The closest pedestrian door belonged to Carey and I walked up to it as if were my own, taking the skeleton keys from my pocket. I'd decided to try and effect a clandestine entry as I didn't want to put the mask on in the street, even though there was no one about. I started with the first key, gently and gradually.

No luck.

Expecting the door to be pulled open by an irate manservant at any second, I tried again, and achieved the same result.

Then the third and fourth keys — no luck either. I dared not glance over my shoulder to see if anyone was watching from a window; it would only have drawn further attention to me.

Still no success with the fifth key.

Attempting to expedite the procedure, I made rather a racket with the sixth, and readied myself to burst in the moment I felt the handle being turned from inside.

It wasn't, and a very loud click heralded success with the seventh key.

I crossed the threshold, closed the door silently behind me, and put the mask on. The entrance hall was dominated by a huge pair of elephant tusks, forming an arch a few feet from the door. The chances were that the house was empty: any occupants would've had to have been deaf not to hear my clumsy entrance. I took the Mauser from my rig and moved from the hall to a wainscoted corridor, treading quietly in case someone was lying in wait.

There were stairs leading up; two doors to the left, and a third at the end of the passage. I tried the first door and looked into what was obviously the servants' quarters. One servant only, the chap I'd spoken to on the telephone. I didn't waste time examining his chambers, but moved quickly to the door at the end. I found myself in a curious kind of stable, with a coach door leading to an inner courtyard. Then I remembered Carey was an automobile enthusiast and realised that this was in fact a stable, a stable for a horseless carriage — which Carey had presumably taken to his destination this morning.

I mounted the stairs for the first floor. Four doors off the landing led to a small kitchen, a similarly-sized library, the parlour, and what seemed to be a cupboard. I wasn't too sure about the last, as it was locked, but I calculated it had to be a very small room. The parlour was decorated in an oriental style, with a luxurious Chinese carpet, ottomans, and a huge tiger skin rug in front of the fireplace. Opposite, mounted on the wall, was a stuffed tiger's head. Not the same beast, but another, for this one was white in colour. The hunting trophies were interspersed with weapons: a Khyber knife, Boxer sword and kukri, amongst others.

I ascended to the second floor, which had only two doors on the landing. One led to a dining room, the other to a smoking room and roof terrace. This floor was decorated with artefacts from the Americas: a bear skin, a mounted bison head, a pair of tomahawks, and a cavalry sabre. I was still concerned that Carey's man might be preparing an ambush, and with all these weapons to hand, I was worried I'd have to wound him. The third floor was smaller than the second, and I perceived the apartment was pyramidal in shape. There were two rooms, a billiards room and a study, both adorned with African curios. Finally, the fourth floor held two bedrooms and a bathroom. The second bedroom appeared to be a spare.

I opted to begin my search in the study and retraced my steps to the third floor.

Having decided I was alone, I replaced my Mauser and removed the mask. The study was more like a den, with a rich oak floor and panelled walls; there were paintings, photographs, and trophies all over. A leopard skin lay in front of the fireplace, and pairs of horns belonging to a buffalo, rhino and kudu surrounded a mounted lion's head. Underneath was a photograph of Carey with two other hunters. I recognised both of them: one was Frederick Selous, the most famous living African explorer and adventurer; the other was Colonel Frank Rhodes.

On the opposite wall was a locked cabinet filled with firearms: a set of Napoleonic duelling pistols, a Mauser similar to my own but with an extended magazine, a long-barrelled Remington .44, a Navy Colt, a double-action Bulldog, a Galand pocket pistol and a Swiss crossbow. A mahogany bureau stood next to the cabinet. I moved over to the matching desk, a rust-coloured monster with feet carved to resemble a lion's. The top was clear except for a writing set. I sat down on the chair and tried the first of four drawers: they were locked. I reached for my skeleton keys, but the slots were far too small. This required either a delicate touch, or brute force. I rose and looked at the tools on display, reaching for a set of spears and assegais, before remembering the Asian weapons downstairs.

I returned with a kukri, which I'd not used before, but seemed perfectly suited to the task. I moved the chair out of the way first. Then I took a firm grip of the curved knife, aimed at the very top of the first drawer, and hacked. There was a crunch as the blade splintered the wood and slid into the gap between drawer and desk. It wasn't in far enough so I took a second swing, achieving greater penetration this time. With several inches of blade inside the drawer, I twisted it around to use the curve as a fulcrum. More wood splintered, but the lock held fast. Once the knife was in position I grabbed the grip with both hands, rested my weight on the desk-top, and heaved.

With an almighty crack, the first drawer sprung open.

The kukri was still intact — very impressive — but I tossed it to the floor and went to work on the contents of the compartment. There was a slim bundle of documents and a lean book with a black leather cover. I flicked through the papers: an invitation from the Duke of Bedford to luncheon at his townhouse in Belgravia, a letter from the Duke of Westminster declining the opportunity to sponsor the proposed hunting expedition, a dozen bills and receipts. Nothing of particular relevance at the moment. The volume was a schedule book, with a full page allotted to each day of the year. I flipped my way through to today. The entry read:

9.30 Auto Club
1.00 D Bedford, Belgrave Sq.
4.00 T.D., Lyons & Co., Butler's Wharf
7.30 Trav Club

All the entries were clear enough, except for the third. I had no idea who or what 'T.D.' was, but presumably it referred to a meeting at a J. Lyons and Company warehouse in Butler's Wharf. I jotted down the details in my notebook, and then went back through August and July. The only item of interest was a series of completely blank pages from Thursday the third of July to Tuesday the eighth of July — the day after Chamberlain's accident. Carey led a hectic existence and these were the only blank days in the schedule book since his return to England on the twenty-eighth of April. Also suggestive was the next mention of T.D., which was on Wednesday the second of July, and read:

11.00 T.D., Bartitsu Club

I'd never heard of the club, but I wondered if it was significant that the meeting was only a day before the blank week. T.D. appeared again on Monday the 9th June:

1.00 T.D., Langham

I made a note of both and continued back through the months. I tensed involuntarily when I reached the twenty-second of May:

7.30 Dr Ellen, ZG

I'd known it would be there, but it still made my blood boil to read it. I fought the fury rising within, and turned back further. T.D.'s final — or first, chronologically speaking — appearance was on Monday the nineteenth of May:

8.00 T.D., Trav Club

There was nothing else of interest in May, nor in the last few days of April. I made a final note, removed the drawer from the desk, and examined the one below. More papers, which I arranged on the desk to speed things up. It was a quarter-past ten already and I probably only had another hour to myself. Carey would be out all day, but his man had no doubt gone to watch the procession. The King and Queen were leaving Buckingham Palace at eleven, due to arrive at the Abbey twenty-five minutes later. If I left at a quarter-past eleven, it should guarantee my escape before anyone returned. There was much to be done in the mean time: the drawers on the left hand side of the desk, the bureau, and then the safe — wherever it was.

The documents from the second drawer were all concerned with Carey's properties. It appeared he owned two other houses, one in Vine Lane in Southwark, and the other in Dibden Street in Hoxton. It confirmed he was up to no good, the latter address especially, as Hoxton had a reputation as the most criminal district in the whole of London. It wasn't the sort of place one would buy as an investment. There didn't seem to be anything noteworthy, so I picked up the kukri.

I took aim at the second pair of drawers — swung back — stopped.

I thought I heard a noise.

I listened.

Nothing.

I waited a few seconds. Still nothing.

I was a little nervous now, and no longer felt comfortable repeating my performance. Instead, I placed the kukri on the desk and walked over to the bureau to see if it was also locked. I tugged at the top drawer —

Footsteps.

They sounded like they were coming from the kitchen, two floors below.

My heart beat a tattoo, blood surging through my veins. I drew the Mauser. Upstairs or downstairs? The roof terrace provided the best escape route, but it was one floor below. What if I met Carey's man on the stairs? There was no time to put the mask back on.

He who hesitates is lost.

I flew from the study, moving as swiftly as I dared. The stairs were thickly carpeted, but I slowed right down — in case they still creaked — and tried my best to ease my weight on to them.

Too late.

As I descended, I heard two men coming up from the first floor.

I could hear their hushed voices: they were speaking Russian.

21. The Russian Connection

When in doubt, maintain forward momentum. I learned that in the war. I kept moving down the stairs — faster — dashed into the smoking room — stopped, dead.

I had a problem.

After looking out into the courtyard earlier, I'd closed the shutters. I'd need two hands to open them, which meant putting the Mauser down. If I opened the shutters, the Russians might hear me. I'd still have to open the French windows before I reached the roof terrace. It was unlikely I'd be quick enough, and the attempt would leave me defenceless.

The Russians reached the landing.

I scoured the room for a place to conceal myself: a card table, four low chairs, two chaise longues, the fireplace, curtains. I crawled under the chaise longue in the corner opposite the fireplace. It was a poor hiding place. I rolled on my back — pulled my legs up as high as I could — and aimed the Mauser at the door.

A pair of feet appeared.

I held my breath. If he gave the room anything more than a cursory look the game was up.

Brown leather boots stepped once — twice — turned and walked out.

I let out a silent sigh.

I heard voices and footsteps. They were going up to the third floor. I'd left the study in a shambles, complete with the kukri on the desk. There was only one thing for it now: I waited until I heard the men reach the next landing and made for the stairs.

There was a shout from above.

I dashed down.

First floor, ground floor.

The door to the stable was open — they must have broken in that way. I reached the entrance hall and thanked Providence I hadn't tried to lock it. I rested my left hand on the doorknob and aimed my pistol at the stairs with my right. Silence from above, no footsteps or shouts. I waited for five seconds, then put the Mauser away. The Russians hadn't realised I was still in the building. I opened the front door and stepped out into King Street. It was still deserted. I closed the door quietly, smiled to myself, and walked away from Blackburn House as if I'd as much right to exit as enter. I sauntered along towards Upper Grosvenor Street without looking back.

A narrow escape.

My next port of call...

Crack — buzz — ping.

A tiny cloud of dust stirred on the road in front of me.

I dived — landed heavily on the sidewalk — and rolled left.

Another crack — a third, fourth, fifth.

I jumped to my feet, put my head down, and sprinted.

There was a final shot — a shout in Russian.

I cut left — for Grosvenor Square. I glanced behind me — no one — and ran down Carlos Street. I received a few curious looks from passers-by, so once I'd made a third change in direction I decelerated to a very brisk walk.

Bastards.

And more fool me. I'd been so pleased at leaving the house without alerting the Russians, I'd relaxed my guard completely. They obviously had heard me, but had decided to snipe from the window rather than chase me into the street. It was exactly what I would've done had our positions been reversed. If I'd been shot in the back, I'd only have had my own carelessness to blame. If our positions were reversed... the Russians hadn't broken in to Carey's rooms to rifle his papers. They were assassins sent to kill either him or me. No one knew I was going to be at Blackburn House, so they must have come for Carey.

As my heart slowed to its more usual rate, I considered the implications of a pair of Russian assassins. All the intelligence Truegood and I had gathered indicated that the Okhrana wanted to eliminate Carey. Whether it was because of the wild allegations about his liaison with the empress or the potential damage to Countess Thécla's reputation hardly mattered. They had first incriminated him in Lowenstein's murder, and then broken into...

It didn't make sense.

The Okhrana would either have framed Carey for Lowenstein's murder and relied on British law to hang him, *or* sent assassins to kill him. They wouldn't have done both. From their sinister reputation, an elaborate plot seemed just as likely as a straightforward slaughter. I was lately convinced that Carey had been deliberately implicated in Lowenstein's murder, but if the Okhrana were to blame, they wouldn't have sent agents to kill him today. The men in his house were Russian, and I had no doubt that they had been sent to kill all the occupants. They weren't necessarily Okhrana, but it seemed probable. If they were, then someone else had manufactured the evidence in Tottenham Street.

My thoughts turned to the more immediate question of my next steps. I had an hour and a half before my meeting with Armstrong and I wanted to visit Whitehall Place en route. It was imperative that I kept the appointment, but on a day when it was going to prove so difficult to get anywhere in London, I couldn't afford to travel back and forth. I wasn't too far from the National Liberal Club. Ellen's reference to 'the chamberlain' in her diary was very likely an innocent allusion to our Colonial Secretary. I believed that Carey had deliberately injured Chamberlain in order to scare him, possibly on behalf of T.D., who was possibly another agent or employee of Milner. What I wanted to know was who Chamberlain had met with on Saturday the twenty-fourth of May. I reckoned I might discover T.D's identity or even a connection between Chamberlain and Rhodes' legacy.

I glanced behind me once more as I crossed the top of Berkeley Square — still no Russians — and made for Piccadilly Circus. The Liberal Club was near enough to Waterloo Bridge for my purposes. It was too far to walk from Northumberland Avenue to the City, but if I crossed Waterloo Bridge for the South Bank, I could probably find a hansom to take me to London Bridge. From there, I could complete the journey on foot, as the Monument was only a short distance from the northern end of the bridge.

The street ahead of me was thick with a stationary crowd. I cursed under my breath. I'd meant to leave Regent Street for Haymarket, but had blundered into Waterloo Place instead. As if to underscore my error, the great guns in Hyde Park issued a salute. This was followed by a fainter sound from the east, as the battery at the Tower of London fired another twenty shots. It was eleven o'clock, and the King was leaving Buckingham Palace. A military band struck up nearby and the multitude, all dressed in their finest attire, broke into Elgar and Benson's *Pomp and Circumstance*:

Dear Land of Hope, thy hope is crowned,
God make thee mightier yet!
On Sov'ran brows, beloved, renowned,
Once more thy crown is set.

Having accidentally arrived closer to the King's route than intended, I compounded my error by attempting to push and shove my way through the press in a futile attempt to reach Charing Cross. All I succeeded in doing was incurring the wrath of most of those around me, and ten minutes later I found myself next to the Duke of York's column. I couldn't see down the steps on to the Mall, but a series of sharp commands to present arms reached my ears seconds before the crowd erupted into cheers.

Long live the king!
Vivat Rex Eduardus!
Three cheers for King Edward!

I assumed the King's carriage was approaching. It would be drawn by eight of His Majesty's creams, ponies bred exclusively for the Royal Mews, and escorted by troopers of the Royal Horse Guards. The passion around me was overwhelming. Rich and poor forgot their differences and shouted ovation after ovation. Even the most steadfast republican would've found it difficult not to cheer, so compelling was the fervour. I looked up the huge granite column supporting the bronze statue of the Grand Old Duke of York, and saw people on the gallery at the top. They would've paid well for what was one of the best views of the King's progress. Lower down, some enthusiastic young chaps had scaled the building at the base of the column, and clung on to the pillar as they waved handkerchiefs and shouted.

The euphoria reached a crescendo as the carriage passed. To my left a young lady in a hat with a brim so lavish it appeared suspended on her head by force of will alone, shrieked in a shrill soprano. To my right an old man with a frayed coat and broken teeth cried, "Bless 'em, bless 'em, bless 'em!" in a deep baritone. About ten feet above me, one of the young men was bawling to a gentleman who had squeezed into a nonexistent space next to me. I watched the chap with concern, for his perch wasn't particularly secure and every time he hailed my neighbour, he tottered precariously.

He turned — swayed for a second — steadied himself. Then he shouted down, "They're here, they're here! The King and Queen! There they go, King Eddie and his lovely lady!"

I reflected that in his zeal the man had used an unfortunate turn of phrase. While Queen Alexandra was indeed a famous beauty, the King was renowned for his unrestrained enjoyment of all the pleasures life had to offer: food, drink, tobacco, gambling... and women. His Majesty's 'lovely lady' could thus have referred to any number of women, Mrs Alice Keppel being the most recent, by all accounts...

Queen Alexandra.

Empress Alexandra.

Empress Alexandra of Russia, born Princess Alix of Hesse and by Rhine.

'A' for Alexandra, 'A' for Alix.

The penang lawyer belonged to Carey, not Armstrong. It had been given to him by the Russian empress. Whatever the exact nature of his relationship with her, he had cherished a gift from so peerless a source. That was why the Russians were in Carey's rooms; he'd made a nuisance of himself with the empress *and* the countess. It was all intuition and hearsay, but it matched the slim evidence afforded by the stick — which was the only trace Lowenstein's murder had left, no matter how sceptical Truegood was. I would need proof before I could present my theory to him or Melville, but the instant I made the connection between the 'A' on the penang lawyer and the homicidal Russians in Blackburn House, I knew the stick belonged to Carey. Never mind how, I just knew.

O'Donnell had been right: someone had deliberately implicated him. Not the Russians, they'd adopted a more direct solution to the problem. I didn't know who else, but I'd just discovered a second route to Lowenstein's murderer: he must not only benefit from Lowenstein's death, but also from Carey's imprisonment and trial. Carey had also murdered Ellen, so he was presumably involved in several schemes at present, and had probably undertaken many others of a similar nature in the past. With each one he could not only have made powerful enemies, but also employers who might later consider him a liability. Then there was his womanising. The Viceroy of India had a reputation for being as dangerous a man to cross as he was a devoted husband. A potentially fatal combination for Carey. In fact, the list of people who might want Carey out of the way seemed inexhaustible.

Somewhere, there was a man who not only had a connection to Carey, but also to one of Rhodes' executors. When I found that man, I'd have Lowenstein's murderer. There was, however, an easier way. Instead of solving the mystery all I needed to do was find Carey, cite the evidence implicating him in Lowenstein's murder, and listen to what he had to say for himself. He might not know who'd killed Lowenstein, but he'd be able to make an educated guess. That was a secondary concern. What I really wanted, the real reason I'd accepted Melville's commission, was to find Ellen's murderer. I was certain Carey had broken her neck, but it was obvious someone had employed him to do it. Carey was the bullet; I wanted the person who'd taken aim and pulled the trigger. If he told me that, I'd let him live. Picking him up would be easy — because I had his list of appointments in my notebook.

May he defend our laws,
And give us ever cause,
To sing with heart and voice:
God save the King!

I was jostled to and fro as people began to move off now that the procession had passed. I decided to try and return the way I'd come and struggled up Regent Street, my pace excruciatingly slow. I'd just turned into St Alban's Place, when I heard another roar of cannon from the west. The King had reached Westminster Abbey, which meant it was twenty-five past eleven. No time for the Liberal Club. I strode into Haymarket, then turned right into Coventry Street, moving as fast as I could without bowling people over. The latter looked busy, so I shot up Rupert Street, aware that the more I tried to avoid the crowds, the more round-about my route became.

I was on the verge of a trot, moving faster than anyone else on the street, when a man on a bicycle raced past me. He stopped outside a mansion opposite the Blue Posts public house, leant his machine against the fence, and ran to the door.

He who hesitates is lost.

In my first ever act of theft, I lifted the bicycle — ironically of the make called 'Honesty' — and propelled it next to me as I ran.

"Oi, that's my bicycle! Oi, you there!"

I ignored the poor chap, hoisted myself on to his machine, and fumbled for the pedals.

"Oi! Stop, thief!"

A false start — my feet found the pedals — I was off.

"Stop him, he's stolen my Honesty!"

I pedalled like a madman, soon outstripping any pursuit. I braked as I approached Shaftesbury Avenue, turned right, and made for the City.

22. Monument

It was a quarter to twelve when I turned off Lower Thames Street to approach the Monument from the east. I'd deliberately taken a circuitous route in order to reconnoitre the scene of a possible ambush before I pedalled into it. I'd already noticed that the viewing platform, similar to that on the Duke of York's column, appeared empty. The whole area was deserted and the City couldn't have presented a greater contrast to the heaving masses and crowds I'd just escaped in Westminster. My caution was in vain, however, for two men stood guard outside the entrance to the fluted Doric column. I was the only other person on the street and they saw me at the same instant I saw them. So much for surprising Armstrong, but at least my safety bicycle would still be there when I came back.

If I came back.

Both of the men wore bowler hats and brown suits. One was portly and middle-aged; the other younger, taller, and more muscular. I kept my eyes on them as I slowed and dismounted. They were both watching me, but neither said anything. I walked right up to them, wheeling the bicycle along next to me. "Good morning, gentlemen." I did not touch my hat. "I wonder if I might trouble to you to look after this pedal cycle while I go up to the top?"

The younger man's lip curled and I readied myself for an attack. The older man said, "Your name, sir?"

"Major Marshall."

He lifted his hat. "Certainly, Major, your bicycle will be safe with us. Mr Armstrong is expecting you."

"Thank you." I propped the pedal cycle against the iron railings.

The men edged away from each other and I passed between them, opened the door, and stepped into the base of the Monument. I closed the door behind me, entered the staircase, and shut that door as well. Seeing as Armstrong had cut off the one and only escape route, the more closed doors between his henchmen and me, the better. The stone staircase was narrow, curling in a tight concertina around an open, central space, which made for less room on the stairway, but better lighting. I pressed my back to the wall and waited, listening for any sounds of company.

Silence.

I unbuttoned my coat, loosened the Mauser in its rig, and felt for the knuckleduster. They were both ready for use, but if Armstrong had more men at the top, there'd be little I could do. I quickly stuck my head out over the stair rail — glanced up — pulled back.

Nothing.

I took a more leisurely look. All I could see were circle upon circle of stairs winding up in a clockwise direction. The spiral seemed without end, though I recalled that it was three hundred and forty-five steps to the viewing platform. The platform itself was a dozen or more feet under the gilded urn of fire at the top, which stood at two hundred and two feet above London. I'd come up here as a schoolboy, paying three pence for the magnificent view it afforded. At the time of its completion in 1677, the Monument was the tallest free-standing stone column in the world, built to commemorate the Great Fire of London eleven years before. Christopher Wren had designed it while he was working on St Paul's Cathedral, half a mile to the west and twice as high.

I waited until five minutes to twelve, when I took a deep breath and began my ascent. I interrupted my progress several times, looking above and below, and listening intently, to no avail. I stopped near the door at the top, pausing to allow my breathing to return to normal. I leant against the wall, and listened again. Nothing. I noted the interior surface of the blocks of Portland stone, worn smooth from the hundreds of thousands of hands and shoulders that had brushed against them. When I was satisfied, I gripped the butt of the Mauser — still under my shoulder — and walked slowly and silently up the last few steps.

The door was open and I could see Armstrong, in top hat and morning dress, standing at the cage. He was looking out over London, with his back to me. I eased the Mauser an inch from the holster — took half a step on to the platform — pulled back quickly.

Nothing.

I stepped forward again — checked left and right. We were alone. I let go of the Mauser, but left my coat open. Once again I closed the door behind me.

When I turned Armstrong was facing me. "Afternoon, Marshall, welcome to the Monument. You have been here before?"

"As a lad."

"A lad? A child would be overwhelmed by the view, perhaps even think he was at the top of the world — yes?" I shrugged. "Yes, he would. But, like so much in life, there is even more to appreciate as an adult. Don't you think?" I didn't reply. "Come, Marshall, stand with me. Look out at the vast metropolis that unfolds below as if for our pleasure alone. Today, it is for us alone; Lord Rothschild has made it so. For me and for you. So that we could have this view, this moment, all to ourselves."

"What is this about?"

He continued without acknowledging my question. "Behold, London. Do you know how far the city extends from its nucleus? No? From six to fifteen miles in every direction. *Fifteen miles* to the edge in some places. From the Square Mile itself to thousands of square miles containing nearly six million people. Can you fathom that, Marshall? Here we are at the very centre, in the beating heart of the greatest city in the world. London, itself, the hub of the Empire. Not *an* empire, but *the* Empire, the most illustrious the world has ever seen. Two percent of its population lives here, underneath us. We stand at the arch of the aorta, one might say."

I couldn't remember if the view differed from my previous visit, but Armstrong was right, it was awe-inspiring. On an overcast, grey day like this, the metropolis was endless, extending as far as the eye could see in all directions.

He raised his cane. "The East End, nearly a million lost souls all on its own. The worker bees, the ants, the foot soldiers; the rats that turn the great wheel of Empire with their toil. They are the scum, the detritus, but everyone has a role to play in the glory that is Great Britain. Come." He walked slowly, and I followed. "More of the common herd, living in grimy hovels in filthy streets in Holborn, Clerkenwell, King's Cross, Finsbury, and Islington. Further, the more salubrious reaches of Hampstead, Highgate, Golder's Green, Muswell Hill. Leafy, green suburbs where respectable citizens enjoy the benefits of the commuter revolution, living miles away from their places of work.

"The dome of St Paul's, caked with the dirt, dust and smoke of Empire. A magnificent monument to the superiority of the Anglo-Saxon, but not nearly as important as the cathedral behind it. Do you see them? The spires of Westminster mark the seat of governance of Empire. Westminster and Whitehall, where even now the King is being crowned. To call Edward the Seventh *king* is a misnomer. He is not a king, he is an *emperor*. Not just Emperor of India, but Emperor of Great Britain. Then, a succession of parks — "

In the distance, the forty-one guns from Hyde Park began their salute. As if in answer, cannon roared close by, from the Tower of London. The noise echoed across the city below, along with bells and the sounds of far away cheers. Sixty-two guns from the Tower. The King had been crowned: it was done. At various strategic points throughout the city, flags waved signals, just in case anyone had failed to hear the salutes.

Armstrong kept walking. "The Thames, the docks and wharves. This is the most important view. Not the undistinguished sprawl that is South London — that has no more significance than any other part of the whole — but *that*," he hit the cage with his cane, "that thin stretch of water that lies between us and the South Bank. The Thames winds its way to the sea, to even the remotest corner of the Empire. That unimpressive, foul-smelling stream is the life-blood of Empire, providing the essential, umbilical connection to the heart and the hub. From the Empire to London, back again, and to the rest of the world beyond. A world over which the Empire already holds an important sway, but a world that will one day be synonymous with Empire."

He stopped and I followed his gaze: Custom House, the river, London Bridge, Southwark. "What do you want?" I asked.

"What do I want? What *I* want is unimportant at the moment — at the moment, mark you — I am nothing more than an implement of the will of a greater man. It is not what I want, but what the Viscount Milner of St James' and Cape Town wants. And what My Lord wants is *you*."

"Me?" I was surprised.

"Yes, Major Alec Marshall VC, late Natal Mounted Rifles, hero of Ladysmith."

"What does he want with me?"

"Not only does Lord Milner have the ear of the King, but he is also about to inherit the greatest fortune in the Empire. The King and Mr Balfour's government in Whitehall may be the public face of Empire, but the power behind the institutions belongs to men like him. Men like

Viscount Milner, Viscount Palmer, Baron Rothschild, and the Earl Grey. Men who constitute the brain of the head of state. Of all these leaders of men, Lord Milner's star is in ascendance above the rest. In his wisdom and foresight he has gathered about him young men with potential and ability. Young men who will one day assist him in ruling the Empire."

"Men like you?"

"Men like me, Duncan, Dawson, Curtis, Brand; men who are destined to inherit the Empire. I communicated the details of our first meeting to Lord Milner, but he wasn't offended by your impudence. He sees further than other men. He looks not to the present, but to the future, and he has had very favourable reports of you. Lord Milner considers you one of the best men of our generation. He has instructed me to offer you a place at his side. He wants you to come back to Cape Town with me. He has a position for you in his new administration." Armstrong paused and let the import of his words sink in.

"He sees himself as the architect of Empire, does he?"

"Yes, you have it exactly! Lord Milner is the architect responsible for the greatest edifice ever constructed — ever conceived." He waved his arm across the vista below us, and whispered, "All this could be yours one day. To be the brain of an Empire that will rule the whole world; what more could any man ask?"

What more indeed.

Although I didn't like him, Armstrong's words cast a kind of a spell on me. I felt that up here we really were at the centre of London, Empire, and Earth. I was dizzy with power. I closed my eyes for a second, opening them to the illusion that all this really was mine. I was master of all I surveyed. A lord of the Empire, a man with nations under his command. I closed my eyes again and savoured the sensation, so palpable I could almost taste it on my lips.

Some megalomaniac like Milner had been responsible for Ellen's death.

I opened my eyes and saw Armstrong smile. "Yes, that's what it will feel like."

But the moment had passed. "Are you offering me membership of the Society of the Elect?"

He frowned. "The what?"

I spoke slowly and clearly. "The Society of the Elect. Milner and Rhodes."

"What the hell do you mean? Are you talking about Mr Rhodes' *Confession*?"

"Yes."

He made a dismissive gesture. "Fantasy, pure fantasy. A great idea — *the* Idea — but it would never work. That's not how things are done. Lord Milner has his own plans."

"Are you saying that there is no Society of the Elect?"

"Not that I've ever bloody heard of!"

I was sure he was telling the truth. "You speak as if Milner were the sole beneficiary of Rhodes' fortune, but at the moment Jameson stands to inherit everything. Even if he manages to invalidate the codicil, Milner will still have to share the legacy with half a dozen others."

"Lanner! I wouldn't give him another thought. He is nothing without Mr Rhodes, nothing. His pathetic attempt to succeed Mr Rhodes has already been outmanoeuvred."

Rhodes had given all of his inner circle nicknames. Jameson had two: 'Doctor Jim' and 'Lanner'. "Are you saying that Milner had Lowenstein killed and Drayton is next?"

Armstrong shook his head. "Don't be a damned fool, man. Lanner is so completely out-matched that the life and death of Lowenstein and of Drayton are insignificant. Drayton will board his steamer tomorrow and do you know what he'll find when he arrives in Cape Town? He's already too late. Lord Milner has invalidated the alleged final codicil. Have you read the latest news about the will?"

"On Wednesday?"

"Yes. Lanner doesn't know it yet, but Lord Milner foiled his plan on Tuesday. Drayton will arrive to find Lanner one of seven executors, and an isolated one at that. No one trusts him anymore, and his pathetic attempt at a coup d'état played right into Lord Milner's hands. My Lord is the true inheritor of Mr Rhodes' fortune, and he will use the power it puts at his disposal to lead the Empire to everlasting glory. You can be a part of that."

"Did he have Lowenstein killed?"

"Lowenstein! Lowenstein? Why should anyone care at all that some Jewish banking clerk is dead?"

"I care."

Armstrong shook his head again. "I feared as much. You still have the petty concerns of the policeman at heart. You may be a leader of men, but only on a small scale, and you will never aspire to lead the leaders. I suggested as much to Lord Milner."

"Did he have Lowenstein killed?" I demanded.

"No, he did not. He didn't need to, just as he doesn't need to delay Drayton. Can't your simple, narrow-minded brain grasp that?"

"Do you know a man called Carey, Francis Carey?"

Confusion spread over his freckled face. "Who the Devil is Francis Carey? Dammit, man, I'm here to offer you an opportunity for greatness — to rule the bloody Empire — not suffer another interrogation!"

"You don't know Carey?"

"No, I don't know this blasted Carey, whoever he is. This is your last chance. Come with me, with Lord Milner. Join us in Cape Town." He reached for me.

Once again, I thought he was telling the truth. I stepped away, and made for the stairs. "No thank you. You're quite right, I am a simple policeman, and I like being one. I don't want to be a soldier again and I certainly don't want to be Milner's lackey. Good day, Armstrong."

"Marshall!"

I stopped — reached for the Mauser — kept my hand on it as I slowly turned around. "Yes?"

"When you arrive at the bottom of the stairs, knock twice and wait for Moser to open the door."

I let my hand fall to my side, empty. "Or else?"

"You will not leave the Monument alive."

23. Empire Day

"Good afternoon, sir, begging your pardon — "

"There's no need for that, but I require three things from you rather quickly," I said to the attendant at the National Liberal Club as I wheeled in the pedal cycle. "First, could you find somewhere to keep this? Somewhere safe, there are plenty of thieves about today. Second, a telephone and some privacy. Third, I'd like a word with the senior member of staff who was on duty on Saturday the twenty-fourth of May."

"I'm sorry, sir, but I'm afraid —"

"Major Marshall, Scotland Yard." I leant the bicycle against the counter. "I'm on police business, so I'd appreciate if you step to it."

He pressed an electric buzzer. "Certainly, sir. One moment, please."

Several guests passed me on the way in and I caught part of a comment about uppity servants, which no doubt referred to my dress — I was still in my suit — and the Honesty. A few seconds later an under-manager by the name of Barnes appeared. After a brief explanation from the attendant and confirmation from me, the bicycle was removed to the cloakroom, and Barnes asked me to follow him.

I was taken to an office below stairs which looked as if it was shared by several under-managers or clerks. "There you are, sir. I was on duty on the date in question. May I help?"

"Was Mr Chamberlain here with a party of guests?"

"Yes, sir, he was."

"Very good. If you could return in ten minutes, I'd like to ask you a few questions."

"As you wish, sir."

When he left, I gave the operator the number for Rochester Row police station, and asked for Truegood once I was connected.

"Truegood."

"It's Marshall, anything new?"

"No joy. As I thought, Rose hasn't a clue. Lamb's torn the Otter's Pocket to pieces, but there's nothing there either. You just caught me.

I'm going to give it one more hour, then I'll let the CID here get on with it. When I'm done I'm going to take Lamb and start on Murgatroyd's other haunts — not that I expect him to be in any of them. You survived Armstrong?"

"Yes, and I think I've got a better idea for this afternoon."

"Go on."

"I broke into Carey's rooms this morning."

"I'm not sure I want to hear this."

"I wasn't the only one in there. A couple of Russian chaps arrived shortly after me. Having heard that the Russian sense of humour isn't quite up to the Scots standard, I decided discretion was the better part of valour and beat a hasty retreat. They didn't see the funny side, and took a few shots at me as I departed."

"Bloody hell!"

"I'm convinced that Carey is the man behind the Chamberlain incident, and that he may have been working for the same person who set him up for Lowenstein."

"Not the Russians?" he said.

"No. I reckon if they set him up to be arrested on Tuesday, they wouldn't be trying to kill him on Saturday. It must be someone else. We have more than enough circumstantial evidence to bring Carey in for questioning about Lowenstein. When we've got him, we can find out about Chamberlain."

"It sounds good to me. There's just one problem: I don't want to have to haul him out of some duke's mansion. Not after our battle in Devil's Acre — and you shooting up Grosvenor Square — on coronation day. Christ, I've got enough to explain to Mr M as it is."

"According to Carey's schedule book, he's meeting someone at Lyons & Co., Butler's Wharf, at four o'clock. I assume that's the tea company and they have a warehouse there?"

"Yeah, on Shad Thames. Who's he meeting?"

"That's the good news. I think he's meeting the same man who arranged Chamberlain's accident."

"Who's that?"

"Does T.D. mean anything to you?"

"Who?"

"'T' as in Lyons & Co.; 'D' as in drink. All I have are the initials."

"Nothing."

"What about Rose and Murgatroyd? Any T.D. they might know?"

Truegood didn't answer for a few seconds. "I'll ask Rose politely, shall I? Where are you?"

"The National Liberal Club."

"I'll meet you at the Yard at two — no, better make it three."

"I'll be there."

Rose appeared to be a dead end, which made Aitken's sacrifice in vain, though we'd had no way of knowing beforehand. Whoever employed Murgatroyd had killed Lowenstein and arranged the evidence to point to Carey; someone had employed Carey to kill or scare Chamberlain; it looked like both employers were T.D. Who wanted Chamberlain frightened and Lowenstein dead? Then there was Ellen. For whom had Carey killed her? The elusive T.D. was a possibility, but once again there was the question of motive.

There was a knock at the door and Barnes entered. "If it's convenient, sir... "

"Of course. Sit down, Barnes, it's your office. Did I miss the guns?"

He sat down, ramrod straight. "No, sir. It appears there's been a delay at the Abbey. His Majesty hasn't left yet."

I wondered why, as the coronation had run like clockwork so far. "I'm going to ask you some questions about Mr Chamberlain and his guests on the twenty-fourth of May. Before I start I want you to know that the matter is of the utmost importance and may even involve the safety of His Majesty himself. Holding anything — *anything* — back from me is tantamount to treason. Do you understand?"

He paled and stammered, "Y — yes, sir. I wouldn't —"

"Of course you wouldn't, but I wanted to make that clear. Similarly, our conversation must remain entirely confidential."

"Yes, sir." He nodded so hard I thought he'd do himself an injury.

"Good. Please tell me everything you can about Mr Chamberlain's visit to the club on the day in question."

"All right, sir. Mr Chamberlain arrived just after half-past eleven. He had booked the Earl Russell Room, and went up at once. He instructed that his guests be directed there on arrival. He had arranged a luncheon for seven, to start at half-past twelve, but required complete privacy from the time the last guest arrived until the luncheon started."

"Does that mean he was alone in the room with his party?" I asked.

"Yes, sir. The guests began arriving at a quarter to twelve. There were five gentlemen and a lady, but I'm afraid the only one I knew was His Grace, the Duke of Devonshire."

"Can you describe the others?"

"Yes, sir."

"Then do so please, in the order of their arrival."

"The first was a major of cavalry. I do not know the gentleman's name, but his regiment was the New South Wales Lancers, I remember that much. He also had a scar on his face." Barnes touched his cheek, just under his left ear.

"Was the major blonde, with a thick moustache?"

"He was, sir. Shortly after came a tall middle-aged gentleman wearing spectacles. He was soft-spoken and very polite. Then the lady, who was also middle-aged, and — if I may say so… "

"Yes, this is important."

"The lady was rather forthright considering she was a guest at a gentlemen's club, sir."

"Did she have any distinguishing features?"

"I'm afraid not, sir."

"Please continue."

"After the lady, an older gentleman arrived. Once again I did not know who he was, nor was there any particular feature that I could use to describe him. He was perhaps about Mr Chamberlain's age and he walked with a slight stoop. The last guest was His Grace. He arrived with a very fashionably dressed young gentleman with a waxed moustache and a… " He touched his chin.

"A chin puff?"

"Yes, sir."

"What happened next?"

"I took His Grace and the young gentleman up myself. That was at about five minutes to twelve. Once all his guests were in the Earl Russell Room, I locked the doors. At exactly half-past twelve, I unlocked them, and the staff served luncheon. At two o'clock all Mr Chamberlain's guests left, except for His Grace. His Grace and Mr Chamberlain withdrew to the Smoking Room and remained there until just after three o'clock, when they both left."

"Thank you, Barnes, you've been most helpful. I've just one more request. Miss Roberta Paterson is a guest of Lord Morley's. Could you send her my compliments and ask her to join me at her convenience?"

"Yes, sir, I'll see to it immediately."

"Thank you."

Barnes departed, closing the door behind him.

I took out my pencil and notebook and jotted down Chamberlain's guest list. The Australian officer was almost certainly Major John Binstead, one of Lord Kitchener's aides-de-camp. The Duke of Devonshire's companion was obviously my friend Drayton. Then two other men and a woman. A New Woman by the sound of it. I didn't think I'd have a hope of finding out who the latter three were today. Perhaps tomorrow, when I could speak to the waiters who'd served them. I'd have to concentrate on the four I did know.

Joseph Chamberlain was Secretary of State for the Colonies. A fanatical imperialist, Rhodes' co-conspirator in the Jameson Raid, and his ally in the expansion of the Empire at all costs.

I'd met Jack Binstead twice, but knew little about him except that he'd come to South Africa as a captain in the New South Wales Lancers. When his regiment had been sent back to Australia, he'd been retained by Kitchener as an ADC, one of his band of boys.

Spencer Cavendish, the eighth Duke of Devonshire, was the president of the British Empire League, which aimed to bind the Colonies closer together in a commonwealth, to the benefit of all. I didn't know if Rhodes had known Cavendish, but Rhodes' main concern after the expansion of the Empire, was its federation.

Morgan Drayton, private secretary to Jameson and Jameson was Rhodes' most notorious henchman and a close friend of his brother; he had made a play for Rhodes' fortune, enlisting the aid of Drayton and Lowenstein.

One man linked all four.

Cecil John Rhodes was Chamberlain's partner, Kitchener's friend and Jameson's employer. His goal — after world conquest — was Imperial federation, shared with Cavendish. Rhodes had proposed a secret society to rule first the Empire, and then the world…

The woman was Flora Shaw, Rhodes' friend, Chamberlain's ally, and another of the Jameson Raid conspirators. According to Ellen's diary she had been in London that week. Shaw was as ardent an imperialist as Rhodes, she was middle-aged, and she was a New Woman.

Chamberlain, Kitchener, Cavendish, Jameson, and Shaw…

The secret society.

Chamberlain and his party had inaugurated Rhodes' secret society. It made perfect sense. It wasn't just Milner and his kindergarten who wanted to rule the world, it was Chamberlain and Jameson as well. Chamberlain with the political power of his office and Jameson with the financial power of Rhodes' fortune — or so he hoped. Seven years ago they'd planned the Jameson Raid together; now, their aim was far more ambitious. That was why Jameson had kept Drayton in London for the coronation, because of the newly-formed society.

I considered the implications of my explanation and the more I thought about it, the more confident I felt that I'd uncovered the truth. Yet my insight — if it could accurately be described as such — still failed to solve the three mysteries: who had employed Carey to kill Ellen; who had employed Carey to frighten Chamberlain; and who had murdered Lowenstein? Carey was the only link amongst three otherwise unrelated crimes. It was imperative that I speak to him this afternoon.

There was a knock at the door. "Enter!" It was Roberta, wearing a crimson Gibson Girl outfit with a floral hat. I stood. "Good afternoon, Roberta, you're looking particularly lovely, if you don't mind my saying so."

"Hello. I do not mind."

I pulled out a chair for her and sat down once she'd made herself comfortable. "I found another entry in Ellen's diary that might have something to do with her death. It involves Flora Shaw."

Roberta gasped and put her hand to her mouth. "Miss Shaw, surely you must be mistaken!"

I took her into my confidence, advising her about the Lowenstein murder and the intrigue surrounding the execution of Rhodes' will. She was well-informed on the latter, and told me that she'd spent some time this morning in the company of W.T. Stead, who was one of her editors, and whose latest literary work was entitled *The Last Will and Testament of Cecil John Rhodes*. Once Stead's publication was in circulation, all London and the Empire would know of Rhodes' dream to conquer the world. Few would know that Chamberlain and Jameson had already set it in motion. I skipped Carey's involvement in Chamberlain's accident, and moved directly to the luncheon in May.

"I may be wrong, but I think Chamberlain was inaugurating Rhodes' secret society. Meanwhile, in the Cape, Jameson was wrangling for control of Rhodes' fortune." As I voiced my suspicions, my certainty ebbed. With each word I felt more ridiculous. "Er, now that I've said it, I'm not so sure anymore… " I tailed off sheepishly.

Roberta wasn't looking at me, nor was she listening. Her eyes were unfocused and she appeared deep in thought. I waited in silence. Eventually she said, simply, "No."

"It seemed like a good idea, but you're probably — "

"No. Do you know what the twenty-fourth of May was?"

"Er, wasn't it Queen Victoria's birthday?"

"Yes, but that's not what I mean. I'm talking about the twenty-fourth of May 1902?"

"I'm sorry, I don't follow you," I said.

"It was the first widespread celebration of Empire Day."

"Empire Day?"

"Yes, Empire Day, the day that has been set aside to celebrate the establishment of the British Empire. And you're absolutely right: what better occasion to launch Mr Rhodes' secret society?" she concluded.

"Damn — pardon me, but this is one occasion where I'd much rather you'd proved me wrong."

"I think I feel the same way." From the floors above we heard cheering and clapping. The King had evidently left the Abbey at last. "Do you think Mr Chamberlain is the leader of the society?"

"It seems so. Why do you ask?"

"Just something Mr Stead said earlier. He was talking about men of the late Mr Rhodes' ilk, men who seek power and personal glory above all else. He said that it would be difficult for them to form the kind of cabal of which Mr Rhodes dreamed, because they have an overwhelming tendency to fight amongst themselves. He used the examples of Mr Chamberlain and Lord Milner, and then Mr Chamberlain and Dr Jameson."

I raised my eyebrows. "Chamberlain and Jameson?"

"That's what Mr Stead said, and he should know. Apparently they are rivals in almost everything. The expression he used was that each wanted to be the 'cock in the henhouse.'"

"The henhouse being the Empire."

"It's just like the plot of some *Penny Blood*, but it's really rather frightening if it's all true. I've thought of something else, as well."

"Tell me."

"Have you considered that Mr Lowenstein might have been murdered by one of his own?"

"What do you mean?"

"Isn't that the detective's maxim? To look to the victim's relatives and friends. That's what you told me when we met, isn't it?"

"It is, but I don't quite follow your line of reasoning."

"Everyone knows there's no honour amongst thieves. Perhaps Mr Lowenstein fell out with Dr Jameson? Or perhaps he had a pang of conscience and changed his mind?"

"It's possible," I said.

"I don't know if that's helpful, but I can see why you've been so busy. How does this all involve Ellen?"

I hesitated. "I'm not sure yet, but I am sure that Carey murdered her. You were right."

Her mouth formed an almost perfect circle, and the colour drained from her angelic face. She said nothing and I watched her expression change in a series of conflicting emotions. Slowly, she covered her mouth with her hand again. Then tears flowed down her cheeks and she started to whimper quietly.

I moved around to her, gave her my handkerchief, and put my hand on her shoulder. I wasn't sure what to say. All I could think of was, "I'm sorry I doubted you."

Roberta cried for a few moments more, then dabbed her eyes dry and gave a very delicate sniff. She looked up at me and I saw the pain had been replaced by a steely determination. "Are you going to kill him?"

"No, I'm going to find out who hired him and why."

"Who on earth would have employed Lieutenant Carey to kill Ellen?"

"I don't know yet, but I will soon; don't worry about that."

"I'm not. I know you'll find whoever's responsible." She stood and my hand slid from her shoulder. Our faces were only inches apart. I could see her pearly white teeth between her red lips, and feel her breath on my face. "Do I look presentable?" she asked as she handed my handkerchief back.

I took both her hands in mine. "No, you look beautiful."

"Thank you. I wore this for you, Alec."

"For me?"

"It's crimson, the same colour as the ribbon of your Victoria Cross."

"Thank you, I'm honoured. It becomes you. Not only beautiful, but intelligent too. If you hadn't told me about Empire Day, I'd probably have changed my mind. Now I know I'm right. Chamberlain and Jameson were forming their society. You must be an excellent journalist. Perhaps you'll let me read some of your work when we have the time."

"I'm glad to have been of assistance, and you're very welcome to read my articles if you don't think they would bore you." She squeezed my hands before letting go. "Are you going to join me at the luncheon?"

"I'm afraid not. I have to get back to Scotland Yard. I'm hoping I'll be able to convince Inspector True good to arrest Carey."

"I understand. Let me show you out, at least."

I opened the door for her, and she led me upstairs to the hall, now full of people. Some were milling about, and others leaving, but most were coming back in having watched the procession.

"After what you've told me, I don't suppose you'll be able to dine with us tonight either?"

I rested my hand on her arm. "No, I'm afraid not. Once Carey's been taken into custody I'm hoping we'll be able to coerce him into telling us who employed him to kill Ellen. She's still my main concern."

"I've never doubted it." She looked up at me and smiled.

As we were in public, I took her hand and brushed my lips over it. "I'll telephone you tomorrow, if I may, by which time I should have some news."

"I look forward to it. Goodbye, Alec."

"Goodbye." I watched her return to her party. Then I retrieved my bicycle and pushed it outside to strains of Elgar:

Land of hope and glory, mother of the free,
How shall we extol thee, who are born of thee?
Wider still, and wider, shall thy bounds be set;
God, who made thee mighty, make thee mightier yet!

I tried to arrange my thoughts into some sort of order as I walked, but it was impossible. There was just too much to think about. Rhodes, Chamberlain, Jameson, Milner, Carey, Armstrong, Drayton, Colonel Rhodes... the connections were myriad and complex.

It was a few minutes to three when I was escorted up to Truegood's office. I thanked the constable and entered without knocking.

Truegood looked up from his desk, jumped to his feet, and pointed at me, "You fucking lied to me, Marshall! You like taking me for a fool? You've got another thing coming if you think I'm going to let you get away with it!"

24. Rendezvous in Shad Thames

It had already been a rather trying day. What with Murgatroyd, the Russians, and Armstrong, I was in no mood for Truegood. I threw my hat on the nearest desk, reached my left hand into my side pocket, and gripped the brass knuckles. As Truegood surged towards me, I stepped forward with my left leg, increasing my reach and minimising my size as a target. "Come on. If you want a fight, let's fight. Otherwise, tell me what the hell you're talking about!"

Truegood stopped three feet from me, well out of reach, hands on hips. His chest and shoulders rippled with muscle. "This is all about your sister, isn't it? She was riding with Carey when she died. You think there was foul play, and you want Carey questioned. You want him questioned about her, so you've twisted everything so it points to him: Lowenstein, Chamberlain, the lot."

"I'm warning you now: unless you want to explain to Melville why both of us are unfit for duty, you'll show my late sister the proper respect. It's Dr Marshall, for a start."

"Dr Marshall, if you bloody like!" He threw his hands in the air, turned, and stomped back to his seat. I let go of the brass knuckles. "When Mr M hears about this, it'll be you off the payroll, sharpish. Fit for duty or fucking not." He sat down heavily. "I should never have trusted an amateur."

I sat on the edge of a desk. Once again, to give him his due, Truegood was thorough. He'd obviously cross-referenced the Yard's records for mention of Carey's name. "Yes, I think Carey was hired to kill Dr Marshall. Your own surgeon, Dr Maycock, thinks the scene of the offence was contrived to make a murder look like an accident. You suspect that Carey offers his services for hire; I just don't know who employed him to kill Dr Marshall, or why, but Carey was definitely Chamberlain's cab driver. When I looked at his schedule book, the third of July to the eighth of July were blank. They were the only blank days since his return from East Africa."

Truegood's anger disappeared in an instant. "The third to the eighth?"

"Yes. The day before, on the second of July, he met with T.D. at the Bartitsu Club, whatever that is."

"It's Barton-Wright's self-defence club in Shaftesbury Avenue. He teaches boxing, wrestling, singlestick, fencing — all forms of single combat. The second of July?"

"That's right."

"Christ in heaven!" He brought his huge fist down on the desk. "That's it, that's bloody it! The Colonial Conference started on the Tuesday. This T.D. villain or his superiors don't like something Chamberlain says. T.D. meets Carey the next day; Carey becomes Tom Stringer on the Thursday, and takes the first opportunity that presents itself — Monday morning. He waits one more day for appearances sake, then returns to Mayfair, and Stringer is no more. Yeah, I like it — no, hold on a minute. What about the hat? Why would he wear his own hat while he was doing the business on Chamberlain?"

I explained why I thought Carey might prefer to keep some identifying feature when working in disguise.

Truegood scratched his chin. "I like it; I like it a lot. I can't believe I spoke to the man and didn't realise it was Carey."

"Why would you?"

"True. What's your plan? We bring Carey in for questioning about Lowenstein, using the eyewitness and the penang lawyer as evidence. Is the stick his?"

"Yes, I think it was given to him by the Empress of Russia."

"Yeah, that would explain the Okhrana agents this morning. Are you sure they didn't set him up for Lowenstein?"

"As certain as I can be about anything. If the Russians I met this morning were Okhrana — and I can't think who else they'd be — then there was no need, was there?"

"You're right, yeah. Why risk blowing the Lischinskys' cover when they can just gun Carey down in his own house? Not by half. Right, we bring Carey in for Lowenstein, put your sis — Dr Marshall's — murder on him as well, and tell him we know he's Stringer. That'll be easy, I'll just say I recognise him. You said something about the ears being difficult to disguise, didn't you?"

"That's right."

"I'll use that then. What next?"

"With two murder and one espionage charge against him, I'm hoping he'll tell us everything: who employed him to kill Dr Marshall, who employed him to scare Chamberlain, and who wanted us to think he had killed Lowenstein. With any luck, he'll give us a name with which we're already familiar. Once we find out who wanted him arrested for Lowenstein's murder, then we'll know who the real killer is."

"This T.D. fella?"

"Possibly. There's one other thing I've got to tell you."

"Go on," he said.

"Do you know of the rumours about Rhodes' secret society?"

"The one based on the Jesuits?"

"Yes, with the aim of expanding the Empire until it rules the whole world. Well the society — I don't know what they call themselves — exists. I'm pretty sure it was inaugurated at the National Liberal Club on Empire Day."

"Christ, you're serious, aren't you?"

"Yes. I don't know all of the leaders, but we've got Chamberlain, Jameson, Cavendish, Kitchener and Flora Shaw for a start."

"How did you find that out?"

"It's a long story."

"Cavendish, Chamberlain, Kitchener… bloody hell, if I wasn't such a bellicose bastard, I'd resign now. Save them the trouble of sacking me later."

"You're right about that." I smiled.

"What?"

"You are a bellicose bastard."

"If I wasn't, I'd sit back and wait for orders from Mr M — but he won't be available until tonight, and we need to get Carey now. What about T.D., are we going to pick him up as well?"

"I don't think we have enough cause. Yet."

"I agree. You said Lyons & Co., didn't you?"

I took out my watch. "In half an hour. We'd better get going and hope we can find a hansom in Southwark."

"We can do better than that, sir," said Lamb as he entered the office. "I've got a growler waiting outside."

"Right, let's go." Truegood grabbed his hat. "You're both armed? Good."

A four-wheeler was waiting on the Victoria Embankment. Truegood left the driver in no doubt of the urgency of our mission, and we bounced off at a brisk pace, crossing Westminster Bridge into Lambeth. He briefed Lamb about Carey, but didn't mention the secret society. When Truegood was finished — by which time we were leaving the wide, clean streets of Lambeth for Southwark — he turned back to me.

"Lyons and Co. have several warehouses in Shad Thames, on Butler's Wharf, the other side of Tower Bridge. We'll have to find the right one when we get there. Regarding Murgatroyd, we think he might also be in Bermondsey. One of his adams is a ponce called Boustred. Boustred runs a whorehouse in the warren off Snowsfields, which is only a stone's throw away from Shad Thames. Problem is there's just the three of us until tomorrow. If Murgatroyd is there, the place is bound to be defended, and I'm not planning another raid until I've got all the men I need."

"Yes, quite right."

"When we're done with Carey and this other gent, I'll put my docker's togs on again, and go and have a look," said Lamb.

We lapsed into silence as we rattled through Southwark. The streets weren't as busy as Westminster, for obvious reasons, but there were still plenty of people celebrating as well as occasional signs of commerce, despite the bank holiday. We drove through Newington and turned north. Even though the factories were closed, the caustic smell of glue hung thick, like an invisible fog. As we neared the South Bank, the foul odour of decaying flesh and drying skin replaced the glue.

"The Leather Market," said Lamb in response to my grimace. "No market today, but the tanners will have their skins out to dry."

We passed Guy's Hospital and crossed Tooley Street. The character of the air altered again, the smell of the tanneries mingling with the reek of the Thames, raw sewage and rotten fish. No wonder so many Britons chose to move to the fresh air and open spaces of the colonies.

"The driver will stop at the bridge and wait for us," said Truegood. "All of the Lyons & Co. buildings are this side of the dockyard, so we'll just have to take them one by one and hope Carey doesn't see us coming."

Tower Bridge came into view, a Victorian gothic folly marking the entrance to the Upper Pool of the Thames. Opposite stood the Tower itself, fortress London, with the Monument to the west, and St Katherine's Dock to the east. Small boats and pleasure cruisers plied their way along the great river. I checked my watch again: five minutes past four. The driver stopped at Horselydown, where Shad Thames began, and we alighted. I'd never been here before, and I was astonished at the huge warehouses — some of them seven or more stories high — on either side of the narrow, cobbled street. Above, a maze of metal walkways connected the buildings, evenly spaced between cranes and winches. It looked like something out of the future, an alien landscape from the pen of Mr Wells.

The street was completely deserted.

"Come on," said Truegood, striding ahead, "the first one is just around that corner."

A few paces later, we could see around the bend: on the left, about a hundred and fifty yards ahead, a single vehicle sat in the street. It was a horseless carriage. "That's Carey's," I said. "He's an automobile enthusiast."

"Lamb, duck down into Maggie Blake's, and cover the front. And keep your revolver handy, I don't want any mistakes this time."

Lamb darted ahead of us, then disappeared through a cause to the left, on to the front of the wharf. Truegood and I stepped up our pace. We approached the horseless carriage, resting on its thick india-rubber tyres, its polished brass horn and wheel gleaming.

My thoughts of time travel were disturbed by the muffled sound of a shot.

Truegood and I reached for our weapons simultaneously.

The Panhard-Levassar was parked immediately outside a door. I followed Truegood around the front of the automobile, feeling the warmth of the engine as I passed. The door was closed, but unlocked. Truegood opened it — I heard a shout — another — we dashed inside.

The warehouse was long and narrow, with plenty of light from a row of riverside windows. It was full of tea chests and sacks, stacked right up to the low ceiling in many cases. Another shout — to the right; and movement — to the left.

Truegood sprinted forward and turned left into an aisle. I turned right, making for the cry.

"Stop, police!" I heard from behind. A stifled shout — then a groan ahead.

I found a Bowie knife with a nine inch blade lying on the floor, a bloodstain, and bloody footprints.

I gritted my teeth and charged around a stack of chests: Carey, lying prone, arm outstretched. More blood: from his arm up and over several chests.

"Police, stay where you are!"

A crash, then running feet.

I crouched next to Carey — kept an eye in front — and turned him over. He'd been shot in the face and stabbed twice in the torso. His eyes flickered and blinked, he made a tight fist with his right hand, and then he was gone.

A figure appeared above the blood trail — I raised the Mauser — aimed.

"It's me, sir!"

"Where's Truegood?" Lamb shrugged. "He went that way." I left Carey and sprinted back to where I'd last seen the inspector. There were no more sounds. "How did you get in?" I shouted over my shoulder.

"From the wharf. The doors were unlocked."

The warehouse had two sets of doors on either side, which was how Lamb had missed the murderer. I turned towards the river and saw an open door ahead. I burst out onto the wharf, turned left, and picked up the blood trail. It was intermittent; the bleeder was moving fast. No sign of Truegood or the suspect. I glanced over the railing towards Tower Bridge — boats and cranes, but no Truegood. I ran into Maggie Blake's Cause, emerged onto Shad Thames, and heard a shot from somewhere ahead.

And another.

We dashed up Horselydown — reached Tooley Street — followed the raised arms and voices of pedestrians — ran past St John's, and under a railway bridge.

Lamb blew his whistle — as if in answer there was another shot, closer this time.

We reached Tanner Street and a group of loafers outside the Bermondsey Workhouse pointed right, towards the leather market. We crossed Bermondsey Street — I heard another whistle — saw two constables running towards us.

The road ahead forked.

I shouted to Lamb to go right, and went left into Underpass Street.

The leather market — empty stalls. No Truegood, no suspect, just the stench of meat and skin.

I continued, arriving in a wide terrace, the houses decorated with Union flags and streamers.

Nothing here either.

I heard a whistle from behind and ran back — along the north side of the market this time.

Another policeman came towards me from Bermondsey Street. At about twenty yards distance, he saw my pistol and stopped.

"It's all right, I'm from the Yard!"

He nodded. "This way, sir!"

I followed him up a narrow alley to my left. A constable was in the middle of the street, kneeling over Truegood. The constable saw us and shouted to his colleague. "Up there, Sarge, an' be careful there's another plainclothesman on the loose!"

The sergeant continued up the alley, but I stopped: the constable had Truegood's head propped up on his thigh, and his hand was covering the inspector's throat. "He's been shot!" Blood oozed from under the man's fingers. Truegood's eyes were closed, and he was groaning.

"You're doing a good job, Constable, do you need help?"

"No, sir, I've got 'im. They've gone for the ambulance."

"Good. Just keep the pressure on the wound. Did he say anything?"

"No, sir, 'e was like this when I found 'im."

I continued up the alley, but soon met Lamb on his way back with the sergeant and another constable. "How's the guvnor, sir?"

"Not good. Did you see who it was?"

"No, sir, and he's gone now."

"Gone where?" I asked.

"Snowsfields." He pointed back the way he'd come. "That's Snowsfields, sir, where Murgatroyd is."

25. The Empire Loyalist League

"What did he look like?" I asked.

"I only caught a flash as he went round the corner, then he was gone. He was dressed like a gentleman, and he was carryin' a stick in his left hand. I'm afraid that's all, sir."

"What about the others?" I indicated the uniformed policemen.

"No one else got a look in, sir."

"Listen carefully. I want you to send a couple of constables over to the warehouse to prevent anyone from interfering with the scene of the offence until a detective arrives. Carey is already dead so they needn't go inside. Then you can take me to the nearest police station and help me track down Melville."

"But, sir, he's — "

"At the Palace, I know. It doesn't matter. Even if he can't come out here, I need to speak to him — now."

"Yes, sir."

We left Truegood in the care of the sergeant and two constables. An ambulance was en route from Guy's Hospital. Lamb directed another two constables to secure the scene of the offence, and led me to the Bermondsey Street station, only a short distance away. I waited while he gave the duty inspector, a middle-aged man by the name of Jones, a summarised version of events. Jones contacted M Division headquarters, in Borough, to request a detective, and then left us alone.

"You sure about this, sir?"

"I am," I replied.

"I think it might be better comin' from you, sir. This telephone contraption is all about how a person sounds, and they can tell — well, I think an educated accent like yours might go further, sir."

"But I don't know the protocol. I'll tell you what, Lamb. You make a start and I'll take over when you need me to. And don't worry about speaking to Melville, I'll do that."

"Yes, sir."

More than half an hour later I was alone in the office, earpiece in hand, still trying to penetrate the privacy of Buckingham Palace. After doing his bit, Lamb had left to meet Inspector Hughes, from district headquarters. I was wondering if the telephone was such a useful invention after all, and if it wouldn't have been quicker to appear in person and trust to my military rank and VC. For the umpteenth time I heard muted voices from the other end and prepared to repeat my request yet again.

"Melville."

At last. "It's Marshall, I'm sorry to bother you, but it's urgent."

"Make it quick."

"First, Truegood has been shot in Snowsfields."

"Is he alive?"

"He was when the ambulance took him. You recall Lieutenant Francis Carey?"

"Yes."

"We found evidence suggesting that Carey was hired to frighten Chamberlain last month, and that he was falsely implicated in Lowenstein's murder. He was meeting a man with the initials T.D. today in Butler's Wharf. It is likely that this man was involved in both crimes. When we arrived Carey was dead. The unidentified suspect escaped after shooting Truegood. Do you know about the raid this morning in Devil's Acre?"

"Yes."

"The intelligence subsequently received was that Murgatroyd had gone to ground in Snowsfields with a man named Boustred. It's possible that our suspect, whether it's T.D. or not, is hiding with them."

"Carey was dead when you found him?"

"Dying, but he didn't say anything. I would've telephoned you about Truegood anyway, but this afternoon I worked out that Rhodes' secret society exists. It's not Milner or the Society of the Elect — that was nonsense. Chamberlain and Jameson inaugurated the real society this year, on the twenty-fourth of May."

"Empire Day."

"Exactly. The Duke of Devonshire and Flora Shaw were present. Lord Kitchener sent a representative, Drayton stood in for Jameson, and there were two other unidentified men."

Melville was silent. I was about to try and persuade him I was right when he said, "The Empire Loyalist League."

"Excuse me?"

"The Empire Loyalist League. That's what they call themselves. When Chamberlain was in hospital, he kept repeating the phrase to the constable who assisted him. He was concussed at the time and I thought he was referring to the British Empire League or the Colonial Conference. I've been a complete idiot, I should've realised — do you think one or more of these individuals had Lowenstein murdered?"

"I'm not sure."

"It doesn't matter at the minute, anyway. What we need now is to lay our hands on Murgatroyd, and whoever else is with him. Who have you got there with you?"

"Lamb, the duty inspector, and a detective from Borough."

"Let them know I'll be over to take charge as soon as I can. In the interim, I want a cordon around Snowsfields, whatever it takes. Put the duty inspector on — and thank you for letting me know."

I found Inspector Jones and hurried back to the warehouse, where the constable on duty refused me entry until he'd summoned Lamb. Lamb introduced me to Hughes, who'd arrived with a detective constable whom he'd instructed to sketch the scene. Carey's body lay undisturbed. "My congratulations on your offence scene work, Inspector."

"I've asked Wright to draw a plan before we touch anything. Mr Henry's a stickler for procedure these days, and I can't say he's wrong in many a case."

"Melville is on his way over," I said to Lamb. "He's going to organise a man hunt for Murgatroyd." I looked back and saw the bloody Bowie knife, and further behind that a top hat. "You said the suspect was dressed like a gentleman. Was he wearing a hat?"

"No, sir, he wasn't."

"Do you mind, Inspector?" I indicated hat, knife, and corpse.

"Not at all. If you're one of Melville's Gang, that's good enough for me."

I knelt down and examined the top hat. Carey was a practical man and the initials F.F.C. were embroidered in tiny letters in the lining. "Lamb, follow the bloodstains, but be careful not to disturb any footprints. I want you to look for a hat, probably another top hat. It may be some distance from the trail."

"Yes, sir."

I remained where I was. T.D. had arranged to meet Carey. Had he come himself, or sent an agent? Probably come himself, so as not to arouse Carey's suspicions. After employing Carey on at least one nefarious enterprise, T.D. had murdered Lowenstein, wearing a broad-brimmed hat and leaving Carey's stick at the scene of the offence. Then he decided to do away with the man who could implicate him in the Chamberlain matter and end the police investigation of Lowenstein's murder at the same time. He lured Carey to the warehouse to kill him. What would the police think of Carey's murder? A dissatisfied customer, the Okhrana, an underworld contact, a jealous husband; the list would be long indeed.

In front of me the Bowie knife lay in a pool of blood. Carey hadn't been easy to kill. He was himself a hunter and killer. He'd come prepared, and managed to stab his assailant in the struggle. I replaced the top hat and walked past the knife, keeping clear of the blood. There were partial footprints in it, but they were smeared and it looked as if more than one set was superimposed over another. Some would be mine, and I didn't think we'd be able to reproduce a clear imprint from the mess.

I tried to picture the sequence of events. T.D. had arrived first. He knew Carey would enter from Shad Thames, so he'd prepared his exit on the riverside. He'd unlocked both doors, the one he'd used to escape, and the one Lamb had used to enter. Carey arrived and the two men met where the knife lay. T.D. had attacked first, but Carey fought back. The blood was pooled in only two places, under the knife and around the corpse. The stain under the corpse was to be expected; the stain under the knife suggested a prolonged initial struggle. They had perhaps been grappling, then one of the combatants had broken away, and the fight had become fluid. It ended with Carey's death on the other side of the stack of tea chests, where I'd found him. The trail of blood Lamb and I had followed confirmed that his killer had not escaped unscathed.

"Could you find me a large piece of cloth, please, Inspector? Or a sack or tarpaulin — there must be something in here." Hughes nodded, disappeared, and returned with an empty burlap sack. I thanked him and spread it out over the blood next to Carey's body.

He was lying on his back, as I'd left him. I'd heard a shot, but Carey had also been stabbed twice. The bullet had shattered his right cheekbone a couple of inches under the eye. There was no exit wound, so it had either lodged in the skull, or the scalp, possibly following the curve of the cranium. There were powder burns on his skin, so the shot had been at close range. The wound was on the right hand side, suggesting the murderer was left-handed — but that didn't take into account his blade.

One of the puncture wounds was to Carey's stomach, in the region of the navel. The other was direct to his heart. Inside his topcoat, in a similar fashion to the holster I wore for my Mauser, Carey had a leather rig for the sheath holding the Bowie knife. It hung upside down, under his left shoulder, with a clip over the guard to ensure it didn't fall out. I rolled his body over and saw that the killer's weapon had not only penetrated his ribcage, but his entire torso, causing a second — smaller — wound in his back. The blade must therefore have been even longer than the Bowie knife; longer and thinner.

I looked back to the trail leading around more of the chests and through the warehouse. I thought I could read the scene with some accuracy. T.D. had attacked Carey with a concealed sword. Carey was too quick: the first strike caught him in the stomach, wounding but not incapacitating him, and he drew his knife and struck. His blow must also have landed in a non-critical region. Realising that he was now fighting for his life, T.D. abandoned stealth and drew a pistol. He must have used his left hand, because he was right-handed — like Lowenstein's murderer — and had his sword in his right hand. He shot Carey in the face. Carey dropped his knife, but managed to stay on his feet and grasp hold of T.D. T.D. retreated in order to create enough space to use his sword. When he succeeded, he stabbed Carey again, making sure this time by piercing his heart.

I turned to where Lamb had made his initial appearance. A trail of spattered blood ran from Carey's body over a pile of crates. I followed. The blood led to an aisle running next to the windows, then out the door to the wharf itself. Whoever T.D. was, he was a very cool customer. By the time he'd administered the coup de grace, he would've realised that the police had arrived. Instead of bolting for the wharf, he'd stopped to listen, established where Lamb was, and used the second set of doors. All while Carey was gasping his last, and Truegood and I were already blundering around inside the building. Not only had T.D. taken a second to establish where his pursuers were, he'd also retrieved his hat, which had more than likely fallen during the struggle. It was an astonishing performance.

I walked out onto the wharf, to which only two small boats were moored. There was no sign of the hat anywhere and there were several different sets of partial footprints in the blood. Truegood, Lamb, and I had all contributed to the confusion while in hot pursuit. The blood splashes led along the front of the wharf into the narrow cause. I'd just entered it when Lamb appeared from Shad Thames.

"I went to the end of Horselydown, but I didn't find anything."

"We're looking for a sword as well," I responded.

"Is that what he was stabbed with?"

"Either a sword or a knife with a very long blade." Lamb and I walked back onto the wharf. As we approached the warehouse, I had an idea. "What about the river?"

"The river, sir?"

"The hat. I'm betting he threw his hat into the river."

Lamb shrugged. "Maybe he wasn't wearing a hat, sir?"

"He was. A lack of headgear would have drawn attention to him, and no murderer wants that. We'll have to do a thorough search of the warehouse —"

"There it is!" Lamb pointed down at the strip of shingle below us. "That's a silk hat, sir, I'm sure of it."

While he went to retrieve the evidence, I returned to Carey's corpse, taking a different route this time. I found Wright sitting well away from the blood and body, smoking his pipe.

He stood as soon as he saw me. "Inspector Hughes' compliments, Major. He's been called back to the station and instructed me to allow you and Sergeant Lamb to finish your investigation before I arrange for the removal of the deceased."

"That's very kind of him. Are you finished sketching?"

"Yes, sir."

"Have you searched the body yet?"

"No, sir. The guvnor said to leave it until you were finished."

"I'm much obliged, Wright."

"Don't mention it, sir," he said, resuming his perch.

I knelt next to Carey again, on the sack. My clothes were already bloody — for the second time today — but I didn't want to disturb the scene any more than necessary. Carey was lying on his front, as I'd left him. I took off my coat and rolled up my sleeves. It was time to go through his pockets, which would be soaked with blood.

Lamb arrived with a dented, soggy, silk top hat. "I've got it, sir. Well done! No sign of the sword, though. It must've sunk to the bottom."

"Does the hat give us any clue as to the owner's identity? And don't tell me it has the initials T.D."

Lamb smiled. "No, sir, it doesn't. All it says is, 'by Alfred Overdale and Sons'. I know the firm, they've a shop in Borough High Street."

"Then let's hope they can remember who they made it for."

"I'll see to it directly."

"You'd better wait for Melville. Inspector Jones is setting up a cordon around Snowsfields, and I'm sure your chief will want you there. Murgatroyd is our priority at the moment."

"Of course, sir. Do you think the villain we were chasin' is holed up with him?"

"It looks that way."

Carey's right hand was still bunched in a fist. I opened it and something fell out. I retrieved the object from the floor, stood, and reached for my coat. Outside, the heavens finally opened and rain poured down in a noisy torrent. "I'm going back to my hotel," I said. "I'll wait there until I hear from you. Look after the hat, and this as well."

Lamb opened his palm. "What's that, sir?"

"It belongs to the murderer." I dropped a cufflink into his hand.

A diamond cufflink.

26. Cat-and-Mouse

It was after six when I arrived at the Windsor; the rain had eased off to a drizzle, so I was uncomfortably damp rather than completely sodden. There were no messages. I told the attendant I was expecting one shortly, and went up to my rooms. I removed my coat and necktie, hung the rig with the Mauser over the back of one of the chairs, and rolled up my sleeves. I packed my meerschaum, set the last of the tobacco and the matches in reach, and made myself comfortable in an armchair. I puffed the pipe alight, relaxed in the cloud of spicy smoke, and attempted to unravel the mystery before me.

Where to begin? At the beginning, of course. Wasn't that what the detectives always said in magazines? The problem in real police work is that beginnings aren't always clearly defined. Where did the story of Lowenstein's murder begin? The inauguration of the Empire Loyalist League, the forging of the will, the Jameson Raid, or Rhodes' *Confession*? I decided to start on the twenty-second of March this year, four days before Rhodes' death.

When Jameson was sure Rhodes was dying, he faked a final codicil with the complicity of Lowenstein and Drayton. As soon as the forgery was complete, he sent Drayton to London. There could only be one purpose important enough for Jameson to risk sending one of his witnesses so far away, and that was the creation of the Empire Loyalist League itself. In which case it appeared that Jameson was the leader, rather than Chamberlain. Meanwhile, Milner and the other executors contested the forgery, and Lowenstein fled to England for fear of the consequences of being caught between his employer and Jameson.

Jameson now required a witness to confirm Rhodes' signature. He couldn't recall Drayton because Drayton had to remain in London on League business, so he ordered Drayton to send Lowenstein back to Cape Town. Drayton would've passed on the instructions in person, given the fortune at stake. Lowenstein had no intention of returning to the field of battle. He'd booked the return journey for the fifth of May to buy himself some time, and hidden himself in London's little Bohemia.

His deception probably wouldn't have been discovered until the ship arrived in Cape Town twenty days later.

As soon as Jameson realised Lowenstein hadn't followed orders, he wired Drayton, who hired Littlechild, Slater, and Murgatroyd to find the missing clerk. Lowenstein wrote to Colonel Rhodes, very likely begging him for advice, assistance, or both, and was very likely ignored. With Jameson in Cape Town, Chamberlain pursued his own agenda at the Colonial Conference, and Drayton had to remind him he was the monkey, not the organ-grinder. Carey performed the job with characteristic flair and skill. As soon as I saw the initials 'T.D', I should've known. They referred to 'The Doctor', Rhodes' nickname for Drayton.

What I didn't know, was why Drayton hadn't returned to Cape Town as soon as Chamberlain had been warned, but Carey's part in the Colonial Secretary's accident was further confirmation that Jameson was the ringleader. A month later, Rose found Lowenstein. Drayton had obviously planned to dispose of Carey earlier, and stolen his penang lawyer in order to put the police on a false trail. Drayton then broke into Mrs Curran's establishment, conducted an interview with Lowenstein, and killed him.

Roberta was quite right: Lowenstein was murdered by one of his own in order to keep him quiet. Drayton made sure Lowenstein's identity would be discovered by leaving his hiding place under the floor uncovered. Jameson needed the knowledge of Lowenstein's death to be made public, because the solicitors had to be aware that Drayton was now the only witness to the codicil. Drayton left the scene of the offence wearing the wideawake hat, and deposited the murder weapon in the dust-bin, where he knew it would be found.

Carey was Drayton's only remaining loose end. Drayton arranged to meet him in a secluded setting, where he could kill him in relative safety, and where his corpse was unlikely to be discovered until Drayton was already out of the country. Killing Carey not only removed a potential threat to Drayton, but also ensured that further inquiry into Lowenstein's murder would be improbable. Carey had so many enemies that the police wouldn't have to look too far for a credible suspect. There was the Okhrana, just for starters.

Drayton met Carey this afternoon, and struck with his sword-stick. Twenty-seven inches was long enough to produce the puncture wounds I'd seen. I knew Drayton never went anywhere without his Derringer, and I'd no doubt that the post-mortem examination would reveal the bullet in Carey's head to be a point-four-one calibre round. The pistol had a two shot capacity; the second bullet was in Truegood's throat. Despite Drayton's remarkable composure in action, Carey had still scuppered his plans. He was too tough to be killed cleanly, and resourceful enough to grab a cufflink from his killer when he knew he was dying.

Was it enough to arrest Drayton when he boarded his steamer tomorrow? No, not for a man under the protection of the Duke of Devonshire. If I found him tonight, his wound perhaps untreated, his cufflink missing, traces of blood on his blade… that would be completely different. Drayton would have a contingency plan for every eventuality anyway, including sustaining a wound. He wouldn't return to Devonshire House covered in blood for fear of implicating Cavendish, so Boustred's brothel in Snowsfields seemed a strong possibility. I wasn't entirely convinced, but Melville was already dealing with Snowsfields, so it was logical for me to begin my own search at the home of the victim.

I put my pipe down and checked my watch: nearly half-past seven. I dressed, made sure that the Mauser was fully loaded, and left the Windsor for King Street. The rain had stopped and the streets were busy, although not as crowded as they would be shortly, when night fell and the illuminations were switched on. I made good time to Upper Grosvenor Street and opted to approach Blackburn House with caution. I was sure the Russian gentlemen would be long gone, but once bitten, twice shy. My vigilance was unnecessary: as soon as I turned into King Street, I saw a policeman standing sentry outside Carey's rooms. I identified myself and was told Lamb was inside.

I found him on the fourth floor, in the master bedroom, spreading the contents of Carey's safe on the four-poster bed. "Evenin', Major, care to lend a hand?"

"Certainly, any news?"

"Yes, sir. The guvnor is goin' to be all right. The surgeon did a fine job, aside from which Mr Truegood is built like a bull. Probably be back at work before he's mended, knowin' him. Inspector Hughes and the lads from Borough raided Boustred's bawdy-house, but they didn't find him, Murgatroyd, or the missing gentleman."

That was unfortunate. "Drayton."

"Dr Drayton?"

"Yes, T.D. stands for 'The Doctor'. It's Drayton's nickname in South Africa."

"If Drayton killed Carey, then who killed Lowenstein?"

"Drayton again, although he arranged the evidence to point to Carey."

Lamb's puzzled expression eased. "Ah, I see. That explains the stick."

"The stick?"

"Yes, sir. You were right about the penang lawyer, it belonged to Carey. It looks like his valet has scarpered, but I spoke to the butler next door. He remembered Carey's stick — and his floppy hat of course."

"Did you open the safe?" I asked.

"Mr M has a cracksman he uses for jobs like this. I brought him with me. He helped me find it and then popped it open."

"Where are we taking all this?"

"Down to the study, to put with the rest." I followed Lamb downstairs, carrying neatly tied bundles of paper and cash. "How did you know it was Drayton, sir?"

"The diamond cufflink. Truegood and I saw him wearing them on Thursday. I also know him from Bechuanaland: he carries a sword-stick and a Derringer. I had to think it through, but I'm absolutely certain. Drayton set up Carey for Lowenstein's murder and then killed him. I'm also certain Drayton isn't at Devonshire House at present, not after the bedlam this afternoon. Did you do all this?" In the den, the drawers of the desk and bureau were all open, with stacks of papers piled on every available surface.

"Yes, sir. Except for one of the desk drawers. It had been forced with that curved knife over there."

"Do you know where Melville is now?"

"Yes, sir. He's in Bermondsey Street with Inspector Hughes."

"I'll telephone him there, but I want to have another look at Carey's papers first."

"These are the ones from the desk; those are from the bureau; I haven't had the time to look at any of them, yet. Just the one thing, sir. If you're sure it's Drayton, can't we just collar him when he boards his ship tomorrow?"

"Only if we find some hard evidence. And I mean something more than a cufflink. Don't forget he's under the protection of the Duke of Devonshire."

"Ah, yes, you're probably right about that. I don't s'pose His Grace would look too kindly upon us causin' his guest to miss his passage."

"Do you know if Truegood's talking yet?"

"I don't, sir. Last I heard he was in the clear, but still out cold."

"Then we better get a move on."

I started with the documents on the desk, skipping the schedule book and the other items I recognised, and concentrating on what must have been in the second set of drawers. I sat down at the desk and flicked through them: a ledger, several letters sealed in envelopes, a blank notebook, and some more papers concerning his properties. Nothing of particular interest. The stack from the bureau was huge: a series of weather-beaten notebooks bound in wrinkled leather, dozens of maps and charts covering most of the world, and several hundred loose pages of what looked like a rough draft of a manuscript. I recalled that in addition to his many other skills and accomplishments, Carey was a successful author. The notebooks all appeared to be from his travels, but I didn't examine them in detail. I picked up his appointments book again.

"Did you say Drayton is T.D., sir?"

"Yes, why?"

Lamb was kneeling on the floor, more papers and notebooks scattered around him. "There's a dossier on him here. It looks pretty thorough. There you are." He handed me a folder with the initials T.D. on it, and half a dozen loose sheets inside. I paged through them. Carey had obviously researched his employer:

1884 University College Hospital London

1891 General practitioner, Pitsani, Bechuanaland Protectorate

1896 Jameson Raid

Second Matabeleland War

Various positions in BSAC, Salisbury, Southern Rhodesia

1898 Private secretary, Dr L.S. Jameson (Chief Mag, S. Rhodesia 91-93; Administrator, S. Rhodesia 94-96; SAR Raid — Rhodes/Chamberlain)

There were also notes on his associates and haunts in London:

...resident Devonshire House, apparently has patronage of Cavendish... Gen Sir Evelyn Wood VC ...dines at the Savoy, Claridge's... frequents the Café Royal and American Bar (Criterion)... Bartitsu Club, Soho...

And some cautionary notes:

...an expert swordsman by all accounts... crack shot... A killing gentleman.

The latter characterisation was ironic, in view of how Carey had died.

There wasn't much in the dossier that I didn't already know from either my earlier acquaintance with Drayton or my recent inquiries. It was, however, comprehensive, and it gave me an idea. Carey was nobody's fool. He'd spent a large proportion of his life hunting beasts and men. He was quick-witted and savvy, and had probably kept a dossier on all his employers as a form of insurance. He would've known there was always the possibility at least one of them would try to get rid of him as a precautionary measure. Up until he decided to work for Drayton, he'd outfoxed them all. The shikari and The Doctor were in fact very well matched, and each had proved the other's undoing. Drayton had killed Carey, but Carey had unmasked him as a murderer and conspirator.

They had stalked each other, Drayton knowing from the very beginning that the time would come when he must eliminate Carey. The theft of the penang lawyer — whenever it had been carried out — was proof that Drayton had been thinking ahead, but I knew him far too well to require evidence of his foresight. My idea took shape. First, Drayton would've known as much about Carey as Carey knew about him. Second, although he'd been over-confident this afternoon, he'd planned the murder with meticulous care. Drayton never left anything to chance, and always prepared for every eventuality. He would've anticipated pursuit and injury, and established a convenient bolthole nearby. It would be somewhere without a connection to him, Cavendish, or Murgatroyd; a place where he knew he wouldn't be disturbed until he left for the docks. I wasn't sure if it was intuition or my intimate knowledge of Drayton, but I knew the answer was within my grasp...

With mounting excitement, I rifled through the original papers I'd removed from the desk drawer. Property. Carey had property in Hoxton and Southwark. I found the Vine Lane address. Then I returned to the stack from the cabinet and started on the maps and charts. Central Africa, the Central Provinces of India, East Africa, Afghanistan... I flung them all aside. Eastern Europe, Gujarat, Punjab, Southern Africa... none of them any good to me. Lamb had interrupted his perusal to watch my performance. "Have you seen a map of London anywhere here?" I demanded.

"Can't say I have, sir, what're you after?"

"How well do you know the South Bank?"

"About the same as the rest of The Smoke. Try me."

"Vine Lane, Southwark?"

"I know it."

"It doesn't happen to be anywhere near Butler's Wharf, does it?"

"Yes, it does. It's a couple of hundred yards the other side of Tower Bridge from the warehouse where we found Carey."

"That's it!" I punched the air. Carey has rooms there as well. That's where he went!"

"You mean to say he doubled back, sir?"

"If that would've taken him to Vine Lane, then that's exactly what I mean. Clever, too, because the logical conclusion would be that he was at the brothel."

"If he's the one who employed Murgatroyd, sir."

"He is. Do you have the number for Bermondsey-street station?"

Lamb gave it to me and I raced downstairs to Carey's telephone.

In less than a minute I heard a deep, reassuring voice say, "Is that you, Marshall?"

"Yes, I know who killed Carey and Lowenstein."

"Dr Morgan Drayton would be my guess."

"That's right. I also know where he is now."

"That is very welcome news. Inspector Hughes and a squad of men from Bermondsey Street raided Boustred's brothel in Snowsfields, but there was no sign of Drayton, Murgatroyd, or even Boustred. Do you think he might have gone to roost in Devonshire House?"

"No, he'll be at Carey's rooms in Vine Lane. Lamb just told me it's close to Shad Thames. Murgatroyd and Boustred are probably with him."

"Lamb? So you're in Upper Grosvenor Street?" asked Melville.

"Yes. Drayton and Carey were playing a game of cat-and-mouse with each other. I'm not a betting man, but I'll bet all I have that Drayton planned to use Carey's own rooms as a rendezvous after killing him. I reckon he'll stay there until the steamer leaves tomorrow."

"Yes, it makes sense. The scoundrel would want somewhere close, especially after Carey made a mess of him with the Bowie knife."

"That's what I thought. The address is 32B Vine Lane."

"I'll send a couple of men there now to keep the place under observation, but I need time, and the men need a break; some of them have been on duty for nearly eighteen hours. Tell Lamb to secure Carey's rooms, leave a constable on guard, and report back to Bermondsey Street. You can go back to your hotel and take a couple of hours rest. I'll meet you at half-past ten at Simpson's."

"Simpson's?"

"Simpson's in the Strand."

"The restaurant, whatever for?"

"For supper, my dear sir. Supper and a good cigar!"

27. Supper at Simpson's

I arrived at Simpson's Grand Divan Tavern a few minutes late, but I was expected, and the maitre d' escorted me across the coloured tile floor to a corner alcove. We passed a great bar window and a giant dumbwaiter laden with glasses and decanters, and I marvelled at the candelabra, twice as tall as me, which stood on either side of the dining area. The room was nearly full, even at this late hour, hazy with smoke, and noisy with the hum of excited conversation and the clinking of cutlery and crockery. Melville was waiting for me in a wood-panelled booth for two, made snug with a little curtain and brass rails. He rose as soon as he saw me and extended his flipper again. "Marshall, I'm so glad you could join me!"

"I've always wanted to eat at Simpson's — ever since I was at Westminster."

We shook and sat; then Melville poured me a glass of wine from the bottle of Liebfraumilch on the table. "No chess tonight?" I asked. Simpson's was famous as the home of European chess.

"There's always chess being played here, but the tables are upstairs, next to the ladies' dining room. I'll show you afterwards, if we have time. First, His Majesty King Edward the Seventh!"

"King Edward the Seventh!" I raised my glass.

"Now that the crown is at last firmly upon His Majesty's royal head, and he and his guests are safe and sound in the Palace, I can turn my attention to the problems Mr Rhodes has caused for us. Please accept my thanks for looking after the Empire Loyalist League while I was otherwise occupied. Your very good health, and congratulations!"

"Thank you. Good health!" I replied.

Melville glanced to the side to check that our conversation was indeed private. "You were right. There're at least two occupants in 32B Vine Lane, and I've no doubt one of them is the elusive Dr Drayton. Let's order, then you can tell me how you solved this very complex case."

We decided on a fish starter, cod for Melville, and turbot for me. Simpson's beef and mutton were legendary, so I welcomed his suggestion of sirloin of beef for two. As soon as the waiter left, he continued. "As far as I can make out, everything seems to hinge on this Carey fellow, but how on earth did you construe that? Was it because of his involvement with your late sister?"

Melville was asking for more than I was prepared to divulge; I wasn't ready to share everything with him yet. "That was what initially brought the man to my attention, but when Truegood and I questioned O'Donnell he suggested the Okhrana had set Carey up for Lowenstein's murder."

"That proved incorrect?" Melville took another drink from his glass.

"It did, but the wideawake hat pointed to the possibility that Carey had been involved in Lowenstein's murder as well as Chamberlain's accident during the Colonial Conference. It seemed to me that the accident was just the type of job Carey would take pride in."

"His second accident in two months."

I ignored the reference to Ellen. "Even though it turned out Carey had been falsely implicated for Lowenstein, I didn't know that at first, so a connection was established in my mind."

"Yes, I'm told you burgled Carey's house. Rather risky, but an opportunity not to be missed."

I smiled and took a small sip of wine. "By the time I realised the evidence in Tottenham Street pointed to Carey, I already knew he'd been in Bedfordshire when the crime was committed. Therefore, someone had manufactured the evidence to point to him, and who better than the man who'd employed him on the Chamberlain job? But I was a complete fool, for two reasons. First, I should've realised that whoever set up Carey intended to kill him. It would never do to have him stand trial and perhaps call some woman he'd spent the night with at Woburn to prove he never left. So I should've guessed Carey's days were numbered. Second, I should've known that the initials 'T.D.' referred to Drayton. All of Rhodes' cronies had nicknames, and I knew 'The Doctor' was Drayton's. I didn't realise it was him until I found the cufflink clutched in Carey's fist."

Melville nodded, but said nothing as the waiter appeared with our starters. Both dishes had large cuts of the fish, covered in steaming sauce. "Have some more wine."

"No thank you. I'm going to restrict myself to the one glass. We have some dangerous work ahead of us if we're going to take Drayton."

Melville sliced off a large portion of his cod. "Yes, but don't worry, I have three dozen men, counting ourselves." He took his first bite. "Delicious as always. Yes, Hughes has nineteen men armed with rifles, revolvers, and shotguns, and there're another dozen unarmed constables to secure the perimeter. Lamb and Macaulay — another of my gang — will join us as well. There'll be no mistakes this time."

The conversation ebbed as we did justice to the victuals. Once the waiter had cleared the table, Melville resumed. "It's curious, but nearly eighteen months ago, I was in this very same place with a German gentleman. A couple of hours later, my hat was shot through in Whitechapel." He grinned and poured another glass of wine for himself. "You sure I can't tempt you to another? No? Then I won't press you."

"I don't expect Drayton to come quietly."

"With any luck we'll collar him and Murgatroyd. Drayton for the murder of Lowenstein and Carey, and the attempted murder of Truegood; Murgatroyd as an accessory to the murder of Lowenstein and Sergeant Aitken. Murgatroyd is wanted for various other crimes as well, so there's no doubt he'll hang. As for Drayton, I'm not quite sure what we're going to do with him...it's a nasty business this League. Thank God so few know about it."

"I didn't mention the Society of the Elect to Truegood because I wasn't sure if he was in your full confidence, but I had to tell him about the League to convince him of the need for Carey's arrest."

Melville smiled again. "No one is in my full confidence. Taciturnity is essential in this line of work. I make it my practice to pass on to my superiors and subordinates only as much as they require to perform their duties. It wasn't necessary for Truegood to know about the Society of the Elect; it was necessary for him to know about the League. There's no harm done. As for the Society, you think we were misinformed?"

"I thought so when I spoke to Armstrong; I'm certain of it now."

"I shall have to have a word with Mr Akers-Douglas about that. Never mind, let's toast to the success of our joint venture."

I took up my glass again. "And our continued good health."

"I agree!"

The waiter refreshed our plates and cutlery and then a portly chap dressed in a white coat wheeled over an immense joint of beef on a trolley. He ran the sharpener twice over his carving knife with a flourish, and asked where we would like our meat sliced. It was only because of the energetic work ahead that I decided not to join Melville in a second cut.

"There is no place to compare with Simpson's when it comes to traditional English food," said Melville. "Their beef, saddle of mutton, and steak and kidney pie are all the finest in the metropolis. My compliments to the chef as always," he said to the carver. "I can recommend the syrup roly-poly for dessert. Yes? Two of those please, Charles. Thank you."

As soon as Charles departed we continued the conversation in between mouthfuls of succulent meat and flavoursome vegetables.

"My initial comment was to focus on the murder rather than the will, and you did so admirably. Once you had a suspect for the murder — albeit the wrong one — and learned of his connection to Chamberlain, you then turned your attention to the League?"

"Yes. I found out about Chamberlain's meeting at the Liberal Club on Empire Day, and that was when everything fell into place. Or it would've, if only I'd realised who T.D. was."

"You say that Chamberlain and six others inaugurated the League?"

"Yes. Chamberlain and Cavendish were identified by name. From the descriptions I was given, I'm quite sure of the identity of two of the others. Drayton is clearly recognisable as Cavendish's guest and Jameson's secretary. His work with the League was what kept him in London, and why Jameson wanted Lowenstein to return to Cape Town instead."

"Lowenstein must have changed his mind," Melville said, almost to himself.

"That's something else I was slow to realise. Lowenstein had bitten off more than he could chew. He went into hiding, petitioned Colonel Rhodes for assistance, and... and probably prayed a lot. So we have Chamberlain and Cavendish, with Drayton in Jameson's place. From the description of the soldier, I'm certain it was Major Binstead, who is one of Kitchener's band of boys."

"Britain's greatest soldier, another fine recruit."

"As for the woman, I'm pretty sure it was Flora Shaw — another one involved in the Jameson Raid. I believe she's engaged to Frederick Lugard, a high-ranking official in West Africa. So, aside from her own influence, she has her fiancé's official status as well. As to the other two," I shrugged, "two middle-aged men. I've no idea who they were."

"I do, but let's return to Miss Shaw for a moment. You're quite right, it was her. Miss Shaw is engaged to the High Commissioner for the Protectorate of Northern Nigeria. But she wasn't representing him, she was representing Alfred Lyttelton."

"The sportsman turned politician?"

"Yes, famous as a footballer and cricketer, and now Chamberlain's protégé. Two years ago Chamberlain sent him out to the Cape as his head of the committee for the reconstruction of South Africa after the war. Of course, like the rest of those who wanted the war, Chamberlain had no idea it would take so long to win. In the interim Lyttelton has impressed not only his patron, but also Milner. With the pair of them at loggerheads, Lyttelton is probably one of no more than two men who can still boast the support of both. He'll go far, mark my words.

"The other man who enjoys such esteemed friendship is one of the middle-aged men, a Canadian gentleman by the name of Dr George Parkin. Unlike the other doctors involved, Parkin's title is academic, and he's a schoolmaster at Upper Canada College, Toronto. Like so many of the characters who keep cropping up, Parkin is an Oxford man. Twenty years ago he was one of the founders of the Imperial Federation League; ten years ago he became Milner's mentor. He's an associate of the late Mr Rhodes, Dr Jameson, and Mr Chamberlain, and a very influential figure in Canadian and British politics. As to the identity of the seventh man at that meeting, I can only guess... I'm sure you can too."

I ignored this last statement. "How on earth do you know all of this?"

"It is my job to know things that others do not, but seeing as we might have a future together, I'll break my first rule and tell you a secret you do not need to know." He paused and I leant closer. "The telephone."

"The telephone?"

"Yes, a wonderful invention, don't you agree?"

"I do. I don't know how I'd have managed without it today — the whole week, actually. The potential for subterfuge hasn't been lost on me, but I still can't see how you've come by all this intelligence."

Melville lowered his voice. "It is possible to eavesdrop on conversations from the exchange."

"Good God! It...it's so obvious, of course."

"Yes, like all the best ideas, it is dead simple. And like so many of the best ideas, it has been overlooked by almost everyone. Make sure that stays between the two of us, by the way; it's one of my most successful methods of information gathering, and there very few who know about it."

"This telephone has great potential for crime fighting, doesn't it?

"In a word, yes. Amongst other things it enabled me to confirm that Miss Shaw is currently acting as Lyttelton's agent. Combined with your intelligence about the inauguration of the League at the Liberal Club — here comes our dessert."

The waiter placed our final course on the table, and we interrupted our conversation again as we set about the fare. Afterwards, Melville ordered coffee and cigars. As I'd no pipe tobacco left, I joined him. We both opted for Havanas, an H. Upmann for Melville, and a Sancho Panza for me. Our small clouds of aromatic smoke wafted upwards, thickening the haze over the dining room.

"I find a concentrated atmosphere facilitates mental concentration. I read that somewhere recently, but I can't think where," said Melville

"I never thought of it like that myself."

"Now, to the business at hand. How did you establish that Drayton was in Vine Lane?"

"I'm not sure how to describe it without sounding absurd," I replied.

"Try."

"From Carey's papers it was obvious he'd researched Drayton comprehensively. Similarly, Drayton had followed Carey; he needed to if he was to implicate him in a murder, and then kill him. Carey kept two other sets of rooms, one in Hoxton and one in Southwark. When Lamb told me where Vine Lane was... I just knew it. Intuition, maybe? Or perhaps because I know Drayton so well? I could be wrong; he might not be one of the occupants your men have seen."

"He's there all right, and it's probably a little of both where you're concerned. There's nothing wrong with intuition bred of experience, but combined with a personal knowledge of the suspect, I'd say it's conclusive. You have score to settle with Drayton, don't you?"

Once again, Melville was probing at knowledge I wasn't prepared to share. "Yes." I drew on my cigar and changed the subject. "That reminds me: did I mention that Armstrong offered me a place in Milner's kindergarten?"

"No. Do tell!"

"Apparently I'm just the sort of man Lord Milner wants — hardly a character reference, I'm afraid. Anyway, Armstrong presented a very convincing argument for Milner's control of the Empire via his kindergarten. Also, he has apparently outmanoeuvred Jameson as far as the will is concerned."

"So even if Drayton were to board his ship tomorrow, all is lost?"

"If Armstrong was right. But it doesn't do to underestimate men like Jameson and Drayton. Jameson may have another card up his sleeve and Drayton is at his most lethal when he's desperate. I've seen it first hand in Bechuanaland. Drayton may be on the run and wounded, but that will only make him more deadly."

Melville withdrew his watch. "Speaking of which, it's eleven minutes past midnight. We've just time to finish these excellent cigars, then we must be off to Carey's crib. In about twenty minutes Hughes and his men will take up their positions. We'll wait at the back of the house with Lamb and Macaulay. When the uniforms go in... "

"Drayton and Murgatroyd will come out the back, straight into our arms."

Melville chuckled. "That's the idea. You're armed, of course?"

"I have my Mauser."

"Good. I have a black scarf for you — to cover your face and shirt — and a hansom waiting outside. Hughes will launch the raid at one o'clock precisely."

Five minutes later we left Simpson's and boarded the hansom. The lower part of the driver's face was wrapped up, but he grinned and tipped his hat.

"Are you ready?" Melville asked as he pulled the leather curtain closed.

"I am," I replied, similarly obscuring the view from the window at my side.

"Vine Lane it is, then." Melville lifted the trap door above us. "Let's go, Lamb!"

28. A Riverside Duel

Our passage along the Strand was slow and tedious. Lamb was an accomplished cabby, but there were throngs of people admiring the brilliant illuminations, and they took possession of both the pavement and the road. After what seemed an interminable interval, we eventually passed the turrets and arches of the Royal Courts of Justice, crossed Temple Bar, and entered the City. Whereas the Strand literally blazed with lights of all colours, the buildings in Fleet Street were adorned with lanterns that glowed a soft yellow. As the lights became dimmer and fewer, Lamb picked up the pace. I could tell Melville was impatient, for although he said nothing, he fidgeted in his seat. When we approached London Bridge, Lamb slowed once again. The bridge shone with muted gaslight and a host of revellers were enjoying the views of the City, Blackfriars Bridge, and Westminster.

Melville muttered under his breath, removing his watch anxiously. We crossed to the South Bank and entered Borough High Street. Melville muttered again as he replaced his watch, and seemed to notice me at his side for the first time since we'd started. The strain in his face eased and he smiled. "There's a lesson for us both: always leave plenty of time when you're trying to get anywhere in London. You'd think I'd have learned that by now, after policing the place for thirty years. Thirty years exactly, in two months' time. Never mind, the next turn brings us to Morgan Lane, which is two streets behind our destination. We still have ten minutes."

"Thirty years, that's a long time. No thoughts on retirement?"

"Retirement! What in God's name would I do with myself?"

"I don't know. I just thought you might fancy a rest from all this. I reckon you've earned it several times over."

"Very good of you to say, but I don't want a rest. What would I do? Lurk about the house and annoy Mrs Melville, or become a private detective like Littlechild and Moser? Not on your life, old fellow, it's not for me. And there's plenty of fight left in this old dog." He patted my arm.

"I don't doubt it," I answered.

Lamb turned off Tooley Street and we found ourselves on the riverside, at the western end of Pickle Herring Street. The wharf was dimly lit and deserted. A few hundred yards ahead the lights on Tower Bridge cast a pallid gleam, but the area in between was murky. There were only two lampposts to dispel the darkness, and their beams were obscured by wispy tendrils of mist rising from the river. Across the water, the Tower of London sat stately and solid. I was conscious of the racket we made as we rattled along in the hansom, and grateful when Lamb halted.

We all alighted and two figures emerged from the gloom, silent and sinister.

"Come along," said Melville. "That's Stoney Lane, the rear entrance."

The men were police constables, both very tall, and both wearing cutlasses. They saluted Melville, and he ducked down the narrow lane. I was about to follow when I glanced at Tower Bridge once more, and saw a man making haste towards it. He was on the opposite side of the road from the gas lamp, but I caught a brief glimpse of him before he disappeared into the night. He wore a bowler hat and his build was slim. He carried a valise in one hand and a cane in the other.

And he was limping.

"Melville — that's Drayton! He's heading for the bridge!" I gave chase.

"Lamb, stay with Hughes! Cobb, come with me!"

I drew my Mauser as I sprinted along the wharf. I reached the light of the lamp — Drayton was gone — there was an alley off to the right. I dashed into it. I was just in time to see a shadow flit from light to dark about fifty yards ahead.

I charged headlong — arrived at a ginnel — realised too late that I was bathed in lamplight...

I dived across the mouth of the alley as a shot rang out into the night.

I tumbled, rolled, and staggered to my feet. I switched the Mauser to my left hand, thrust it around the corner, and fired three times without aiming. Suppressing fire, we called it in the war.

As I fired the third shot, I ducked down low, switched the pistol back to my right hand, and darted into the ginnel. I bounced off a wall — the coal alley was only a few inches wider than my shoulders — and looked for a target as I crouched on my haunches. There were high walls on either side, their tops covered with creeper plants and illuminated by lights from the warehouses beyond.

No Drayton.

I kept low, turned slightly to my left, and ran as fast as I could in such an awkward position.

Another lesson from the war came to me as I ran: I remembered to take stock of my ammunition. I had seven rounds left.

There was more light ahead — the alley turned left — I was expecting Drayton to appear and fire at any and every moment.

He didn't.

I slowed, knelt, had a quick look around the corner. Nothing, but the alley turned sharply again — to the right. I continued for a few more paces. I repeated my performance and found myself on another lane running between Tooley Street and Pickle Herring Wharf.

I saw Drayton's back — raised the Mauser — fired once.

I missed.

The bullet pinged off the corner of a brick building as Drayton ducked into yet another alleyway.

I had six rounds left.

The blood pounded through my veins and the familiar rage of battle consumed me. Drayton must be stopped. It was just me and him, man to man.

I forgot all caution and stormed into the alleyway.

It was wide, turned to the left, and opened out onto the riverside. Tower Bridge soared above and to the right; ahead, in the distance, the Tower itself. Twenty yards in front of me there was a gap in the wall, with steps leading down to the river.

I made for it.

A bowler hat popped up from the steps, a pale face beneath it. The face was obscured by a hand holding something metallic. Face and pistol disappeared in a flash of flame.

I kept charging forward.

I heard the buzz of the bullet pass my left cheek. I don't know how Drayton missed me at such close range.

I reached the stairs. I heard footsteps behind me — turned and raised the Mauser — one of the constables, cutlass drawn. "Come on!" I shouted.

Below, Drayton lurched towards a skiff that was landing on the dirty stretch of shingle. There were two men in it, but I ignored them and took aim at my quarry.

I fired — he slipped on the smooth stones, dropping to one knee — missed again.

Five rounds left.

I started down the stairs, felt myself sliding on the slime, and made a jump for the beach. I landed heavily, rolled to my right, and leapt up. Drayton threw his valise into the boat as a giant anthropomorphic silhouette appeared above him. The titan pointed at me…

A streak of metal flew through the air.

I dodged — heard a cry and thud from behind.

I looked back: the harpoon had impaled the constable clean through and stuck fast in the stone behind him. He twitched and gurgled on the steps, dropping his cutlass with a clatter. His legs crumpled, but he remained upright, pinned to the wharf like a dead butterfly.

The gentle splash of the river was drowned by a roar and the titan jumped ashore and charged towards me. He was the biggest the man I'd ever seen. He was bare-chested, and his massive muscles swelled as he ran. His face and torso were covered in what looked like woad, or blue tattoos, and he wielded a whalebone club. I absorbed all of this in less than a second, and realised he must be a Maori. I'd never met one before, but their reputation as a warrior nation was legendary throughout the Empire, greater even than that of the Zulus.

He bore down on me, Drayton following behind.

I raised the Mauser, aiming for the centre of the Maori's chest. Even if my shot went wide, it was bound to hit him somewhere.

I fired.

The Maori kept coming.

He was ten yards away; it was impossible I'd missed.

I fired again.

The Maori was five yards away.

I fired twice in rapid succession — his chest twitched, but he stepped forward and pulled his flat, edged weapon back to strike.

I lifted the Mauser higher.

The whalebone club descended towards my head, enough strength behind it to hack my skull in half.

I squeezed the trigger — shot the Maori directly between the eyes.

He jerked back, staggered, and dropped to his knees.

I turned the Mauser on Drayton — cursed — cast it aside.

Drayton smiled, his thin lips cruel under his perfect moustaches. He gripped his ebony stick by the silver skull handle and slid out the sword. The steel sang, thirsty for blood.

I looked down for the Maori's club, but it was attached to his wrist by a leather thong. I saw a shimmer of reflected light — the constable's cutlass — and picked it up instead. It was a clumsy weapon, a couple of inches shorter than Drayton's sword-stick, but sharp and heavy.

I stepped back as I raised my guard.

The Maori, still kneeling, bawled his death rattle. Drayton kicked him in the back and stepped over him as he pitched forward. He raised his sword in salute, keeping the hollow cane in his left hand as a second weapon.

Drayton was wounded, but he'd studied under an Italian master at Livorno, and taught me almost everything I knew about fencing. Added to which, I'd not wielded a blade since before the war. This was not likely to end well, but my blood was up. I found the knuckleduster in my pocket, and slipped my fist through it. If nothing else, it would protect the fingers of my left hand.

"This is about seven years overdue, my friend," he said. "I should not have allowed your perfidy to go unpunished."

We both felt betrayed: me, because he'd joined Jameson, the man who'd appropriated my Border Police squadron for his private army; him, because I'd refused to accept Jameson's leadership and left for Natal. We despised each other all the more because we'd once enjoyed such a close friendship. Brotherly love had turned to hate, and the duel was to the death. He was right, it was long overdue.

"We should have fought in 'ninety-five. If I'd killed you then, Ellen might still be alive."

"You've worked that out, have you? I'm pleased."

"Come on, Doctor! Come on. Leave him!" I heard from the skiff.

Drayton sprang forward and cut a figure of eight in the air.

I retreated, and he pressed the attack home, his blade a blur. I stepped back again, raising the cutlass in attempt to guard my face and chest.

He feinted with a moulinet from the left, whipped his blade under mine, and thrust for my heart.

I turned my blade down, parried, and raised my left arm as the cane sailed towards me.

"Come on, Doc! Last chance, I'm leavin'... damn you to hell!"

Drayton stabbed at my head — I pushed the blade to the right — the cane caught me on the scalp. Blood cascaded down my face. I'd no time for fear as the sword was pulled back and thrust at my chest. I deflected it to the left — not enough — felt the tip of the blade pierce my skin.

Drayton hesitated for a second, confused at my invulnerability.

I slashed at his face.

He parried — riposted — I lifted my blade — felt his part my hair. For an instant I was inside his guard. I ducked under the cane and punched him in the face with my left fist. The blow hit him above the right eye, the brass knuckles doing their work.

He dropped the cane, spun around, and slashed wildly with a backhanded cut.

I pulled away and then thrust as his blade flew past my head.

Drayton leapt to the right, flicked his sword up, and very nearly sliced my throat open.

I jumped back, slipped on a stone — lost my balance.

He cried, "*Avança!*" and stamped his foot in anticipation of running me through. The move is called 'appel' in fencing, is often accompanied by a shout, and is used to distract an opponent. It can be very effective, but is not recommended when one's thigh has recently been opened by a Bowie knife. If Drayton's head hadn't been ringing from the contact with my brass knuckles, he would've realised that.

He didn't.

He stamped, stumbled, and dropped his guard.

I steadied myself and drove the cutlass straight into his sternum — as far as it would go.

He growled through grit teeth.

I twisted the blade and withdrew it, a spray of blood spattering the shingles. Drayton surged forward, swinging wildly.

I kicked him between the legs — his head dipped — I hit him in the skull with the brass knuckles again.

He dropped his sword, and I flicked it away with the cutlass.

The skiff was leaving the shore. The occupant, whom I now saw had a wooden leg, was fumbling with the oars. I started for him — stopped when I reached the water's edge. I wanted Drayton's valise, but the boat was too far off, and Peg Leg rowed better than he walked. I looked out over the dark, foul-smelling river, and watched him disappear under Tower Bridge. Suddenly, I felt very tired.

A shot echoed from behind me.

I spun around — blood poured into my eyes. I crouched and raised the cutlass.

I couldn't see anything. I wiped some of the blood from my eyes with my sleeve.

Melville stood over Drayton's body, a smoking revolver in his hand.

I dropped the cutlass and walked to him. Two uniformed policemen with rifles appeared at the top of the steps. They ran to help their wounded colleague, who was still pinned to the wall, although no longer moving.

"Are you all right?" Melville asked as he holstered his revolver.

"Just a tap on the scalp; you know how they bleed."

"I'm sorry about that, but I couldn't risk Drayton talking. I think you'd put paid to him anyway, but the League's existence must remain secret, and that wouldn't happen in a court of law. Chamberlain, Cavendish, Kitchener…it is a story for which the Empire is not yet prepared — and perhaps never will be. You'll agree?"

"You don't have to apologise to me," I said, looking down at Drayton's corpse, blood seeping from a hole in his forehead. "I would've shot him in the first place, but I had to empty the whole magazine at that chap over there." I indicated the Maori as I opened my coat, waistcoat, and shirt. There was a tiny cut, about half an inch wide and no deeper, in the flesh over my heart.

Melville surveyed the scene as more policemen arrived, then turned back to me. He squinted at my wound. "Stone the crows, that was close!"

"It was. I was saved by the best advice Superintendent Alexander ever gave me."

"What was that?"

I withdrew my notebook from inside my coat pocket. It was skewered. "Never go anywhere without your pocketbook, it's the most important piece of equipment you have."

Melville's broad face shook with laughter.

I laughed with him, but not at my lame joke. It was nervous tension evaporating: I couldn't believe I'd survived.

29. The Seventh Conspirator

Melville had been thorough. Peg Leg, whose name was John Smart, had been stopped by a police launch from Wapping. There had also been two patrols of mounted men waiting in Tooley Street. Exactly how Drayton had managed to slip the police cordon remained a mystery. The evidence indicated he'd not realised the rooms were about to be raided and had simply walked out to meet the boat on the wharf. Before he'd left Vine Lane, however, he'd been just as thorough himself: Murgatroyd and Boustred were both found stabbed to death when Melville's men burst into Carey's house. I wasn't surprised; their usefulness had expired.

Melville and Constable Cobb had attempted to follow me through the warren of ginnels and alleys when I'd dashed off after Drayton. Cobb became the second police casualty of the affair after Aitken, and died before he reached Guy's Hospital. Smart and his accomplice, the giant Maori he called Raw, were both well known to the police. They were former whalers who made a living plying various illegal services along the Upper Pool, operating from the Prospect of Whitby, a dive across the river in Wapping. All four of my shots had in fact hit the man in the chest, but his size, strength, and ferocity kept him going. If I hadn't put the final round between his eyes, he'd have brained me with the first blow from his whalebone club.

I kept it as a memento.

Smart confessed he'd been hired to pick up Drayton in Southwark, ferry him across to Wapping, and conceal him in the Prospect. His commission would've been completed had he delivered him to the Royal Albert Dock in time to catch the Union and Castle steamship that was sailing at midday on Sunday. Melville planned to keep Drayton's death quiet for a while. For twenty days, in fact. The murder of the two policemen and the death of Murgatroyd and his men would be attributed to warfare between rival criminal factions. A particularly violent example of such, but then what did one expect of the man who ran Devil's Acre? Smart was released at seven o'clock on Sunday morning. The Crown had very little to charge him with, and even less to gain from his prosecution. On the other hand, all those who'd been in the Otter's Pocket would face a judge and jury for being accomplices in the murder of a policeman.

Two hours after Smart's release I was in a hansom, passing Buckingham Palace as I was ferried from Victoria to Mayfair. I didn't have time to walk. I was still tired, but the war had trained me for campaigning, and a few hours of snatched sleep, combined with a hot bath and a shave, had refreshed me for the day's work. The driver stopped outside my father's townhouse. I took a deep breath to compose myself and marched to the front door. I pressed the bell and put my hand in my side pocket. A few seconds later the door was opened by one of the footmen who'd escorted me from the premises four days before.

"Good morning, sir — " His face contorted as he recognised me.

I hit him in the chest with my left palm.

He staggered back — I slipped into the hallway — produced my service revolver. "Tell Mr Marshall I'll be in the study." His jaw dropped open as I trotted up the stairs.

If I'd lost touch with my father over the years, I could still predict what he'd do once he learned of my intrusion. He wouldn't hide from me, and he wouldn't call the police. He would deal with my insolence himself, which was exactly what I wanted. I entered his study, closed the door, and replaced the revolver — a Boer War Model Webley — in my pocket. I heard a shout, doors banging, and more shouting. Exactly three minutes after I'd forced entry into his house, the door to my father's study burst open.

I was standing with my back to it, hands behind me, so it was obvious I'd set aside the weapon. I was examining the map of the British Empire.

"What the fuck do you think you're doing in my house!"

I waited for a second, then turned slowly.

My father, the footman, and the butler were arrayed before me. My father was wearing morning dress, but hadn't had time to fasten his necktie or collar. The butler carried a revolver, another Webley by the look of it, and the footman a fowling piece. The footman stepped to one side and pointed the shotgun at me.

"I said — "

"The Empire Loyalist League."

My father stopped in mid-sentence then — quietly — said, "Get out."

Nobody moved.

He looked at the butler. "I said, get out."

"Sir?"

"Damn your eyes, Graham, get out! Both of you. And don't let me catch you lurking in the corridor either. Get out this instant!"

The footman stared at the butler in bewilderment, but when the latter jerked his head, he followed without a word. As soon as they were gone, my father closed the door behind them, and turned the key in the lock. Then he stomped over to his desk, sat down, and placed his hands flat on the leather top. I could see he'd regained some of his hubris, and felt he was back in control of the situation.

"What about this Empire Loyalist League?"

I walked over to his desk and stood directly in front of him. "You've not heard the name before?"

He smiled, baring long, white teeth. "Not that I can immediately recall."

"Then you won't be interested to know that I ran Morgan Drayton through with a cutlass a few hours ago."

The smile disappeared instantly. "If that's true, I'll have you charged with murder!"

"I'm not here about the League; that was just to get your attention."

"You've got it. Continue."

I walked slowly around the room as I spoke, pausing here and there to look at the pictures and photographs on the wall.

"I came back to England for one reason only: Ellen. As you were so quick to remind me, I was a little late for that. I knew it before I left, but there are times when one must follow the dictates of one's heart, even though they make no sense. On Wednesday I came here to ask what you knew of Ellen's death. Your reaction convinced me — as you intended — that there was nothing more to it. Ellen's particular friend, Miss Paterson, assured me foul play was involved. I was inclined to dismiss it all as coming from the heart, rather than the head, except for one point. Why would you want an inquest? Such a public examination of your private affairs was completely out of character for a man as cold and aloof as I know you to be. There could've been several reasons, but it nonetheless prevented me from dismissing Miss Paterson's suspicions completely out of hand."

"You're obviously enjoying a soliloquy at my expense," he remarked. "Is there a point to this, other than allaying your guilt at abandoning your kith and kin?"

"There is, but I want you to see exactly how I reached it, so you understand the certainty with which I speak. You may or may not have known that Ellen kept a diary. Because of the suspicion your conduct had raised, I read her later entries with a view to searching for a possible motive for her murder. There were only two singular occurrences in the last week of her life, discounting Carey's fatal invitation. First, Ellen was due to expose malpractice at the Zoological Gardens to a gentleman from the Humanitarian League on the Friday. Second, she overheard a conversation between you and an unidentified man regarding Alfred Lyttelton, Joseph Chamberlain, and a meeting at the Liberal Club on the Saturday. I'll admit I was preoccupied with the former when I realised that the scandal might implicate the Duke of Bedford, who happened to be the very man Carey was petitioning to sponsor his next expedition.

"I discovered a little more about Carey and visited the scene of the offence in Regent's Park. I was convinced that he had killed Ellen, and also that he'd arranged an accident to befall Chamberlain six weeks later. I'd no clear idea of the motive for either, nor did I know if they were related. Unfortunately for you, a short while before I made my first appearance here, I was recruited by Scotland Yard to find out what Drayton was up to regarding Rhodes' will. My next step was to make inquiries at the Liberal Club, where I discovered that Chamberlain had held a private luncheon on Saturday the twenty-fourth of May, with five male guests and a lady."

"If you're going to pretend you know what was discussed at that luncheon, you're even more of a cretin than I thought. It was completely confidential."

"It was. In fact, only Chamberlain and Cavendish were recognised by the staff; I deduced the identity of the rest from their descriptions. As to the nature of the meeting, that was quite obvious to anyone who knew the real purpose behind Rhodes' will, and the significance of the date: Empire Day. It was equally obvious that Chamberlain acted against the wishes of Jameson and the League when he chaired the Colonial Conference. Drayton was instructed to take care of the problem and employed Carey to stage a coach accident. Then he killed Carey, yesterday afternoon.

"Why kill Carey?" I continued. "There is only one reason: he knew too much, because he was the common denominator in all three escapades." I enumerated the points on my fingers. "He was there when Ellen died, he was there when Chamberlain had his accident, and his penang lawyer was left at the scene of Lowenstein's murder. But Carey couldn't have murdered Lowenstein because he was in Bedfordshire when the crime was committed. Therefore, someone had deliberately incriminated him. Once again, I asked myself why.

"What you and Drayton didn't take into account was me. I know Drayton and his methods, and I know you — albeit that we haven't spoken in eleven years. Drayton had to kill Carey because he'd already used him twice. Once to kill Ellen and once to scare Chamberlain. Carey was a very dangerous man who was now privy to too much information about Drayton's private affairs. Carey's murder also closed the police investigation into Lowenstein."

I stopped in front of a photograph.

"You, personally, made just one error."

"Is this where I'm supposed to beg for enlightenment?" he snarled.

"Don't bother, because I'm going to tell you anyway. This," I pointed to the photo in front of me, "this was your mistake. The J. Lyons and Company warehouse on Butler's Wharf. One of your many business enterprises. You should've told Drayton to transact his second murder elsewhere."

"Are you telling me that a murder was committed in one of the scores of business premises I own?"

"I am."

"And this was — when — yesterday afternoon?"

"Yes."

"And you think that the fact a man was killed on my premises incriminates me? You've come to arrest me as — what, a murderer, an accomplice — when I celebrated the coronation with a dozen or more peers of the realm! You are a disappointment to me, in all possible respects." He laughed without humour.

"I'm not here to arrest you."

"Then what?"

"To lay a series of conclusions before you, the results of my investigation. One, you received Drayton here on Monday the twentieth of May. Did you know that Drayton and I had shared lodgings in Bechuanaland?"

"No, he never mentioned you to me."

"I'm sure he knew best not to, in case you mistook us for friends. Two, the servant — who was new — failed to let you know that he'd shown Ellen into the parlour. You were escorting Drayton out at the time of her arrival, and — knowing your views on New Women — I would guess you were complaining that Lyttelton had sent a lady to take his place at the inauguration of the League."

My father's smirk faded.

"You noticed the parlour door was open, went to close it, and were startled to find Ellen waiting for you. Unfortunately, she made the innocent mistake of mentioning Lyttelton because of his fame as a sportsman. Ellen was trying to assist Miss Paterson, who makes her living from interviewing celebrities. Finally, number three. A few minutes after you joined Ellen, you realised that if she'd heard you mention Lyttelton, then she'd also heard the details of your secret meeting. Correct?"

He said nothing.

"She wrote that you suddenly appeared as if you'd received a shock, and terminated the interview. You realised that your completely confidential luncheon was no longer so. My guess is that you communicated with Drayton as quickly as possible, even though you knew that you were signing Ellen's death warrant. You knew Drayton would have her killed, but you told him anyway. He didn't wait. He met Carey the next day, and Carey made arrangements to meet Ellen on Thursday evening. I wonder if Drayton selected Carey because he already knew Ellen, or if that was just propitious? It doesn't matter. If you didn't know before, you knew afterwards. That's why you wanted the inquest, to ensure everything appeared above board. It was your alibi."

I'd returned to my position in front of the desk now, hands at my sides.

"I did know Drayton was going to have Ellen killed. In fact, I recommended it."

"You had your own daughter killed because she overheard the details a luncheon engagement?" Despite my contempt for my father, I was shocked.

"You are a damned fool! The future of the Empire was at stake, not some fucking luncheon. Rhodes laid the foundation for the expansion of the Empire to rule the globe. Do you think I would hesitate to protect that with my own life, or the lives of my family? The rule of Empire demands sacrifice! Personal and public sacrifice. Much blood will need to be shed, and what sort of example would I be if I was too squeamish to allow the first obstacle to be removed? It was an unfortunate that the idleness of some worthless flunkey resulted in Ellen becoming a threat to the League, but she had to be eliminated. It was necessary." A thick strand of saliva joined his lips, stretching and shortening as they moved.

"Sacrifice? Every time I hear someone extol the virtues of sacrifice, it seems to be from behind a desk in Cape Town, or Whitehall, or Berkeley Square. Soldiers who make the ultimate sacrifice don't talk as if it was some sacred ideal — they just get on with it."

"And what would you know of sacrifice for the Empire?"

I wanted to tell him about the war and all the brave men I'd seen die, but I was too disgusted by him. I had no qualms about the lies I told next.

"The game is up. You can't be brought to trial for Ellen's murder, but there'll be a committee of inquiry into the Empire Loyalist League. Aside from Ellen, five others died because of it: Lowenstein, Carey, and three policemen, one of whom was an inspector. Superintendent Melville has amassed enough evidence to guarantee that Mr Balfour convenes the committee. It will be a repeat of the performance after the Jameson Raid. Jameson himself will be called from the Cape to give evidence, as will Lyttelton. Chamberlain, Cavendish, Kitchener, Parkin, and you will all be required to appear. I say a repeat performance, but that's not quite accurate. The difference between now and then will be that this time they won't be looking to exonerate the conspirators."

"That's imbecilic — all of it!" He leapt to his feet.

"The deaths of a celebrity veterinary surgeon, a famous hunter, and a police inspector won't be swept under the carpet. Not when they happened in London, and not when the very same names from the Jameson Raid are called all over again. I happen to know that the Duke of Bedford has already been selected to chair the committee. I hear he has a reputation as a man with a highly developed sense of public duty and ducal responsibility. No doubt he'll also want to distance himself from any involvement with Carey, who was a guest of his this week."

"You!" He shook his fist. "Don't you ever think of anyone but your bloody self? Not your family or your country, just yourself. The Empire! Rhodes was the architect of the greatest empire the world will ever know. An empire that will rule forever, and make the Earth England, and England the Earth. Rhodes conceived of it, drafted the plans, and spent the rest of his life making sure the means were left for posterity. All we had to do was build the federation, stone by stone, generation by generation. But what have you and this Melville done? Destroyed it! Fucking torn it down before it's even been built, you damned ingrate!" He sprayed spittle all over his desk and reached for the buzzer.

I removed the Webley from my pocket for the second time that morning.

He froze.

Carefully, I placed it on the desk in front of him and stepped back.

He grabbed it, and pointed it at me.

"One!" I shouted, holding up my index finger to reinforce my words.

"What?"

"One." I shook my finger. "There is only one bullet in the revolver. Your choice."

I turned my back, walked to the door, and unlocked it.

Never mind Caesar's Camp, the VC, Groenkop, or what came later, that — turning my back on my father in his study — was the bravest thing I ever did.

I opened the door, stepped into the corridor, and closed it behind me. I descended the stairs and let myself out.

I heard the shot as I closed the front door.

An hour and three quarters later, I boarded the steamer for Cape Town using Drayton's first class ticket. I was carrying his valise and his cane, complete with sword-stick and silver skull pommel. My only regret was that I'd not had an opportunity to say goodbye to Roberta. This time, I hoped I was leaving someone behind.

Good-bye Dolly I must leave you, though it breaks my heart to go,
Something tells me I am needed, at the front to fight the foe,
See, the boys in blue are marching and I can no longer stay,

Hark, I hear the bugle calling, good-bye Dolly Gray.

30. Doctor Leander Starr Jameson

I was one of the first passengers to disembark, in the middle of the afternoon on Saturday the thirtieth of August. I'd given away all my light suits when I'd left for London, but my tweed was not out of place: the temperature was about fifty degrees and, as is usual for the Cape winter, there was a steady downpour. In front of me, beyond the city, Table Mountain was covered with a 'tablecloth' of flat cloud, grey as opposed to the more picturesque white artists are so fond of depicting. To the left of Table Mountain, the summit of Devil's Peak was completely shrouded. I walked down the gangway to the Cape Town dockside with Drayton's valise in my left hand and his cane in my right. The Mauser was snug in its rig, and the brass knuckles were in my left side pocket.

Another lesson from the war: be prepared.

Less than half a minute after setting foot on solid ground, it became obvious I was indeed behind enemy lines when two large men, both smartly dressed and sporting military moustaches, approached me. I'd noticed them prior to coming ashore and suspected they were police detectives.

"Dr Drayton?" said the slimmer of the two.

"Yes, how may I help you?"

"Chief Inspector Maguire, Cape Constabulary Criminal Investigation Department. This is Sergeant Neesom. We'd like you to come with us, sir." Like most of Cape Town's policemen, Maguire was Irish. He reminded me of a younger Melville.

"Certainly. I have a suitcase — "

"That will be taken care of, sir. This way, please."

Neesom held out his hand for Drayton's valise and I gave it to him. I was escorted, with a detective on either side, to an automobile, a 12/14 h.p. Wolseley. Maguire directed me to the tonneau and I climbed in behind the driver's seat. A canvas roof had been raised above us and there was a window at the front to protect the driver. I'd never seen a window screen before and I thought it was a good idea. Actually, I thought the invention as a whole was a useful one, and I'd already made up my mind to learn more about them as soon as possible. Maguire squeezed in next to me and Neesom started the carriage. It was my first ride in an automobile, but I didn't mention that — or anything else — to the policemen.

The differences between Cape Town and London were so numerous that I couldn't but wonder they were part of the same Empire. Notwithstanding the weather, the air was clean and fresh, and many of the buildings — constructed in the distinctive Cape Dutch style — were a dazzling white. There was smoke from the odd kitchen fire, but nothing compared to London. Perhaps that was why so many doctors still advised their patients to go to the colonies for their health. Rhodes had of course come to the Cape for that very reason, exactly thirty years before. We drove over several tram lines — banned from central London — and it seemed as though there were more horseless carriages as well. I wondered if this would be the pattern of cities in the future.

My knowledge of Cape Town was extremely limited, being restricted to two short visits. I spent a week there in 'ninety-nine with Ellen, and then two days in July of this year, en route to England. Nonetheless, the geography of the city made it easy to find my bearings. Cape Town was built on a peninsula between Table Bay in the west and False Bay in the east; Table Mountain provided a three and a half thousand foot high point of reference above the former, with Devil's Peak a couple of hundred feet lower and a couple of miles closer to the latter. Even with the rain and my impeded view, it was obvious we weren't going to police headquarters.

We were in fact driving away from the city, towards Devil's Peak. If we continued in this direction I knew we'd shortly reach Rondebosch ('round bush' in Dutch). Somewhere in Rondebosch was Rhodes' home, Groote Schuur ('big barn'). Rhodes had bequeathed the Groote Schuur estate to the premier of the Cape Colony, currently Sir John Sprigg. South of Rondebosch was Muizenberg — on the more temperate east coast — where Rhodes had chosen to spend his last days.

We left the city behind and began the climb up the eastern side of Devil's Peak. I recalled from my visit with Ellen that the area was one of the greenest I'd ever seen in Africa, even more so than the Valley of a Thousand Hills in the Natal Midlands. To the north-east of us, towards Stellenbosch, were acre upon acre of vineyards. To the south-east, the scenic Cape Flats extended to the coast. All around, there were orchards of pine trees — maritime and stone — and small but striking silverleaf evergreens.

Shortly, we entered Rhodes' estate, and I caught my first glimpse of Groote Schuur. Behind thick hedges covered with light blue flowers, I saw barley sugar chimneys, ornate gables, whitewashed walls, a red roof, and colonnaded verandas. The house was formerly the Dutch East India Company's granary, and had been rebuilt to Rhodes' order by an unknown architect named Herbert Baker. He'd done a magnificent job, and the design had been heralded as the beginning of a new vernacular Cape style. Rhodes, being a self-made man, didn't stand on ceremony. He looked for energy and ability, and rewarded them wherever they were found. They were two qualities which Morgan Drayton had possessed in abundance, and accounted for his rapid rise in the ranks of Rhodes' inner circle.

Neesom drove to the rear of the stately home, and stopped the Wolseley next to a long portico supported by marble columns. The rain had eased to a gentle drizzle and I climbed from the carriage after Maguire. "Will I need that?" I asked, pointing to the valise on the front passenger seat.

"No," Maguire replied.

I followed him into the house, Neesom close behind.

Inside, Groote Schuur was a forest of teak woodwork. Every room I saw was panelled, and filled with curiosities and souvenirs collected by Rhodes on his travels through Africa and Europe. At another time I would probably have been fascinated by the marvels on display, but I was aware that with each step forward, I had less chance of emerging alive. I wasn't being taken to meet Sir John. Until the will had been proved, this was still the lion's den, and the lion himself — Dr Leander Starr Jameson — awaited me.

I was ushered into a commodious study with a lofty ceiling. Across from a delft tile fireplace, arched windows revealed a rose garden apparently without end. Jameson was standing behind a russet-coloured stinkwood desk so large it could've been a dinner table. He'd put on some weight in the last two years. So had I, and considering we'd been suffering from enteric fever at the time, we were probably both the better for it. Jameson had also lost hair, however, and the monk's tonsure that remained didn't suit him. His moustache was thick, and styled in a neat chevron. He wore a brown coat over a double-breasted blue waistcoat, with a cream necktie and grey trousers. He would've made a gaudy spectacle in London, but here he was the archetypal colonial gentleman.

Jameson's smile was hearty, which I thought ominous, coming from a man who'd just lost the Empire's greatest fortune. Nor, I noted, was he surprised to see me in place of his private secretary. "Good afternoon to you all, gentlemen."

"Afternoon, Doctor. This gentleman was travelling under Dr Drayton's name."

"Thank you very much, Maguire. And you too, Neesom. If you'd care to take some refreshment in the drawing room, I'll call for you shortly."

"Are you sure, Doctor?" asked Maguire.

"Absolutely."

"Very good." The policemen left.

"I seem to recall that we've never been formally introduced, even though we know so much about each other. I, of course, am Dr Leander Jameson, and you are Major Alec Marshall. Please sit down." He gestured towards the two antique chairs on my side of the desk, and produced a cigarette case with a flourish. "Cigarette? Cigar? Feel free to light a pipe, if you wish."

I set my homburg down on one of the chairs, and sat on the other, both hands on the pommel of Drayton's cane.

Jameson lit his cigarette, inhaled deeply, and sat in the massive chair behind the desk, a throne fit for an emperor. The expanse of the desk top was bare save for a writing set and an ash-receiver, the latter fashioned from a rhinoceros' foot.

"To what do I owe the honour of a visit from one of our war heroes?"

"I have a message for you."

"A message? From whom?"

"From Superintendent Melville, of Scotland Yard."

"Melville, Melville? Can't say I've heard of the man, but then I don't really follow the English news much."

"Melville is the head of Special Branch."

"The Special Irish Branch?" Jameson sat up in surprise.

"No, their successor. Our equivalent of Europe's secret police, you might say."

"Ah, an important official then. Your presence becomes clearer. Go on, go on, don't let me interrupt."

"First, the Empire Loyalist League is dissolved."

Jameson's hands flew up in the air, and he grinned broadly. "But of course it is, my dear boy! Of course it is, or The Doctor would be here in your stead. Should I infer from his absence, that his soul has departed for a better place?"

"You should."

"That *is* a shame. As I'm sure you recognise, he was a man of exceptional ability. Absolutely exceptional. A more gifted secretary I shall never find. Had Cecil lived longer, I'm sure Morgan would've risen much higher in this world. Now, alas, the keep each other company in the next. How did it happen?"

"I ran him through with a cutlass."

Jameson raised his eyebrows, the movement extending to his bald pate. "Now that really does surprise me. He was an excellent swordsman. You know he studied under Pini?"

"I do."

"And you beat him in a duel?"

"He was wounded prior to our engagement."

"Ah... still, quite remarkable. So, you've killed my private secretary... now I shall have to find another. I will miss him, but life goes on. As far as the League is concerned, you've told me nothing new."

"If you didn't know Drayton was dead, how did you know the League was dissolved?"

"Bloody bankers, damn them all!" He smiled as he cursed and pretended to punch the desktop. "Lawyers are bad enough, but I tell you, Marshall, bankers are the absolute pits." I said nothing, having no inkling as to his meaning. It took him a moment to realise this. "Bankers, eh? Now you've got me wondering exactly how much you do know about the League."

"I know that you and Drayton coerced Lowenstein to sign the codicil you'd faked, and that Lowenstein changed his mind and went into hiding."

He pointed at me with his cigarette. "Yes, that's it! I managed to turn one of Beit's bankers to my way of thinking, but only temporarily — blasted fellow had a change of heart. Either that or he feared one of us was going to kill him — which I did in the end!" He laughed. "Anyway, no it wasn't Eric I meant. I'm talking about Lewis."

"Lewis?"

"Mitchell, Lewis Mitchell. Cecil's banker. I thought I had him firmly in agreement with the League, but he changed his tune at the end of last month. He and Hawkesley pulled some sort of fiddle and now the sixth codicil to the seventh will — Morgan and my effort — has been discounted. I only found out on Tuesday."

"So you no longer inherit everything?"

"Exactly."

"Let me make sure I've got this correct. On Tuesday, you lost the opportunity of being sole heir to the richest man in the Empire — some say the whole world?"

Jameson waved his cigarette again. "Yes, although you exaggerate. Cecil was the richest man in the Empire, but not the world. Far from it. There are several American gentlemen with a lot more money than Cecil ever possessed. He was, however, the richest Briton. The richest Briton ever." He shrugged, drew on his cigarette one last time, and stubbed it out in the ash-receiver.

"You seem to be taking this rather well," I remarked.

"You're a soldier, Marshall, you know how it goes. The fortunes of war, Lady Luck, etcetera. The Lord giveth and the Lord taketh away. If I were a religious man — which I'm not — I'd say that He took away on Tuesday, and gave on Wednesday. Of course, my apologies, how could you possibly know! You've been cooped up on that boat all month. On Thursday I gave my inaugural speech as the Member of Parliament for Kimberley. Cecil would've been ecstatic, seeing as he practically built the place himself. Sort of fate, really."

"You're not concerned about the will and the League?"

He shrugged again. "Of course I'd rather have all the money in the Empire and rule the world, but I'm not one to cry over spilt milk, or let the grass grow under my feet. I have plenty of other goals to pursue. Morgan would've understood, although he'd have been devastated about Lewis. Never mind, there's no more disappointments for him now, eh?" He lit another cigarette. "Are you sure you won't have one? They are superb. Moroccan. No? Suit yourself."

I'd heard that Jameson had a magnetic personality, a charisma that inspired fervour and loyalty in his peers and subordinates. I wasn't sure about all that, but his sanguinity was impressive. "There's one thing I don't understand," I said.

"Ask away, ask away."

"When you realised that Lowenstein wasn't going to return, or hadn't returned — whichever came first — why didn't you call Drayton back immediately?"

"Ah, yes, good question. I only found out that Eric hadn't returned when his ship docked. Another nasty surprise at the quayside, although on that occasion there was nobody, rather than an impostor — if you'll forgive the term. So I could've brought Morgan back, but in doing so I would've risked too much. That was at the end of May. The League had only just been established, and I needed Morgan in London to keep an eye on things. Wisely so, as Joe decided to try and go his own way at the conference."

"But wasn't that a huge risk, not calling Drayton back to Cape Town?"

"Risk! Of course it was, but you should understand that, Marshall. Didn't you risk your very life when you won your Victoria Cross?"

"I did, but I didn't risk it specifically for that purpose."

"I appreciate the distinction, but nothing ventured, nothing gained, and I'm afraid it was a case of all or nothing in this instance. Aside from which, I'd every faith Morgan would find Eric in time — which he did."

"But he'd had a change of heart and wasn't any good to you."

"Yes, although Morgan's one failing was that he was a little overzealous where the League was concerned. I think the whole ruling the world thing went to his head." He waved his hands in the air. "For me it was one avenue of many — and a chance to fulfil Cecil's dream. Poor fellow, for all his practical business expertise, he was such a romantic idealist. But yes, Drayton took it upon himself to kill Eric, and he nearly bloody killed Joe as well. Now, that would've been hell to pay... " He tailed off. "All ancient history now, though."

I stood and drew Drayton's sword, letting the hollow cane fall to the floor.

Jameson started — dropped his cigarette — then recovered. "Ah, this would be the second part of the message from your secret policeman."

The tip of the Wilkinson blade hovered a foot or so from his heart. "It seems I was over-hasty in dismissing Maguire."

"No, this is from me. Several people died because of your Empire Loyalist League. Not as many as on your dash into the Transvaal, but one of the casualties was my sister."

"Ah. That doesn't bode well for me, does it?"

"My sister's name was Ellen, she was twenty-five, and she was a veterinary surgeon. Drayton had her killed because she overheard a conversation about the inauguration ceremony."

"Oh dear, I told you Morgan was over-zealous. I have a Colt in my top drawer, but I suspect you'd be over the desk and have me transfixed to this ridiculous chair before I could open it, let alone take aim and fire." He wasn't smiling anymore, but he was calm.

He was a brave man, although I despised him entirely.

I twisted the blade and slammed it into the teak floor. It quivered and twanged, the silver skull swinging like a reversed pendulum.

"Dr Ellen Marshall. Remember that name."

Jameson swallowed loudly.

I put on my hat. "The second part of Melville's message is this: stay out of England."

He nodded. "I shall."

Epilogue

Jameson was as good as his word. Two years later, he was elected Prime Minister of the Cape Colony. After four years as premier, he led the Unionist Party, and was instrumental in creating the Union of South Africa in 1910. He served under the first Prime Minister of the Union, Louis Botha, who had commanded the Transvaal army during the war. Jameson never was a man to bear a grudge, so long as Empire prevailed. He was created a baronet the year after that, an extraordinary achievement for a man involved in the Jameson Raid and the Empire Loyalist League. Eventually, just before the Great War, he did return to London, but he played no active role in politics.

My mission from Melville was twofold: to warn Jameson, and to remain in Cape Town until Rhodes' will was finally proved. I put up at the Royal Hotel, with no idea how long I'd be staying. I took long walks in the rain, and smoked large amounts of spicy Cavendish tobacco, readily available from the Dutch merchants. On the second Monday I received a letter from Roberta, dated Tuesday the twelfth of August.

It read:

My Dear Alec

Your letter was the kindest I have ever received, and I can't thank you enough for giving it to me with Ellen's diary. Naturally, when I realised the shocking circumstances of her murder, I blamed myself. Were it not for her friendship with me, Ellen wouldn't have to mentioned Mr Lyttelton's name to your father, and he would probably not have done — she would be alive now. My conscience still pains me, but I know I am not to blame. You are right: your father, Dr Drayton, and Lt Carey killed Ellen. It was their doing, and theirs alone, and no one else is in any way responsible.

(I doubt I would ever have been able to write those words, let alone actually believe them, were it not for your eloquence.)

You will probably know by now that your father committed suicide after you left him. You'll forgive me when I say that I am not sorry, for he showed himself to be a hateful and evil man. Please accept my sincerest condolences on what must, for you, have been an even more dreadful revelation than it was for me. With all three of the culpable parties in Ellen's murder deceased, I quite agree with your decision. There is no need to blacken your family name with scandal. Aside from anything else, Ellen would not want it. As her loyal friend, I am content to know the truth myself, and to know that you, whom in all the world she held closest to her heart, were able to uncover such a despicable, cowardly act. I shall never forget what you did for Ellen — and me. I trust your commission will be completed with all expedition, and that you will soon be back in London. Perhaps when you return to your home in Sussex Place, you will call upon me. I should like that very much.

I remain yours affectionately
Miss Roberta Paterson

P.S. I placed your advertisement in the agony columns, and was immediately contacted by a Mr Davidson. He was rather a crosspatch over his Honesty. Regrettably, he is not a very patriotic gentleman either: despite my assurances that the safety bicycle had been commandeered in the service of His Majesty's government, he continued to threaten legal action against the culprit. He was only slightly pacified by the ten pounds you (rather too generously, if I may say) left for him. I reminded him that the donation was more than the price of a brand new Honesty, and sent him on his way. Ungracious, indeed!

I was delighted to read every word printed in Roberta's small, neat longhand. Having survived first my father and then Jameson, I now had every hope of renewing my acquaintance with her on my return to London. The days after the letter seemed even longer than those before.

A week later I attended a meeting on Melville's behalf, concerning the public legacy Rhodes is now associated with, the Oxford scholarships. As early as the first of August, Parkin had been appointed to organise the Rhodes Scholarship Trust. He'd left London the same day as I had, on a world tour, to make the first awards. The Ancient House of Congregation of the University of Oxford initially rejected the scholarships. The Congregation and the Chancellor, who happened to be Lord Curzon, were horrified at the idea of Britain's oldest university being inundated with students whose families couldn't afford to buy their places. Furthermore, they were outraged that the candidates would be colonials and foreigners: of the first two hundred proposed scholarship students, ninety-six were American.

Oxford admitted only twelve scholarship students in 1903, seven from the Southern African colonies, and five from Germany. With the assistance of Earl Grey, Parkin increased the number to sixty-two in 1904, and established the scholarships as a permanent feature for seventy-two men each year thereafter. John Behan, one of the first Canadian Rhodes Scholars, became Dean of University College just before the Great War, and lent some weight to the success of the scheme. Parkin proved an expert administrator of the Rhodes Scholarships, was knighted for his services, and devoted the rest of his life to the work. I couldn't help but wonder how efficiently he would've organised the membership of the League instead. Perhaps, in a way, he was doing just that. Rhodes believed that Oxford was a mystical vortex, the centre of 'Englishness' at the very heart of Empire. The League may have been dissolved, but the scholarships exported Englishness to the world.

On the third Thursday I finally received the news I'd been waiting for: the will had been proved. I went straight from the solicitor's office to telegraph Melville, and I waited there until I received his reply. It came with thanks, included permission to return to London, and a note that Truegood was back at work. I booked a ticket on the next P&O vessel, due to leave on Sunday the twenty-first of September.

I never returned to South Africa.

Melville was right, I was tired of soldiering. I didn't use my testimonial from General Broadwood, and the Twelfth Royal Lancers seemed none the worse without me. Special Branch were somewhat worse off without Melville, however. A year and a month after I returned to London, he shocked all of his colleagues and most of his superiors by resigning from the police and becoming a private investigator. Few could understand why the King's Detective had suddenly decided to retire at a fit and healthy fifty-three. I could, but I had an unfair advantage, because I knew that 'W. Morgan, General Agent' wasn't in fact a private detective agency.

But that is another story.

This one concludes two months after it began, on the afternoon of the eleventh of October. The *Osiris* docked in Southampton harbour and this time I was one of the last passengers to leave. I was elated to be back. At last, after eleven years, the war, Ellen's murder, and the Empire Loyalist League, I was home. I savoured the first step onto the quay, smiling stupidly to myself as the rain beat down. Nothing could've dampened my spirits, but something made them soar. Standing next to Williams, looking like Helen of Troy, was Miss Roberta Paterson.

Hello, Dolly Gray.

About the Author

Rafe McGregor is the author of nine books and two hundred articles, essays, and reviews. His most recent book is *Bloody Reckoning*. He can be found online at @rafemcgregor.

If you enjoyed *The Architect of Murder*, please share your thoughts on Amazon by leaving a review.

For more free and discounted eBooks every week, sign up to the *Endeavour Press* newsletter.

Follow us on Twitter and Instagram.

Printed in Great Britain
by Amazon